W9-BNQ-441

# In Peppermint Peril

## A BOOK TEA SHOP MYSTERY

## Joy Avon

CROOKED
LANE

NEW YORK

Published in the United States by Crooked Lane Books, an imprint of The Quick Brown Fox & Company LLC.

Crooked Lane Books and its logo are trademarks of The Quick Brown Fox & Company LLC.

Library of Congress Catalog-in-Publication data available upon request.

ISBN (hardcover): 978-1-68331-793-7
ISBN (ePub): 978-1-68331-794-4
ISBN (ePDF): 978-1-68331-795-1

Cover illustration by Brandon Dorman
Book design by Jennifer Canzone

Printed in the United States.

www.crookedlanebooks.com

Crooked Lane Books
34 West 27th St., 10th Floor
New York, NY 10001

First Edition: November 2018

10 9 8 7 6 5 4 3 2 1

# Chapter One

T he road ahead had as much frosting as the triple-tiered cake in the back of her station wagon, and delivery to Haywood Hall could be tricky.

Callie Aspen exhaled as she tried to give the car enough gas to keep the engine running without sending it skittering across the road on the slippery surface. The world around her looked like it had come straight out of a fairy-tale illustration: trees laced with frost; every stem of grass, every branch and bramble powdered with the snow that had fallen last night and had been scattered by the strong wind.

That wind was gone now, and a matte golden sun was shining from clear blue skies. Perfect weather for ice skating. The village kids would be having a ball on the meadow at the edge of town, where last night the local chamber of commerce had let the fire department flood the grass so the night's frost would create a natural ice skating rink, which was now surrounded by hastily set up stalls offering hot chocolate, gingerbread men, candied apples, and sausages roasted over open fire. With Christmas only a week away, everybody was in the mood to skate until dusk, when the lanterns along the rink were lit and people left hand in hand across the crunching snow.

As Callie pictured the scene, the smells and sounds filled her head, and she wished she could be there to dig into all the treats and have a whirl on her skates that had been gathering dust—and possibly rust—in her great aunt's attic ever since she had stopped spending her holidays at Heart's Harbor. College had dragged her away, then her exciting job as a tour guide for Travel the Past, an agency specializing in trips to historic venues. Her work had taken her to some of the most iconic sites all over the world. She had seen the huge Christmas tree lit in Trafalgar Square, had welcomed the new year among a festive crowd in Prague.

But this year she was back in good old Maine for the holidays, finding everything comfortably the same, including Great Aunt Iphigeneia's sneaky way of engaging someone in an errand that she herself would rather not run. The weather conditions had demanded a steady hand at the steering wheel and in putting together the masterpiece hidden in the back of the station wagon.

The huge decorated cake was the crowning glory of the tea party Great Aunt Iphy had been talking about ever since Callie had crossed the threshold of her great aunt's vintage tearoom on Main Street. She had barely had time to put her heavy suitcase away or introduce her new companion, the sweet dog that was now snoring in the basket secured in the passenger seat.

Daisy didn't seem to notice the car was skidding on the icy road. With her canine trust in her new owner, she slept straight through the bumpy ride.

Fortunately, from here the drive to Haywood Hall was almost straight, with a broad bend at the end leading to the house. Locals called it "Deception Drive," as you couldn't see anything of the house until you were around that bend. You might think you were still miles away until all of a sudden your destination unrolled in front of you in all its majestic nineteenth-century glory. Would much have changed since she had last seen the Hall? She had always believed the house had a timelessness that could withstand anything.

Callie turned the wheel ever so slightly and let the car find the tracks already made in the road's snowy surface. Guests had to have arrived for the tea party already. Would Stephen Du Bouvrais come?

Her hands clutched the wheel tighter at the thought, and nerves wriggled in her stomach. She tried to reassure herself that Stephen would probably have written a polite email to decline. He could use his diplomatic duties as a reasonable excuse to stay away, even though Christmas was the most family-oriented time of the year and he was Haywood Hall's future heir, the only living relative of its eccentric mistress.

But Stephen had never been big on family. Nobody at Haywood Hall had been. Which made it extra odd that the mistress of the house was now throwing a tea party for her only relative, some old friends, and Heart's Harbor's most distinguished citizens. Not a big affair, but with all the right people present for something . . . memorable.

Callie rounded the bend and gasped.

Haywood Hall's majestic silhouette stood carved out against the tall firs behind it and the blue skies above, the slanting roof covered with a thin layer of snow, the many chimneys breathing smoke into the chilly air. The marble pillars supporting the balcony were decorated from top to bottom with greenery, red velvet bows, and Christmas lights, while the railings along the stone steps leading up to the front door had been entwined in more greenery with silvery accents and a perky robin sitting at the top. Wood or glass, or maybe metal, it looked alive with its dark eyes and round posture, its bright-red breast feathers standing out against the snowy surroundings. Dorothea Finster was Heart Harbor's oldest resident, clocking in at ninety-three, so it was unlikely she had done any of that decorating herself. Had she hired someone to come in to do it for her? It seemed Dorothea had money to spend and needed only to snap her fingers to have people running to do whatever she wanted. But all of those people were strangers to her, who came and went, and she didn't have anybody close to her, to share her hopes and dreams with. Callie supposed that at ninety-three you felt the need for togetherness, especially in December when the darkness came early and the nights were long.

Callie brought the station wagon to a careful stop right in front of the steps and exhaled. She had done it!

A soft sound came from her right. In the basket secured in the passenger seat, Daisy sat up, her floppy, half-hanging ears twitching. Her little nose moved as if to pick up the scent of these new surroundings. She had a white snout in a chocolate-brown face with her lighter-brown undercoat shining through. The Boston terrier stared through the window up at the house as if she was thoroughly impressed with the extensive seasonal decorations.

Grinning, Callie said, "So here we are, Daisy. This is Haywood Hall. I came here a lot as a girl. All those afternoons lying in the apple orchard reading . . ."

She threw a glance up at the windows of the library where the books she had read back then were no doubt still on the shelves and the large writing desk dominated the room. As children, Callie and her friends had sat in the leather swivel chair and searched the desk for hidden compartments, for some lever cleverly concealed in the wood carving that would make a panel slide away.

They had always been treasure hunting, whether in the attic or the cellar, where expensive wine was stocked under the stone arches. Searching for traces of the earlier inhabitants whose faces looked down on them from the portrait gallery, some stern and reproving, others smiling and almost daring them to unlock the house's many secrets.

It was that sense of connection with earlier times and

their people that had drawn Callie to Haywood Hall. Her love of history had been born here, fed by all the stories told by colorful characters like Mr. Leadenby, the eccentric gardener who cultivated his own flower varieties in the conservatory, guarding them like a treasure.

With his deep baritone voice, Leadenby had told them of pirates and bank robberies and of the people who had lived at the estate, lawfully or illegally, long before Callie and her friends had played in the endless woods. With a single voice modulation, he would bring a shiver to their spines or make them laugh out loud. As a tour guide, Callie had always tried to convey that same sense of excitement to her visitors. Nothing was better than seeing a group of people spellbound on the sidewalk, oblivious to the busy city traffic breezing by behind their backs.

Just then, someone came down the icy steps and tapped at her car window. Callie looked up to see the friendly features of Mrs. Keats, Haywood Hall's longtime housekeeper. The elderly lady, dressed in a dark-red velvet gown with a small white lace collar, opened the car door and asked, "Can I help you carry anything inside?"

The back of the station wagon was full of boxes for the tea party, and a helping hand was most welcome, but as a girl Callie had already thought Mrs. Keats was a granny, and these days the woman had to be in her late seventies. The idea of her carrying something up slippery steps, falling and breaking something—a week before Christmas at that!—made her shiver. "Thank you, but I can manage on my own."

"Then I'll go tell Mrs. Du Bouvrais that you're here. She wanted to see the cake first thing."

"Sheila's here?" Callie's mind whirled. Once upon a time Sheila had been in the group of friends Callie had hung out with whenever she was in Heart's Harbor. Sheila had been the natural leader, always with some plan to earn extra pocket money or discover a rare species of bird. Although Sheila was three years older, Callie had never felt she was condescending, and she had actually imagined that that was what it must be like to have a big sister.

But contact between them had broken off after Sheila married Stephen Du Bouvrais, future owner of this entire estate, and moved abroad with him to his diplomatic posts all over the globe. When Sheila had married Stephen, Dorothea Finster had stayed away to show her disapproval of the match. Would Mrs. Finster have suddenly let Sheila take over her household and determine what party to give and what cake to buy for it?

Or had her advanced age persuaded her to make peace with her only family? A Christmas reunion at the Hall? Every little thing would have to be perfect for that.

"Mrs. Du Bouvrais is here with her entire family," the housekeeper said with careful emphasis. Was there also a pointed look in her eyes, a subtle warning?

Callie realized with a little stab of pain that she had hoped to avoid Stephen, but now that he was obviously here, she decided that it had been a childish sentiment. Her close friendship with him was way in the past, and he had not done her any harm by marrying Sheila. He and Sheila had always been much better suited to each other anyway. She had to approach her childhood friends with an open mind and make the best of their sudden reunion.

Forcing a smile, Callie drew back her shoulders. "I look forward to seeing them all again. It's been a long time."

"It has." Mrs. Keats seemed relieved at her cheerful tone and withdrew slowly up the steps. She halted a moment to straighten a bow on one of the pillars, her fingers caressing the velvet.

Callie realized that these bows had to have been attached in the last few hours, or else the overnight snow would have wet the velvet and ruined it. Dorothea had really thought of everything.

She glanced down at Daisy. "It will be up to us, girl, to put the edible touches to this grand party. I can't wait to see what Iphy did with the cake." There had not been time before she left to look closely at anything Iphy had given her to take along.

Callie plucked the doggy from her basket and put her on the ground beside the car.

Daisy snorted as she felt the cold of the snow under her paws, then sniffed it and scratched in it. She turned around and around as if chasing her own tail and then sat on her bottom with a dazed look.

Callie laughed and went to the back of the car. Upon opening the trunk, the dozens of boxes seemed to silently challenge her. Most of them contained fragile items: vintage china, silver cutlery, carefully cleaned and pressed tablecloths with lace decorations.

And three special boxes of various sizes held the three layers of the pièce de résistance: the cake. Fortunately, it wasn't put together yet, so it would be easier to carry inside. Great Aunt Iphy had insisted there was a reason for all of this and that it would become clear once Callie was on the scene. She had acted kind of nervous, wringing her hands, and Callie wondered if Iphy had been worried about Sheila's presence.

Sheila had always been good at springing surprises on people. No doubt she meant well and had the best intentions, but things didn't always pan out like she planned.

With a sigh, Callie picked up the biggest box and looked at Daisy, who was staring up at the house. "Wish me luck, girl."

She walked to the steps and tried the bottom one with her left foot. Not slippery, it seemed. Had her thoughtful hostess instructed some staff member to sprinkle the steps with salt?

"Let me help you with that!" a voice boomed overhead. A stocky man in shirtsleeves came down to her and pulled the box from her hands. His shirt was stained with bright yellowish-orange smudges that looked a lot like plant juice or pollen. His broad jovial face had aged a little, and his white hair had retreated to the back of his skull, but it was still as if she had seen him just the other day.

"Mr. Leadenby!" Callie blinked in disbelief that he was here too. Only minutes ago she had been fondly reminiscing

"Over here." Sheila sailed ahead of her, her back straight, the bun at the back of her head not even moving as she walked, firmly planting her heels into the thick expensive rug. Callie would never have trusted herself with such shoes, but Sheila seemed fully confident in them. She had always been outgoing, risk-taking, and, some might say, slightly manipulative whenever she wanted something. Callie had never resented her for that but had envied the single-mindedness that had taken Sheila so far in life. It hadn't been easy for her to grow up with older brothers who had automatically been taken into the family business while Sheila's wish to study architecture as well had been laughed off as "nothing for girls."

Her wish dashed, Sheila had had to reinvent herself, and she had probably believed that marrying Stephen at just twenty was the best move, as Stephen had been accepted as an exchange student via an international business school, sending him to Paris and Vienna. With him, Sheila could go abroad to all the cities full of the amazing buildings she had wanted to learn about and one day design herself. She had mastered the languages of the countries where they were temporarily living, and after Stephen joined the diplomatic corps, Sheila had made the perfect partner: elegant, adaptable, eager for ever new surroundings and experiences.

Callie caught herself listening for footfalls betraying Stephen's arrival on the scene. Or Amber's. Stephen and Sheila's daughter. Callie wasn't sure whom she wanted to avoid more. Her crush on Stephen was long past, while her coincidental encounter with his daughter had taken place only a few months ago.

Upon the occasion, Callie had not revealed to Amber who she was and that she knew her family and Haywood Hall intimately. It might be painful if Amber addressed that in Sheila's presence. Callie wasn't sure she could explain why she had kept silent about the connection. She didn't even know herself why she had done it. Maybe because she had wanted to avoid explaining why her friendship with Amber's parents had ended in radio silence without even the obligatory polite Christmas card?

But now Amber would have questions, and Sheila would as well, as soon as she found out Callie and Amber already knew each other.

Sweat broke out between Callie's shoulder blades. The venture to Haywood Hall was turning into a tightrope act where one wrong move could send her into an abyss of social disaster. This tea party was an important assignment for the Book Tea, and her personal past with the participants shouldn't ruin that.

For a moment, Callie fervently wished she had refused Great Aunt Iphy's request to deliver the cake and other supplies, at the same time knowing she would never have taken the risk of her lovable great aunt hurting herself. Iphy already had this frustrating tendency to take on more than a woman her age should.

Leadenby put his box on the large table, which had been cleared of anything that had been on it. He huffed and wiped his forehead with his sleeve. "I'll help you with the other boxes, girl."

It was endearing that he still called her "girl" when she was racing toward the big 4-0. She smiled at him. "Fine. I'd better spread the lace table runner across before I set up the cake."

Sheila frowned at Leadenby and whispered, "Change out of that hideous shirt before the guests get here."

Leadenby studied his shirt with an innocent expression. "I've just spent some time with my orchids. They're lovely. You should come and see them."

Sheila barked, "Change. Now."

Leadenby didn't even blink. "I'll get the boxes for Callie."

"Thank you." Callie smiled again.

As Leadenby ambled out of the room, Sheila shook her head at Callie. "No need to make him feel so self-important." Leaning over, she added, "I've told Dorothea countless times to turn Leadenby out of that old caretaker's cottage. He's not paying the proper rent, and he's certainly not earning a living doing anything around the house here. But no home will take him and his orchids. Or rather his stories about exotic poisons. We tried to send him on a group vacation to see if he hit it off with the other participants and might find friends there who would take him in, but he was home again after just two days. They put him in a taxi, paying for the entire ride back here, just to be rid of him."

She nodded firmly as if this incident proved everything she herself believed about Leadenby's character.

"He's harmless," Callie said. "He just likes to tell a good

tale. Whether it's always true is another matter. But I'll go look at his orchids once I'm done setting up the tea supplies and the cake."

"How much do you know about cake anyway?" Sheila asked.

"Enough to be able to put it together," Callie assured her. It was true that she hadn't baked anything in ages, but she didn't want to let Sheila's anxious tone get to her. Even if setting up a tea party was not in her usual day's work, she could pull it off, for the sake of Dorothea Finster and her wish to reunite her family for Christmas.

Sheila leaned back on her heels. "I'm surprised you said you're only here for the holidays. I heard you were back here to stay."

"Really?" Callie was glad Leadenby had come in at that moment with the box containing the table runner. She spread it across the table's shiny surface and smoothed its lacy edges. It was a real vintage piece, like the china and the cutlery. The tea party would have an Agatha Christie vibe, Iphy had confided to her. Callie had caught a glimpse of the mouth-watering cupcakes, topped off with tiny marzipan bow ties and necklaces created from sugar pearls. She wondered what bookish clue her great aunt had hidden in the cake. She always hid one in her pastry creations. Great Aunt Iphy liked nothing better than a puzzle.

And puzzled Callie was when she opened the box holding the largest tier of the cake. It had a big hole cut into its center.

# Chapter Two

Callie studied the cake with half fascination, half panic. She wasn't quite sure why that hole was there. Wouldn't it make the cake unstable?

What if the whole thing collapsed as it was cut?

But Sheila, who was looking over her shoulder, exhaled and said, "Excellent. It's big enough to put the ring box in. But hush hush. Dorothea knows nothing about this. She's too busy with her own charade."

"Charade?" Callie repeated, not understanding any of this.

Sheila whipped back an imaginary strand of hair from her face. "So you haven't seen the invitation to the party?"

"What invitation?"

"It makes sense, considering you're not a guest. You'll just be serving the tea."

Leadenby came in with the other cake boxes, Daisy hard on his heels. The Boston terrier seemed to have taken to the stocky man and was looking up at him with her ears perked up.

Would he take her, perhaps? It was imperative that Callie find a home for Daisy before January rolled around and she had to go out on her trips for Travel the Past again. It was impossible to take a dog along, and she didn't know anyone in her apartment building who could look after Daisy for a longer time.

Not to mention that pets were frowned upon in the building in general, as the landlord feared they would ruin the furnishings or misbehave in the communal spaces. Callie had been lucky that so far nobody had reported Daisy staying with her. If she wanted to maintain a good relationship with her landlord, she had to stick to the rules.

Still, Callie cringed inside when she thought about giving up Daisy. The death of her owner had been a terrible shock to the sensitive dog, and new changes might upset her again.

Besides, the elderly mother of Callie's boss had left Daisy to Callie because she had been afraid her little girl would end up in the pound. Callie had met her boss's mother and Daisy only briefly at a reception when Travel the Past's new office had been officially opened, and on that occasion, standing at the buffet filled with sweet treats, Callie had told the elderly lady about her great aunt's tearoom in Heart's Harbor and her own happy childhood memories there. Apparently those words had inspired the elderly lady, when her health deteriorated, to make a disposition to leave the dog to Callie, asking her to find Daisy a happy home in Heart's Harbor. After all, Callie's boss and Callie herself were traveling for forty-eight of the fifty-two weeks in a year and couldn't possibly take in a dog themselves.

"Here." Sheila went to a cupboard in the corner and opened a drawer to produce a small, black box that she carried over to Callie on the palm of her hand. She snapped up the lid and showed the contents to Callie.

The light reflected off the exquisitely cut stone set in gold. It had a slight bluish glow, while smaller white diamonds formed a circle around it.

Callie held her breath a moment at the sight. "What a beautiful ring."

Sheila studied it dispassionately. "It's a family heirloom. Stephen's great-grandfather bought it in Paris for the woman he loved. She was forced by her family to marry somebody else and returned the ring to him. He never wanted anybody else to have it, but of course he did have to marry to continue the family line, and in the end it ended up with Stephen's grandfather, who gave it to his grandmother when they got engaged. Stephen's parents also exchanged it when they got engaged in Vienna."

Leadenby added, "His father asked his mother to marry him on the Ferris wheel. So romantic."

"Nonsense," Sheila said. "It wasn't on the Ferris wheel at all. I wore it after Stephen asked me to marry him. Later

I took it out on special occasions, but two years ago Stephen brought it back here and stored it in the safe. He's terribly fussy about something happening to it."

Callie nodded. "I can understand that. It has so much family history. And the gold is crafted beautifully. It looks almost like it's woven together."

"It forms strands symbolizing togetherness," Leadenby pointed out.

"The ring will soon change hands again," Sheila said with emphasis, as if to cut him off before he could ramble on. "My daughter will wear it then. In a few hours, Ben will ask Amber to marry him."

"Does Ben already know?" Leadenby asked.

Sheila shot him a murderous look. "I told you to get changed out of that dirty shirt," she hissed. "The mayor is coming, and the president of the chamber of commerce."

Leadenby raised both hands in an apologetic gesture as he backed to the door. "Already going. Still, it's a fair question. I've never seen anything between those two other than genuine friendship."

"Nonsense, they're made for each other." Sheila turned to Callie again. "Ben is such a promising young lawyer. And an excellent golf player. He's everything we could ask for in a son-in-law."

"And how does your daughter feel about him?" It was odd to realize Sheila had a daughter who was getting married, while Callie was still single and traveling the world like she would be twenty-two forever. Her vagabond life suited her, and she never thought much about family except in moments like these when she realized how different her life would have been if she had made different choices. If she had married at a young age, she might have had a daughter like Amber now.

Sheila shrugged off the question as if it hardly mattered what her daughter thought. "She knows he's a good catch," she concluded in a shrill tone.

Outside a car honked.

"That will be Ben." Sheila's tight expression lit. She snapped the ring box shut and handed it to Callie. "Quickly put that box in the cake and place the second layer on top. Nobody can see the box, least of all Ben. He'll cut the cake, and when he finds the box inside, he'll know what to do with it."

Mystified, Callie dropped the box with the ring inside the hole in the base of the cake and opened the medium-sized cake box in a hurry while Sheila left the room to welcome her prospective son-in-law. Callie lifted the middle tier out of the box and placed it carefully on top of the base. It looked amazing with its white marzipan decorated with lots of sparkling ice crystals. Iphy had crafted them one by one, making each look a little different from the other.

And there was still a third tier to add. But Callie needed time for that. She'd better go and give Sheila a hint that she needed more time in here before Ben got in accidentally and saw something he shouldn't.

Callie went to the door and stepped out, closing the

door firmly behind her. Standing in front of it like a sentry, she watched as a tall young man with blond hair leaned down to kiss Sheila on the cheek. He carried a big bouquet of white roses, which he pressed into her hands. "For you."

"I thought they'd be for Amber."

"I have something else for her." Ben patted the pocket of his woolen overcoat. "Is she here yet?" He glanced up at the ceiling as if he expected to hear her footsteps overhead.

"Of course. She flew in this morning. I think she's upstairs. I'll go get her."

Ben looked to his right and spotted Callie. "Hello there. I don't think we've met."

"Callie is an old friend of mine," Sheila said. "We spent summers here together when we were children. She's back in town for the Christmas season. Normally she lives and works in Trenton, whenever she's not in Italy or France, that is."

"A real globetrotter, I see." Ben flashed a charming smile. "For business or pleasure? I'm afraid my knowledge of Paris doesn't extend beyond the airport and the hotel where I stayed for a conference. I had promised myself I'd go see the Louvre, but there was simply no time." He shook Callie's hand. "Ben Matthews."

"Callie Aspen. Next time you're in Paris, you should stay a day longer and go see Versailles. Not just the palace but also the gardens."

Sheila checked her watch ostentatiously. "Callie is working on the tea party buffet," she explained to Ben. "The guests will arrive in less than an hour. You go into the kitchens and ask Mrs. Keats for a cup of that mocha coffee you like so much. Then Callie can finish up without people interfering. And don't go into that room. There's a lot to set up, and we don't want to ruin anything for Dorry."

Dorothea Finster wasn't the sort of person to let anyone call her Dorry, Callie supposed, but then Sheila was a force in her own right. She had been in front the day the gamekeeper had overtaken them on forbidden territory, trying to explore the old watermill that was closed off and at serious risk of collapsing. Sheila had told the irate gamekeeper to write down what grievance he had with them and send it to her father. It had been a bold move, but the anxiously anticipated letter had never arrived and their parents had never known about the risks they had taken.

Smiling at the memory, Callie excused herself and slipped back into the room to finish the cake. Approaching the table, she saw that one of the ice crystals had come loose from the middle tier and was lying on the table's smooth oak surface. She studied the rest with a critical frown. Did others look like they were going to come off? Great Aunt Iphy usually worked very neatly. And Callie had carried the cake box so carefully, not leaning it to one side.

Had it been the cold in the back of the station wagon, having an adverse effect on the cake?

With a worried sigh, Callie picked up the loose crystal and placed it somewhere on top where it could rest on a solid surface and wouldn't fall off again. Iphy took great pride in her creations and would be upset if this cake didn't turn out as perfect as she had planned it.

The sound of an engine outside drew Callie's attention to the large French windows. She saw a van with orange lettering—AFFORDABLE CHIMNEY SWEEPING—drive away from the house at a higher speed than was advisable in these wintry conditions. With as many chimneys as Haywood Hall had, chimney sweeping had better come at affordable prices.

Still, it was odd that a sweeper could work when the fires in the hearths were burning. After all, smoke had been rising from the many chimneys on the roof as Callie had driven up to the house.

Shrugging off this incongruity, Callie opened the smallest cake box and placed the third tier on top of the other two. It looked amazing, with a crown of delicate sugar work that twinkled as if it was natural frost. Great Aunt Iphy could be proud of this. It was very seasonal. What it had to do with Agatha Christie, though, was a mystery to Callie.

"Hello."

Callie almost knocked into the table at the sudden sound of the female voice behind her. She spun around.

A girl with red curls hanging down to her shoulders stared at her with a delighted grin. "We meet again."

Callie couldn't help smiling in return. "Amber! I hadn't heard you come in. Good to see you again."

They stood and surveyed each other, thinking back to their first meeting in Vienna. Callie had been guiding a tour studying Austrian architecture and had been surprised to see an Amber Du Bouvrais on the list. It wasn't exactly a common last name. During a break at an ice cream parlor, she had asked the girl casually where she came from, and, innocently, Amber had told her about Haywood Hall in the small town of Heart's Harbor where she spent all her vacations.

It had been bittersweet for Callie to hear someone else recount her favorite childhood memories of forest hide-and-seek, the hut by the creek, and Christmas caroling along the houses. She hadn't told Amber that she knew her mother, her father, and the house she had described in such loving detail, from the stained-glass windows to the oak beams in the library. She had believed she would never meet Amber again.

Amber said, "My mother mentioned to me you were coming over to see to the tea party preparations on behalf of the Book Tea team. I immediately recognized your name from the trip. Not many people have the last name Aspen."

"Or the first name Calliope." Callie grimaced. "My family just has this thing for long Greek names." With a nervous wriggle in her stomach, she added, "Did you tell your mother I was your tour guide in Vienna?"

"No." Amber's youthful face scrunched up in a frown. She pushed her hands into the pockets of her faded jeans. "I wasn't sure why you hadn't told me when we spoke there that you grew up here as well. Besides, Mom . . ."

Amber flushed. "She seems to think every girl in the village used to be in love with Dad."

Callie took her time to study the cake from all sides. Sheila's assessment was probably right, as Stephen Du Bouvrais had been a heartthrob and a good catch with Haywood Hall attached. Still, Callie had never loved him for that, but rather for his extensive knowledge of books and animals, of all that they had shared, like some invisible connection. She had believed, as children do, that their bond would be forever. When it had ended, it had seemed like the end of the world. But she couldn't explain that to somebody else, especially not Stephen's daughter.

Daisy ambled over to Amber and sniffed at her royal-purple ankle boots.

"Hello there." Amber leaned down to pat her. "She's cute."

Callie nodded. "Her owner died just a few days ago. I'm taking care of her for a little while."

Amber looked up, her hand resting on Daisy's back. "What's going to happen to her then?"

"I don't know yet. I can't take her along when I travel."

"But you won't give her up to a pound, will you?" Amber surveyed her with anxious eyes. "She'd feel totally abandoned."

"Of course I won't. I'm going to find her a home with someone in Heart's Harbor. This is the perfect little town for her to live in." Despite her cheerful tone, Callie's heart clenched when she thought about letting Daisy go. The dog was so cute and such good company. Quickly she opened a box and began to unpack the china, taking off the tissue paper that had protected the gold rims during transport.

Sitting on the floor now, scratching Daisy under her chin, Amber asked, "What's the cake's clue?"

Callie looked at her, pretending not to understand what she meant. The truth was that Iphy hadn't told her much before her hasty departure for Haywood Hall, let alone anything about the cake's clue.

Amber rushed to explain, "Every cake and sweet treat Iphy makes has a clue. I was in the tearoom this morning when I came from the airport, and as it was close to lunchtime, I ordered a high tea for one, called One Cookie Too Many. It's a big plate with several treats on it: chocolates, a brownie, carrot cake, and cookies. I thought One Cookie Too Many was just a cute name, but Iphy pointed out to me that every treat on the plate had a clue that links to the Brother Cadfael mysteries. I think I saw a TV adaptation once and recognized the tiny white roses on one of the bonbons as a reference to the mystery surrounding the rose rent. Oh, and I loved the brownie hollowed out to form a treasure chest filled with jelly beans. So creative. Do you know those books?"

Callie nodded. "You bet I do. I read them all, and I even bought some foreign editions during my travels. The medieval covers are ever so lovely."

Amber nodded. "I love the Middle Ages, went to Europe to see more medieval architecture and manuscripts at museums and libraries. Such skill went into making those letters with gold leaf and the tiny scenes of birds and flowers that entwine them. I'd like to do something in graphic design, but Mom doesn't think it's a real job."

She rolled her eyes. "Iphy gave me a Cadfael mystery to read this morning while I drank my tea and sampled the sweet treats. I thought it would be all murder and mayhem, but it was actually quite romantic. I didn't realize the time until it was past two. Mom was upset I had stayed away so late."

She stared ahead a moment, her eyes wide and questioning as if she was mulling over a difficult problem. Then she refocused on Callie. "Is Ben here yet?"

"Yes, I saw him in the hallway. He went to the kitchen for some coffee. He did want to see you right away. He has a present for you, I think."

Amber scrambled to her feet and dusted off her jeans. "Probably hollyhock seeds from his mother's garden. She harvests seeds and keeps them in her seed cabinet. I asked for them the other day on the phone. Guys usually forget little things like that, but not Ben."

The fondness in Amber's voice seemed fitting for a best friend rather than a future husband. Callie wondered for a moment if Leadenby was right in his assessment that Amber and Ben were friends, not in love with each other. It might be a mistake to marry someone without being really in love.

But Callie could hardly ask a girl she barely knew whether she loved the man who would shortly ask for her hand.

And who knew, maybe a deep, genuine friendship was a better base for a solid marriage than mad feelings of being in love?

Callie bit the inside of her cheek a moment. She had so little relationship experience. And it was none of her business, after all.

Amber muttered that she was going to look for Ben and left the room.

Daisy looked after her and whined at the loss of her newfound friend.

"You'll see her again, girl." Callie gave the dog a quick brush across her soft head. "Now we'd better get everything ready in here."

# Chapter Three

Callie was almost done setting up the long table when Iphy bustled in. Despite her short stature and fragile build, she commanded any room as soon as she entered it. For the occasion, she wore a dark-blue velvet dress with silver jewelry. Nothing conspicuous, but still in line with the tea party's theme. Iphy firmly believed in getting every detail just right. She stood for a moment, surveying the buffet with her sharp, ice-blue eyes. Then she smiled at Callie. "It all looks perfect. Did you put the engagement ring inside the cake?"

"Yes, Sheila gave it to me." Callie checked that the door was closed, but she still whispered as she continued, "You didn't tell me Sheila was back in town. Or that this tea party is an engagement party."

"It is not," Iphy said with emphasis. "Sheila's making her own plans, but Dorothea will beat her to it, believe me."

She closed in on the cake and studied it long and hard.

"Yes, I think Amber should see it. She's clever enough. And determined to be happy. That's important."

Callie leaned back on her heels. "Quit talking in riddles. What exactly is going on here? Sheila mentioned something to me about an invitation?"

"All the guests are, of course, invited to the party. To ensure they would accept, Dorothea made it an invitation they couldn't refuse."

Callie tilted her head. "Go on. I still don't understand."

"Do you know what Ben does? I mean, what he is, in everyday life?"

Callie frowned, recalling her brief exchange with Sheila. "I think Sheila mentioned in passing that he's a lawyer?"

"Exactly. Ben works for the firm that handles all of Dorothea's affairs. That's how he and Amber met."

Iphy leaned over. "Right now, Ben is not in the kitchen with Mrs. Keats drinking her famous mocha coffee and studying photos of her fifth grandson. No, he's upstairs with Dorothea, handing her a sealed envelope with the paperwork."

"Paperwork?"

"There must be paperwork." Iphy looked at Callie as if she was slow to catch on. "That's what this whole tea party is about."

"About what?"

Iphy looked around her as if to ascertain no one was there to overhear her revelation. "The new will."

"Will?" Callie echoed. "Dorothea made a new will?"

"She wants this Agatha Christie vibe: the big gathering, the denouement. Not of a murderer, fortunately, but of the lucky person who will take home part of her fortune."

Iphy's face scrunched up in deep thought. "I doubt she'll leave it all to just one person. I think it's going to be split up."

Callie was surprised at the suggestion. "But I thought Stephen was her sole heir. That he was going to get Haywood Hall and all of her other assets. I mean, you do need assets to keep a big place like this afloat."

"Sheila thought he'd get Haywood Hall and all the rest when she married him." Iphy gave Callie a sharp look. "She only tried so hard for Stephen because of the money."

Callie felt obliged to defend her old friend. "Why can't she have loved him? He was very charming."

"True." Iphy nodded. She looked contrite and chastened at the realization of her prejudice. "I don't really know, of course, what Sheila thought at the time. I could be all wrong about her. But I do know this. She's the type of person who wants to control things. Her life, her future, her daughter. And you can control things better when you have a lot of money."

Callie could hardly deny that. On her travels, she had met many people whose wealth afforded them pretty much anything they wanted.

Iphy stared ahead thoughtfully. "I bet Sheila believes Ben comes around because he wants to make a match with money. Personally, I think Ben doesn't care one bit for Amber's money."

"Does he care for Amber?" Callie asked, a lump in her throat at the idea that he did not.

"Does Amber care for him?" Iphy countered, wagging a finger at Callie. "I talked to her a bit this morning over at the Book Tea, and she has so many plans I doubt she's in a rush to get married and settle down."

"She told you about the graphic design she wants to do?"

"Graphic design and learning Spanish in Spain and seeing the northern lights." Iphy smiled indulgently. "Some of these things you can do together of course, but I doubt that Ben wants to live in Spain. He's building his career here, and he knows much better what he wants in life than Amber does. He's past that stage where you run around looking for experiences and adventure. The farther away from home, the better."

"But if Ben and Amber really aren't at the same point in life, where they can make a successful match out of it, then why did Sheila hide an engagement ring in the cake? She said Ben would find it and know what to do with it. So he's going to propose to Amber."

Slight panic crept up inside Callie. "If you know Ben and Amber aren't actually ready to commit to each other, then why did you work with Sheila to make the proposal possible? You provided this cake, with the hole in it."

"Yes, but there's more to this cake than meets the eye."

Iphy studied her creation with a loving smile. "It can tell Amber something. And who knows, maybe the engagement won't happen."

"What do you mean, won't happen? Ben is going to cut the cake and there's going to be a ring box in it. And there will be people present, watching it all. He can't simply ignore the box, hand out the cake, and get on with it."

Iphy waved a hand at her. "Don't worry about it. It will be fine."

Callie shook her head at her great aunt's cryptic words, but she didn't have a chance to ask any more questions or express any more doubts, as several cars came down the driveway at that moment.

Iphy spied out the window and grimaced. "The town dignitaries. I bet you ten bucks they'll come in squabbling."

Callie watched as the two dark sedans and one bright red compact halted and several men and women got out, well dressed and greeting each other, all smiles. The atmosphere between them seemed relaxed and perfectly friendly.

Callie grinned to herself. This would be the easiest ten bucks she'd ever earned.

However, as Mrs. Keats opened the front door to let the guests in, Callie caught a heavy male voice saying, "If it has to be spent on anything, it should be improvement of Main Street. New lampposts, better pavement. Coordinating colors on the storefronts instead of everybody just choosing what they like. If you want to draw in tourists, you have to show them this town is ready for the future, not stuck in the past."

"The playground at the school hasn't been renovated in decades," a female voice protested. "When we're talking about the future, we should invest in our children. They need new swings, slides, and a climbing wall."

"A climbing wall? You've got to be joking."

Iphy looked at Callie and made a "pay up" gesture with the index finger and thumb of her right hand.

Callie shook her head, half smiling. She should have known that her great aunt would be in the know about town strife and pretty certain that not even the nearness of Christmas could stop these people from squabbling to prove their point.

The guests entered and were introduced to Callie. Mayor Moore and his wife looked at ease in these exalted surroundings, while head teacher Brenda Brink smoothed down her dress as if she wasn't sure whether it was suitable for the occasion. Or maybe she never wore dresses but was more of the sporty jeans type? The mention of a climbing wall suggested she had an interest in adventurous activities. President of the chamber of commerce Frank Smith was suave in his suit and a silk tie printed with golden French lilies.

All the new arrivals shook Callie's hand with obliging smiles while Iphy explained that Callie had come to stay with her for the holidays, but she bet they barely caught her name as their eyes flitted around the room as if they were scoping out hostile territory. With Dorothea's will, and her fortune, at stake, each seemed determined to make sure they left with the spoils. Mrs. Moore complimented the cake, while Brenda Brink and Frank Smith continued to argue about what needed a financial boost more urgently: Main Street or the playground.

Smith said, "If parents want changes to the playground, they should pay for it, or roll up their sleeves and make adjustments themselves."

Brenda smirked at him. "There are safety rules, you know. You can't just carry in a swing from somebody's garden."

The door opened, and Sheila sailed in. She had changed into a mustard silk dress that reached down to her ankles. Her hair was down now, making her look younger and almost excited at the prospect of seeing her daughter engaged soon.

With a stab of sadness, Callie wondered how Sheila would feel when the engagement didn't go as planned like Iphy seemed to expect.

But then again, with the ring hidden in the cake and Ben about to find it, what could prevent the engagement from taking place?

Right behind Sheila, Amber came in, wearing a purple dress and a delicate golden chain around her neck, from which hung a coinlike pendant that didn't seem completely suitable for the occasion. Was it a subtle sign of rebellion? Amber's way of putting her own ambition to travel and see the world into her mother's carefully crafted perfect picture?

Male laughter resounded from the hallway, and there were Ben and Stephen, both in suits with crisp white shirts and impeccable ties, sharing some joke they both found incredibly funny.

Callie steeled herself against the burn she knew she'd feel inside upon seeing Stephen, but she didn't feel anything but a general warm sensation of being home again in a place she had always loved. Something much more connected with Haywood Hall and many happy memories than with the person of Stephen Du Bouvrais in particular.

Suddenly it seemed silly that she had stayed away for so many years, thinking it would be painful, and missed out on all that this wonderful town and this house could offer her. Her teenage crush on Stephen had vanished like melting snow, and although she was glad to see him well, mercifully, she didn't feel any kind of attraction to him anymore.

Iphy nudged her and gave her a smile as if she had read her feelings. Callie was suddenly grateful Iphy had steered her here, forcing her to face a feeling that she had clearly blown out of proportion. She was now free to reconnect with what she had loved about this place and find her way back to the happiness of old.

Stephen shook hands with the mayor and Frank Smith, then caught sight of Callie from the corner of his eye. He came over to her at once, his hand out, laughter wrinkles around his eyes. "Callie! I had no idea you were here."

Callie caught a glimpse of Sheila watching them anxiously and felt relieved that she could genuinely say, "It's been too long, Stephen, but you know how these things go. Busy, busy."

"With too many things that don't really matter, huh?" Stephen held her hand, squeezing. "Last month a friend of mine keeled over while golfing. Heart attack. Nothing they could do anymore. He died there, on the course. Gets you thinking."

His gaze wandered to Amber, who was patting Daisy again, and for a moment Callie wondered if Stephen was the one pushing for the engagement, not Sheila like they all had simply assumed. Maybe the sudden death of his friend had reminded Stephen that life was short and family mattered most of all?

But had he taken the time to talk to Amber and find out what she wanted, instead of arranging for a connection he thought was best?

Sheila appeared beside them, saying, "Brenda Brink left, maybe for the restroom? Could you find her, Callie, and bring her back here? Dorry will be making her grand entrance soon, and she'll be annoyed if all guests aren't present."

Although Callie sensed she was being sent away to end her conversation with Stephen, she accepted the task with a smile and left the room, walking down the hallway to where a door led to the restroom and kitchens. The Christmas trees spread an invigorating scent of pine, mixing with aftershave and perfume left in the wake of the arriving guests.

It was so quiet. Nobody seemed to be around.

Callie remembered Leadenby hadn't been present at the party either and turned to the conservatory door to find him and see if he had changed out of his stained shirt as Sheila had asked. Annoyance over something as simple as a shirt had to be avoided on an afternoon like this.

Opening the door leading into the conservatory, Callie caught raised voices.

Brenda Brink said, "I can't do it. I just can't. I never wanted this in the first place. I told you before."

And Leadenby's baritone countered, "If you don't tell her, I will. Today, at the tea party."

"You can't do that. Don't you care at all about ruining my entire life?"

Callie cringed to hear the heartfelt emotion in the woman's shaking voice and retreated quickly. She had no business intruding upon this very personal moment. Brenda would realize people were waiting for her and would come back of her own accord.

Callie returned to where the others were gathered. Sheila gave her a questioning look, and Callie shrugged to suggest she didn't know where Brenda was.

Sheila's eyes narrowed. She rushed to the door as if hurrying to keep a naughty child from playing a prank.

But before she reached the door, it opened, and Dorothea Finster appeared on the threshold, fragile and regal at the same time in a black gown with a gray pearl necklace. She walked into the room with her head held high as if she still had a nanny telling her not to slouch. Mrs. Keats was right behind her, a protective force. The nervous twitch around the housekeeper's lips suggested she had an idea of what was about to play out here.

Callie guessed the staff knew about the new will being presented today. If only because of rumors in the household, perhaps.

Dorothea halted in the middle of the room and studied the buffet. A smile formed around her thin lips. "Well done, Iphy. Very well done."

Iphy nodded in recognition of the compliment.

Behind Dorothea, Brenda Brink squeezed herself into the room and slunk along the wall to find a place beside Mr. and Mrs. Moore. Callie had expected her to be red in the face after her fierce argument with Leadenby, but she was deathly pale. Her nervous swallowing suggested she was about to burst into tears and only controlled herself with an enormous effort.

Dorothea said, "I suppose you're all very curious why I invited you here. I'm normally not someone who enjoys the dramatic, but Iphy's book teas gave me the idea. Let's play this like a scene from a classic mystery. You have all gathered to hear what I have to say. It concerns my will."

The mere word *will* sent a silent ripple of excitement

through the room. Mr. Moore slipped to the edge of his seat, while Frank Smith uncrossed his legs and leaned forward with his hands on his knees.

Dorothea swayed a moment, and Mrs. Keats stepped up to her employer as if she wanted to support her.

But Dorothea raised a hand to stop the intervention. She stood stiffly and continued, "I've had enough time to think about my fortune and what to do with it. After all, my husband is dead, and I never had any children."

"I hope you feel," Sheila spoke up, "that Stephen and I have been like children to you."

"When?" Dorothea's blue eyes flashed. "You were never here. You were always in some foreign city, meeting important people and buying designer clothes. You kept Amber from me like you were afraid she might love this place and want to live here instead of being dragged all over the world and dumped into international boarding schools."

Amber shrank under these fierce words. She glanced at her mother.

Sheila's face turned fiery red. "My daughter had the benefit of living in some of the most beautiful and stimulating places on earth. She went to the best schools that prepared her for a successful career."

"I never missed anything," Amber said quickly, casting a worried look at her mother.

But Callie remembered Amber's loving descriptions of the short stays at Haywood Hall and wondered if she was telling the truth. She had caught a sort of longing in the girl's words as if she *had* missed something: closeness, intimacy, family.

And the successful career Sheila spoke about had probably all been planned out by her, while Amber had different ambitions, wanting to study graphic design, learn a language in a foreign country, and see the world before ever taking a nine-to-five job. But would she get the chance to do any of that?

Sheila seemed to realize she had sounded too defensive and quickly said to Dorothea, "I appreciate that you love Amber so much you want her happiness above all. We all do. I suggest you sit down for a moment, as you're clearly tired, and allow Ben to cut the cake and pass around some of it to our guests. I'm sure they'd all like a treat before we continue this."

Dorothea seemed shocked by Sheila stealing her moment this way, but Ben, clearly anxious to keep the atmosphere pleasant, had stepped forward already and grabbed the knife that had been put beside the cake.

Sheila nudged Amber to go stand beside him. Looking confused, Amber did.

Ben lifted the knife and let it hover over the cake's base tier. "It's so pretty, it's almost a shame to cut into it." He glanced at Iphy.

Iphy wasn't watching him but studying Amber, as if she expected to see something special in her face. Understanding of what the clue in the cake was, perhaps? But what could Amber do to stop this?

Callie realized she was holding her breath.

"Go on," Sheila nudged Ben. "It's all right."

Ben cut into the cake. He picked up a plate from the stack and scooped out a piece of cake, intending to give it to Amber. Then he froze. "Hey, it appears to be hollow and . . ." He fell silent, flushing down to his collar.

Sheila smiled in satisfaction, while Dorothea seemed confused. Mrs. Keats touched her arm and whispered that she had to sit down, but the elderly lady waved her off, keeping her eyes on the cake and what Ben had found in it.

Ben put the plate with the slice of cake aside so he could use both hands to carefully pull out the ring box. Its blue velvet was still clean, not smudged by any frosting. It rested regally on the palm of his hand. Ben didn't have to ask what it was, as the name of the jeweler was printed prominently on top in golden letters.

Sheila flashed a look at Dorothea.

Callie felt a cold shiver go down her spine. Sheila's words that Dorothea wanted Amber to be happy seemed to take on new meaning. After this moment, where Ben would ask Amber to marry him, Dorothea could hardly cut her family out of her will. It would be embarrassing toward Ben, a social disaster, especially in front of the distinguished local guests. They were all watching with open curiosity.

How clever of Sheila. How well planned. She probably believed she was helping everybody with this move. But was she really?

Ben held the ring box in his hand, staring at it with a slightly panicked look.

Callie thought she heard Amber whisper "Don't," but she wasn't sure if she'd heard it or it was just her imagination in these tense moments. Her heart was pounding and her throat was dry.

Ben looked at Sheila, his brown eyes wide.

Sheila nodded.

One regal, commanding nod.

Ben clicked the ring box open.

Callie felt trapped in a bad dream, the kind where you want to stop what's happening but you can't. It wasn't her place to say or do anything, but still . . . if people were just friends, you couldn't simply force them to make more out of it and get engaged, right?

Ben stared into the box. "It's empty," he croaked.

Amber looked as well. Her facial expression didn't change. She just stood, pale and vulnerable. Her hand came up to touch the pendant on her necklace.

"It's empty," Ben repeated. Suddenly anger flashed in his brown eyes, and he turned on Sheila. "Is this your idea of a message? Let me know in the presence of others that I'm not wanted in your family?"

He clanked the empty ring box onto the table and seemed ready to rush out of the room.

"No!" Sheila cried, horrified. "The ring was in the box. I showed it to Callie. She saw it. She put it inside the cake."

Sheila now focused on Callie, her tone pleading. "You saw it, right? You . . ."

Then her expression changed and she whispered, "You

took it! You wanted this to go wrong. You never could stand . . ."

"Sheila!" Stephen stepped up and arrested his wife's arm. Callie winced under the pressure he seemed to apply. Stephen's voice was cold and controlled. "I'm sure this is all a misunderstanding that neither Ben nor Callie can help."

Callie had found her voice again. "Sheila's right. She showed the ring to me. I placed the box inside the cake. I'm sure that when I put it in the cake, the ring was still in it."

"And then you finished the cake?" Stephen was still grasping Sheila, who didn't seem able to speak at all.

"Yes. Well, partly. Ben arrived and I stepped out of the room for a moment to greet him. Then I went back in and . . ."

Callie's thoughts came to a crashing halt. She saw herself step up to the table again to find the little sparkly ice crystal lying on the table's surface. Fallen off the cake. Not attached properly?

Or the evidence that someone had tampered with the cake, with the ring box inside, while she had been out of the room? She had left for only a few minutes. Could it be?

*Daring, but possible.*

She said in a breathless voice, "I was out of the room for a few minutes. Someone could have come in through the French windows and taken the ring."

Stephen frowned. "How would that person have known the ring was in the cake?" His pointed look at Sheila seemed to say, *I didn't even know it, so how could someone else have known?*

"If he or she had been watching us." Callie was determined to press her point. "I can't vouch that no one was outside looking in while Sheila showed me the ring. How about you?" She gave Sheila a probing stare.

"No, of course not," Sheila said, "but it doesn't seem likely that . . ."

Callie cut her off. "I even saw a van driving away."

The moment she said it, she realized how dangerous this was. She was mentioning something she had seen without having any idea whether it was related to the disappearance of the engagement ring. But it was too late now to take back her words.

"What van?" Stephen asked.

"Of course!" Sheila cried. "The chimney sweep. I said from the moment I saw him here that Dorry should never have hired him."

"Cole is not involved," Amber said quickly. Her voice was strained, and Ben cast her a look that was both surprised and slightly suspicious.

Sheila threw her daughter a warning glance. "That is for the police to decide. We mustn't touch anything here. They can determine whether his fingerprints are on the box."

"Ben already touched the box. Any prints must be smeared." Amber sounded almost relieved.

Ben scanned her expression as if he wondered why she was so defensive of this Cole character. Callie was curious about that herself.

"I'll call the police." Sheila wanted to walk to the old-fashioned black phone on the sideboard.

But Dorothea said, "I'll determine whether the police are notified. This is my house."

It was such a clear slap to Sheila's face that Callie winced again. She noticed that the mayor's wife was following everything with keen attention, as if she were watching a good soap opera. The only thing missing was the popcorn.

Dorothea spat at Sheila, "You meddled in my tea party with your ridiculous idea of an impromptu engagement. You deserve every second of embarrassment you get out of this. Amber is not getting engaged to Ben. Today or any other day."

"You don't decide that," Sheila whispered, deathly pale now.

"Neither do you," Dorothea countered without feeling. "Now let us go on. I want to tell you about my will. That's why we're here."

The mayor cleared his throat. "If you'll allow me, Mrs. Finster, Mrs. Du Bouvrais has a point about the police. If your ring was stolen, the thief could be on his way out of state with it as we speak. You should notify the sheriff so he can do something about it."

Callie checked her watch. "More than an hour passed since I saw the van drive off. If he . . ."

"It wasn't Cole," Amber said. There was a desperate insistence in her eyes. "I'm sure the ring will turn up some-where around the house."

"It can't," Sheila said. "It was in the box when I gave it to Callie, and she put it in the cake. At least she says so."

Callie held her chin high. "Do you want to search me?"

"This is ridiculous." Stephen quickly intervened. "Of course Callie wouldn't steal from us."

"Why is she here then? Lost her job?" Sheila's face crumbled as her voice rose in a desperate attempt to drag someone else down in her own humiliation. "She always believed she . . ."

Sheila didn't say it, but they could all finish her sentence. Callie had believed she would become mistress of Haywood Hall.

Callie fought tears, trying to save some shred of her dignity. She had been so happy to return to Heart's Harbor, spend time with Great Aunt Iphy, and even help out at the Book Tea, but this tea party was a catastrophe. How could she show her face again when people started talking about this?

And she could see by the look on Mrs. Moore's face that the mayor's wife was already mentally calling all of her friends to share the juicy details of this event. The news would be all over town before day's end.

# Chapter Four

"I don't want the police brought in," Dorothea said with determination. "Amber is right, the ring will probably turn up again somewhere around the house."

"How can you treat this so callously?" Sheila's eyes were wide with disbelief. "This is a family heirloom."

"Yes, from *my* family. It doesn't belong to you."

"It belongs to Stephen," Sheila said, "and as I'm married to him, it also belongs to me. I was the last woman to wear it."

Dorothea said, "I want to talk about my will. It's by far the most important document I have ever signed in my life. It will determine the future of Haywood Hall, the seat of my family for many generations."

Her voice picked up strength as she continued, "This is not just a valuable old house. It's not just an example of a certain style or a family legacy. It's a place where people loved and laughed, experienced hard times and pulled through, overcame difficulties and proved themselves stronger than they had ever believed they could be. This place represents so many things I care for."

The elderly lady's passionate words resonated inside Callie. Haywood Hall had always been a place that felt like home to her.

"As a town, we value the nearness of a grand place like Haywood Hall," Mr. Moore said weightily. "And of you as a respected citizen. We think it's very important that the citizens who have a certain position in life contribute to the community."

Callie couldn't believe that the mayor would so blatantly fish for money, but Dorothea's expression was unmoved.

Frank Smith leaned forward. "Haywood Hall would be nothing without the town. If the town thrives, it's good for you as well. We need to update Main Street if we want to keep the tourists coming in. You could open up a wing of this house to the public. Those tourists could also benefit you. Just a few nice lampposts along Main Street, a bigger parking lot. Even a tour that takes the tourists past all highlights?"

"He means past his business," Stephen whispered to Callie. She had to fight a wobbly smile.

Smith continued, "We have to stand together to save the town for future generations. I'm sure that you want to contribute to that. If you leave us some kind of fund, we can even name something after you. The community center. A street if you like. I'm sure the mayor agrees."

Moore nodded eagerly, and Mrs. Moore said, "Dorothea Finster Street has a very nice ring to it."

Dorothea's gaze slipped to Brenda Brink. "Is there any-thing you want to ask for?"

Brenda was still pale and upset, it seemed, but she held her head up. "I'm sure that whatever the school needs can be raised by old-fashioned fundraising."

Smith burst into laughter. "A little old bake sale is not going to get you that climbing wall you were talking about on the way over here. Don't act so self-righteous, Brenda. You also want something out of this."

"No. I don't want anything from her." Brenda said it soft and flat, but still the words had a sting to them.

Callie wondered why Brenda seemed to dislike Doro-thea Finster so much. What could a schoolteacher and an old widow without children or grandchildren in that school have clashed about?

Dorothea blinked a moment. Sheila's surprise with the ring in the cake had already thrown her off balance, and now the people who had been cast as players in her little last will performance were not acting in the way she had wanted them to. Admittedly, Moore and Smith seemed eager enough to cash in, but Brenda Brink was obviously not game.

And would Dorothea really leave her fortune to a town rather than her family? Maybe she had never liked Sheila, but Stephen was her only relative, and Dorothea seemed genuinely fond of Amber.

Dorothea brushed her forehead with a delicate hand, and Iphy said quietly, "Now it's time to sit down." She nodded at Mrs. Keats, and together they moved a chair behind the elderly lady, who sank into it. Her hands were shaking, and she put them on the armrests to hide it.

"I'll pour you some tea." Iphy went over to the table and picked up the teapot, pouring the tea into a cup with a gold rim. "I mixed a special blend this morning. It's like Earl Grey but with more citrus. I'm sure you'll love it. Very refreshing."

She handed the cup to Dorothea, who sipped carefully.

Iphy said, "I'll also pass around some tea to the other guests. Besides this special Earl Grey, I have a green tea flavored with berries and even a white tea that has a hint of grapes. Who wants what?"

A clear chiming filled the room, and Smith dug into his pocket. His brows shot up as he studied the screen of his cell phone. He rose from his seat. "An important call I must take," he muttered, and left the room in a rush.

Iphy invited Mrs. Moore and Brenda to the buffet, pointing out the black-tie cupcakes and the brownies with little marzipan decorations representing a small sheet of paper with handwriting on it. Iphy had to have used a toothpick or something to get such small lettering on them.

Callie handed out the green tea with berry flavoring and inhaled its scent. The warm fruity notes, mixed with something sweet like rose petals, calmed her fluttering heartbeat. Iphy was so right to let things settle a little before they continued. This will announcement obviously meant a lot to Dorothea, and for her sake, they should try to make it memorable—in a good way.

Glancing around, Callie noticed that Sheila and Ben had also left the room. Was Ben still bursting with anger about the empty ring box, and did he want to leave the house in a rush? Was Sheila pleading with him to stay and not make this any worse?

Iphy appeared by her side, whispering, "Are you sure the ring was in the box when you put it inside the cake?"

"Yes. I saw it with my own eyes: Sheila shut the box with the ring inside it and gave it to me."

"There weren't two boxes?"

Callie resisted the urge to roll her eyes. "You read too many books. Why would Sheila swap boxes? She wants Ben to propose to Amber."

"I suppose you're right." Iphy sighed, looking worried. "I'm just afraid it won't be a simple matter of the ring turning up again somewhere around the house. It's very valuable. And some people would do anything for money."

Callie wasn't sure if her great aunt was speaking in general or meant someone in particular.

Amber stood a few feet away from them, not having taken any tea or sweet treats. She nervously gnawed on her lower lip. Then she also dashed out of the room.

Dorothea in her chair looked older and more breakable, her shoulders slumping, as if she realized that her grand will reading had taken a terrible turn.

Iphy picked the biggest black-tie cupcake, put it on a plate, and carried it over to her. "You should really try one of these. They're delicious."

Putting her hand on the elderly lady's arm, she squeezed. "It will be fine, I'm sure."

Dorothea looked up at her. "Where's Sheila? I don't want her to call the police."

"I'll go look for her," Callie offered. She was curious what was happening outside the room.

Glancing back at Dorothea, she saw that Daisy had seated herself beside the elderly lady and was looking up at her with knowing eyes, as if she sensed her distress and wanted to comfort her.

Dorothea leaned down to pat the dog, relaxation slipping across her tense face.

Smiling to herself, Callie left the room.

In the hallway, everything was still deceptively quiet, but there was a cold draft that hadn't been there before. The front door stood ajar.

Callie went over and opened it so she could see outside. A chill bit into her face. As daylight faded, the wind had picked up again. Its gusts sent fine flocks of snow drifting in front of her.

From the right, a figure came toward the house, walking fast and panting. Squinting into the snow drift, she couldn't make out who it was at first. Then, as he took on a solid shape, she recognized Ben. He stepped up to her. The shoulders of his dark suit were stained with snow. He held his hands clenched together as if trying to warm them.

"I needed a breath of fresh air," he said in a tight voice. His brown eyes were full of disbelief and hurt.

"Don't take this out on Amber," Callie pleaded hurriedly. "I'm sure she knew nothing about her mother's plan to have you propose to her."

Ben didn't reply. He brushed past her into the house and stood next to one of the tall Christmas trees flanking the stairs. He stared at the twinkling lights without seeming to see anything.

Callie wondered if she had really heard Amber say "Don't." Was Ben upset about that? About realizing that Amber hadn't wanted him to propose to her? Had he concluded she didn't care for him at all?

But Amber did care. She had never meant to hurt Ben's feelings, Callie was sure.

A door slammed, and Frank Smith reappeared, rubbing his hands. "Just my secretary about a small matter. Nothing important. I told her I was out for a meeting and didn't want to be disturbed, but she forgot. You know how it is before you close down for Christmas. Everybody wants something. Sorry to have disrupted . . ."

He glanced from Callie to Ben and back. "Is it still going to happen? The will reading, I mean?"

His mere interest in the money disgusted Callie, but she tried to sound normal. "I suppose so. But it will be up to Dorothea."

Frank Smith nodded. "Town renovations are really important. We have to stay up-to-date and compete with other towns. Too many young people are already leaving because they don't see a future here. It's really sad to drive around town and see more and more properties empty. If we want to keep Heart's Harbor alive, we need money."

Without waiting for their response to his plea, he went back into the room.

Callie wasn't quite sure what to make of Smith. His determination to fight for the town's survival was a good thing, of course, and he seemed to have the interests of more people than himself at heart. At the same time, he didn't seem to sense the pressure resting on this moment, or care for the feelings of the others involved.

Ben still stood, kneading his hands, as if he were trying to gather courage to face the people inside. His labored breathing filled the quiet hallway. Callie felt sorry for him but didn't know what exactly to say. She didn't want to put the blame on Sheila, who was also totally devastated by the turn things had taken. For a self-conscious woman like her, this humiliation in front of other people was a disaster that would linger in her mind for a long time to come.

Then a piercing scream tore through the silence.

Ben broke to life with a jerk and glanced at Callie. "That's Amber!" He rushed into the corridor leading to the kitchens.

Callie's heart pounded as she followed him. "Are you sure it came from there? I think . . ."

The door leading to the conservatory burst open, and Amber ran at them. Her face was contorted, and her voice came out strangled as she cried, "It's Mr. Leadenby. He's . . . dead!"

Ben grabbed her shoulders. "Dead?" he echoed. "What do you mean?"

"He's lying on the floor and . . ."

"Maybe he had a heart attack or something. Let's look." Ben wanted to push past Amber, but she stopped him. "No. Don't go in there. You don't want to see that. The police have to come *now*. He's not just dead. He was stabbed."

She broke into wild sobbing, and Ben grabbed her again and held her close against him. He patted her back, brushed her hair, and muttered soothing words.

Callie stood with her hand pressed to her throat. The first thought that went through her head, quite illogically, was that Leadenby had asked her to come see his orchids and she hadn't. That now she could never see them with him. Ever.

She hadn't seen him in years, and even as a child she hadn't been close to him, but to her, Leadenby was a part of Haywood Hall and her perfect memories of the place, and the idea that he could be dead, gone, torn away from them, was terrible.

At the same time, her mind reeled with the idea that he had been stabbed, murdered. This wasn't a natural death, a sad case of someone dying, perhaps under strain but not by any foul play. No, someone had deliberately stabbed the poor man. Had consciously killed him.

Why?

Leadenby seemed like the type who wouldn't hurt a fly, who wasn't in any trouble with anybody.

*That is, except . . .*

He had been arguing with Brenda Brink shortly before he died. When Callie had tiptoed away, she had left the two of them alone. Brenda had shown up again later, pale and distressed. Leadenby hadn't returned. Had Brenda stabbed him? To prevent him from coming in for the tea party and revealing her secret, as Leadenby had threatened?

It was an enormous accusation against someone she hardly knew, and Callie went cold at the idea of what was about to happen to her. The police would come and question everybody and she would be faced with a choice: tell them what she had overheard, putting Brenda in the hot seat, or keep it to herself, not knowing if she was protecting a murderer.

Leadenby had always been kind to her, and upon seeing him again, the old feeling of warmth had returned. His death could not go unpunished. She'd have to do something to make sure his killer was caught.

Still, her heart kept pounding at the idea of making a statement that would get someone in trouble. Brenda was the same age as Callie, and falling under suspicion of murder could mean facing a long time in jail.

Of course, the police would look at other information: fingerprints, the weapon, means, motive, the whole thing. But having argued with the victim shortly before he died would immediately put Brenda high on the suspect list.

Callie brushed her forehead. In true Agatha Christie style, the will reading had led to murder. But not of the testator or any of the chosen heirs.

*Or...*

She frowned hard.

Could she be sure Leadenby hadn't been one of Dorothea's chosen heirs? The elderly lady had been prevented from reading her will.

If Leadenby was in it, who would inherit his share now? Would it fall back to the other heirs? Did that give them motive? But who were they?

"What's wrong?" Sheila appeared, descending on Ben, who was holding Amber and whispering reassuring words in her ear. "Are you upset about the missing ring, darling? It will be retrieved, I'm sure."

"Leadenby is dead," Amber muttered against Ben's shoulder. "Killed!"

"What?" Sheila looked incredulous. "That can't be." She stood with her head up, nostrils flaring, as if she dared any killer to commit a murder in what would be her home. "I bet it's just one of his tasteless jokes. He always wants to ruin everything."

"Mom, how can you say that when he's dead?" Amber sobbed again.

Callie closed in on the trio. Her knees were wobbly, her gaze fixed on something dark on Sheila's mustard dress. A stain that hadn't been there earlier.

She said softly to Sheila, "I think you know he's dead, Sheila."

Her former friend turned her head and looked at her

with wide eyes. "How can you suggest something like that? How would I know that?"

Callie swallowed. She lifted a hand and pointed at the dark-red smudge on the dress. "Because that wasn't there earlier. And it looks a lot like blood."

# Chapter Five

Sheila glanced down at the spot on her dress. Her face went even paler. She seemed to struggle for something to say. She cast a quick look at Amber, who was still sobbing against Ben's chest.

Then Sheila pulled back her shoulders. "There's a very simple explanation for that. And an innocent one."

Callie cringed under the implied criticism in Sheila's tone. She wanted to apologize for her blunt words in pointing out the possible bloodstain, but then decided not to until Sheila had explained. Leadenby was dead, and Sheila had apparently been near the body. Not panicking and running off to get help like Amber had . . .

Sheila said, "I saw him lying on the floor and thought he was unwell. Fainted or maybe having a heart attack. I walked over quickly and crouched down to check his vitals. I wanted to help him, but it was too late to do anything. Then the blood must have gotten on my dress."

Joy Avon

"And this was before Amber found the body?" Callie asked. "Why didn't you cry out and raise the alarm?"

"I think . . ." Sheila glanced at Amber again. "I think it was after Amber found the body. Because I heard her scream and came straight over here to see what it was."

"But you said nothing when you came in. You acted like you had no idea Leadenby was dead, when in fact you had already seen his body and even established that he was no longer alive?" Callie's mind was reeling, unable to make any sense of Sheila's statements.

Sheila stammered, "I, uh . . . I saw how upset Amber was and didn't want to make it any worse."

Callie shook her head to herself. Something about Sheila's story didn't ring true. But could she really suspect her former friend of having killed Leadenby? Why?

Besides, it seemed inconceivable that straitlaced Sheila would pick up a knife and stab someone. Yes, she had been annoyed with Leadenby's presence, his bumbling behavior, and his refusal to change into something decent for the distinguished guests' arrival, but was that really a reason to kill someone?

Callie also liked to think that Sheila had too much integrity to take another's life.

But then, she hadn't seen her former friend in many years and had no idea how she might have changed. What might have driven her to act out of character?

Amber said in a trembling voice, "I'm all light-headed."

Ben clutched her tighter, as if he was afraid she would faint and slip away from his grasp.

"You'd better lie down, darling," Sheila said. "You need to recover from this shock."

Ben said, "I'll take her up to her room."

Sheila nodded. "I'm coming with you. She needs a sedative to calm down."

"I don't want a pill," Amber protested.

"Nonsense." Sheila patted her daughter's shoulder. "You just need to sleep a little. When you wake up, you'll feel much better."

Callie raised a hand to stop them from simply walking away. "What about the police? They'll want to talk to everybody. Probably to Amber first, since she discovered the body."

"The police?" Sheila echoed, eyes wide, as if it hadn't occurred to her at all that a murder should be reported to the police.

"Yes. The conservatory is a crime scene now. Nothing can be touched or moved there. The police will have to come out here right away and take care of everything. They have to secure the area so nothing is lost."

Sheila seemed to want to protest. Callie could see the alarm in her eyes: *Police in my home? While there are guests here?* The social disaster.

Callie pressed, "If we don't call them right away, they might conclude we had something to hide. If evidence does get lost, Dorothea could be found liable. It is her home, after all."

"It must have been a burglar," Sheila suggested feebly.

"In the daytime? With guests around? All their cars are parked right in front of the house. Besides, what would there be to steal in the conservatory? There's nothing of value there. Just lots of plants, I imagine."

"Maybe the burglar wanted to come in through the conservatory doors so he'd go unnoticed while we were all in the sitting room listening to the will reading. He wanted to go via the conservatory into the rest of the house and take whatever he could grab quickly. However, Leadenby was in the conservatory and saw him. Then the burglar had to stab him to get away."

"Wouldn't he just have turned and run? Leadenby wasn't the youngest man. Why would the burglar have assumed he couldn't outrun an old man? Resorting to violence seems so drastic. Unnecessary."

Sheila seemed to scramble for an answer. "Leadenby recognized him. That's it. He saw the burglar's face. It was a local. Leadenby could have turned him in to the police. So he had to act, lash out and silence him. Forever."

Callie wanted to protest that these were all very far-fetched assumptions and that, even if it had been a burglar, the police would still have to know about Leadenby's death. But before she could say anything, Stephen came into the hallway. He said quietly, "The police are on their way."

Sheila glared at him. "Did you call them? How could you do that? Didn't you hear Dorothea say she didn't want police in her house?"

"That was about the missing ring. Now we have a murder on our hands. And I didn't call. The mayor did."

"How did Mr. Moore know that the police needed to be called?" Callie asked at once.

"He heard Amber screaming, and his wife overheard something about someone being dead."

*Aha.* Mrs. Moore had apparently sneaked to the door upon hearing the scream and had listened in on their conversation in the hallway.

Callie flushed. Had Mrs. Moore also heard about the bloodstain on Sheila's dress? Would word of it get around, branding Sheila a murderer before anything about Leadenby's sudden death had been properly investigated?

Cringing at the idea, Callie glanced at Sheila, but she didn't seem unduly worried or upset. She just stood there like a statue, posture straight and unmovable in her indignation. "Amber's going to bed anyway," she said. "The police can talk to her later. She's not feeling well. I'm not letting her stand around until she faints."

"Let's go." Ben ushered Amber toward the foot of the stairs to take her up to her room, supporting her as she gingerly put one foot in front of the other. Sheila turned on her heel and followed them. Her hand on the railing clenched a moment, turning her knuckles white. But her voice was calm as she repeated that Amber should sleep a little and would feel better then.

In a low, rushed tone, Stephen said to Callie, "Is Leadenby really dead?"

"I haven't seen his body myself, but Sheila checked on him and she says he is, so it must be true."

"Sheila was in there with . . . *she* screamed?" Stephen seemed confused now.

"No. Amber found the body, but apparently Sheila had already been in the conservatory as well." Callie realized how lame it sounded. The police would never buy this.

Stephen rubbed his forehead. "Maybe I'd better call a lawyer."

"Do you think you need one?"

He shrugged. "You never know. I have no idea how the local law operates around here, but . . . maybe they'll simply go with the first clue they can find?"

Callie held his gaze, trying to read the emotion in his eyes. "And that first clue would be?"

Stephen sighed. He looked down with a frown. His fingers played with the leather band of his wristwatch, pulling it up, pushing it down, pulling it up, pushing it down.

"Stephen?" Callie pressed. "What are you thinking?"

Keeping his eyes on the floor, he seemed to search for the right words to phrase his concern. "When we came to stay here, Sheila took charge of the household. It's her way. Dorothea wasn't really pleased with it, and Leadenby took it even worse. He still saw us as the children of old to whom he told far-fetched stories about the estate. He didn't take Sheila seriously, didn't listen when she asked something, and it made her mad."

Callie tilted her head, trying to understand the implication of his word choice. "Mad? You mean, angry to the point of lashing out? I had the impression that Sheila just thought Leadenby was an old fool. Yes, his obstinate behavior seemed to frustrate her perfect little tea party here, but . . ."

Stephen looked up with a jerk. "Perfect little tea party? This was Dorothea's will reading. She was going to decide all of our lives!"

Callie was shocked by the violent feeling behind his words, in his gesture as he reached up to rake back his hair. His normally friendly face was contorted with an emotion she couldn't quite place. Anxiety?

Fear?

"But . . . you have your own lives. Whatever Dorothea was about to decide, what did it matter to you?"

Sudden suspicions raced through her. Maybe Stephen had financial problems and had hoped for help from Dorothea? Maybe Sheila knew nothing about those problems yet and Stephen had hoped he could keep it that way?

Maybe Stephen was afraid to tell Sheila about mistakes he had made and hurt their marriage? Had this will reading been his last chance to save his entire future?

Outside a siren resounded, drawing near. Stephen startled upright. "That was fast," he whispered. "Very fast. As if they were in the neighborhood already, as if they knew!"

He turned away from her with a jolt and disappeared into the back of the house.

The siren stopped abruptly, and moments later the front doorbell rang. Callie looked at the door to the sitting room, expecting Mrs. Keats to appear to answer the door. But nobody stirred. Maybe the housekeeper was tending to Dorothea? Several shocks so close together had to have shaken the elderly lady.

*Seems to be up to me, then.* Callie took a deep breath and stepped forward. The door's brass handle felt cold in her palm. She struggled to pull the heavy door open.

"Good afternoon." A tall man with dark hair smiled at her. His black leather jacket hung open, revealing a checkered flannel shirt. Black jeans and hiking boots completed this sporty ensemble. "There's a problem here?"

Callie glanced past him to find a large black-and-white police car parked right in front of the steps. The blue lights on top were still flashing and reflected in the silvery Christmas decorations on the steps' railings.

She asked, "Umm, you're with the police?"

The man glanced down at his casual clothes. "Yeah, sorry about that. I was about to go skating with my nephews when the call came in. The mayor was rather vague about what had happened, so I just thought I'd drop by and see what the matter was. Probably a misunderstanding, right? I can't imagine a dead body at an old lady's tea party."

Callie now detected two blond heads behind the window in the back of the police car. Little faces were pressed against the window in an attempt to take in the entirety of the impressive house.

"Those are your nephews?" she asked, horrified at the idea of children near a crime scene.

"Yeah, Jimmy and Tate." The man's face split in a wide grin. "They think they're the fastest skaters in the world. I let them win, of course."

"Of course. But uh, Sheriff, don't you think–"

He raised a hand to stop her. "Deputy. The sheriff is out of town to visit his in-laws. I thought everybody around here knew that." He studied her with renewed interest.

"I haven't been here in years. And when I did drop by regularly, I can't remember ever having anything to do with the law."

He grinned again, little laugh lines around his brown eyes. "Good for you." He reached out his hand. "Deputy Falk, at your service."

Callie put her hand in his. His grasp was warm and reassuring, a sharp contrast with the cold feeling inside about Leadenby's sudden death. "Callie Aspen. I'm here with my great aunt to organize the tea party for Mrs. Finster. But I'm afraid the mayor was right when he called you. We do have a dead body here."

Deputy Falk squeezed her hand. "I'm sorry to hear that. Dorothea? She's not the youngest, of course, and the strain of entertaining guests . . . not to mention Christmas. All the fuss seems to have a bad effect on some people."

It didn't sound like the deputy was a big fan of the season. "Not Mrs. Finster, no," Callie rushed to explain. "Fortunately. But I'm afraid it wasn't a natural death either. Mr. Leadenby was stabbed."

Falk let go of her hand. "Stabbed?" He glanced back at

the police car as if he was worried the words had drifted over to the two little boys inside.

The window rolled down, and a high-pitched voice called, "Are we going now? We want to skate! And you promised us hot cocoa!"

"And cookies!" another voice added.

"I'll have to call my sister to come get the kids." Falk pulled a cell phone from his pocket. "And I'll have to get some people in here to take pictures of the body and check for fingerprints and everything. Plus a doctor to establish the cause of death. I mean, he might look like he was stabbed, but we do need more official results for the investigation."

He looked her over. "What a thing to happen so shortly before Christmas." He narrowed his eyes. "Are you OK? You look very pale. Maybe you should sit down or something."

He glanced back at the police car and the two blond heads now sticking out the rolled-down window. One boy wore a blue knitted cap, the other a yellow one. They looked a lot alike, but one was obviously a little older. The door opened a crack, as if the boys weren't quite sure whether diving out was a risk worth taking with their uncle holding access to the promised treats.

"Stay there!" Falk called to them at once. Keeping his eyes on the boys, he said to Callie, "I'd go in with you so you could sit down if it wasn't for the kids."

"I understand."

"Yes," Falk spoke into the phone, "it's me. I've got a case. Something serious. Can you come and get Jimmy and Tate? No, I can't go skating with them now. Yes, I know you're at the hairdresser's. But they can't stay here. This is . . ."

He fell silent. "What?" He checked his watch. "Fifteen minutes? Yes, I understand you can't run around with curlers in, but . . ."

Callie reached out and put her hand on his arm to draw his attention. "They want hot cocoa, right? I can take them into the kitchen and give them some, with cookies."

He nodded at her and spoke into the phone, "Fifteen minutes is fine, then. But not longer. This is serious business here. What? No, I'm not . . ."

His face flushed. "Just come out here, OK? Dorothea Finster's estate. And don't mention it to anybody at the hairdresser's!"

He disconnected and looked at Callie. "She thinks I'm trying to get out of taking care of the boys. She heard a female voice, she said. Well, you can imagine the rest."

His sister thought he was dating someone while he pretended to be looking after her kids? Did Deputy Falk have that kind of reputation? He was good-looking enough to turn heads, she supposed.

Callie focused on the boys in the car and quickly observed, "A bit late in the day to go skating with them."

"They wanted to skate by the light of the lanterns. Besides, Tate is too young to skate for hours. It's just for fun."

"I see. If your sister is going to take fifteen minutes to get here, I'll take them inside now."

"Yes, but you're sure they won't see anything . . . ? Peggy would never forgive me if they did."

"I'd never forgive myself if they did. But the body is in the conservatory, and I'll take them straight into the kitchen."

"Thanks, that's very nice of you. I'll go get them."

Falk trotted to the police car and opened the door wide. The two boys tumbled out of the back seat. The bigger one picked up some snow and started to shower it over the other one, who screamed and then picked up his own handful to throw back at his older brother.

Falk grabbed each by a shoulder and marched them up the steps. "Now this is a very fancy house," he warned them in a stern voice, "so you'd better behave yourselves. You don't touch anything and you do exactly as this nice lady says. You're getting hot cocoa and cookies, but only if you're good."

The bigger boy looked at Callie. "Do you live here?" he asked in awe.

Callie shook her head. Judging by his height, she'd say he was about six. The other one had to be about four. He seemed a little shy, trying to hide behind Falk's legs.

"Do you work here?" The elder's expression scrunched up. "Your dress isn't for working."

"We're having a very fancy tea party here, so even though I'm working, I did dress up."

70

Callie added to the deputy, "The tea party had an Agatha Christie theme, so Great Aunt Iphy asked me to put on something festive and appropriate for the 1920s feel." Glancing down, she felt uncomfortable thinking of poor Leadenby dead in the conservatory.

The smaller boy stepped forward and offered her a hand still dusted with snow. "Cocoa and cookies," he said in a commanding tone.

Callie had to smile at his sudden audacity and took his hand. His older brother was too dignified for that and walked beside her, cocking his head to take in everything around them. "You have two trees!" he exclaimed. He ran over and reached out to a glittery bauble, then seemed to remember Falk's words and retracted his hand as if burned. He scanned the empty spaces underneath the trees. "But there aren't any presents here. Won't you have presents?"

"I'm sure they'll be put there later. It's not Christmas Eve yet, right?"

"At the community center, the presents are already under the tree. They're all wrapped up in silver and blue. I don't know who they're for. Nobody lives there. And the mayor doesn't need them. He has enough, Miss Brink is always saying. She's our teacher."

Falk followed them and whispered, "Can I leave them with you now and go find the . . . what I'm here for?"

"Of course." She glanced at him over her shoulder. "I think I got the best end of the deal."

Falk smiled at her a moment, a dimple appearing in his

right cheek, then disappeared into the room where the others were probably still waiting. The moment he went in, a shadow slipped out and came for Callie.

It was Daisy, rubbing her head against Callie's leg as if to say she had missed her.

"A doggy!" the smallest boy cried, and he crouched down to pat Daisy. She let him and even closed her eyes as his little fingers scratched behind her ears.

"She's cute," the older boy said, looking on. "Is she yours?"

"Yes. She can come with us into the kitchen."

"Can she have cocoa too?" the small boy asked.

"No, chocolate is bad for dogs. But she loves to be patted. You can even hold her in your lap if you want to."

\* \* \*

"And then the head fell off, and Mom was really angry." Jimmy reached for another cookie, but Callie pulled the platter out of his reach. "Finish your cocoa," she admonished. He had been so busy telling her all of these stories about what he could make out of snow that he had barely taken a sip.

A quick glance at her watch told her it had been twenty minutes since Falk had called his sister. Did Peggy really think he had been lying about being on a case and was taking the opportunity to woo some female he'd met at the rink? Had his sister decided not to show up at all?

Callie glanced at Tate, who sat with Daisy in his lap,

running his finger again and again across her soft fur. His jeans had patches on the knees, either some impromptu repairs or a precaution to ensure he didn't tear them. Little boys had to go through their clothes fast.

The kitchen door opened, and Falk came in with a woman who was about as tall as he was, but blonde. Her locks were freshly permed, and the scent of the chemicals wafted around her. She gestured at the boys. "Come along, quickly." Her voice was rushed, a little sharp. "I have to find someone else to look after you."

Falk said, "You're done at the hairdresser's now. Where else do you need to go where you can't take them?"

Peggy's eyes flashed at his question. "None of your business. You're ducking out of our agreement. I thought you'd be true to your word."

She looked Callie up and down, and again Callie realized how odd her festive clothing must look. She said quickly, "I'm sorry that the deputy has to work. But I can assure you that it's not pleasant for any one of us that . . . the tea party was interrupted by a crime." She didn't want to mention the word death or murder in front of the children.

Falk's sister pulled the strap of her purse farther onto her shoulder and gestured at the boys again. "Say good-bye to the nice lady."

Tate didn't look at his mother. He kept patting Daisy.

Jimmy remained seated, crossing his arms over his chest. "Why can't you have cocoa with us? There's enough for everybody."

"I thought you wanted to go ice skating. If we don't hurry, it will be too late for that. I'll drop you off. Someone can look after you."

Falk leaned over to his sister, whispering, "You can't just let them loose on their own. Tate's only four."

"I said I'll find someone to look after them. There are enough little old ladies manning those stalls. You'd have known that if you had ever gone there."

"Peggy . . ." Falk protested, but his sister leaned down and took Tate's shoulder. "Put the dog down now."

"It's not just a dog," Jimmy protested from the other side of the table. "She's called Daisy. Can we have a dog too?"

"Yes, Mommy," Tate joined in. "A puppy? Please?"

Peggy looked at Callie. "Can you please remove your dog?"

Callie leaned over to lift Daisy off Tate's lap. He wanted to hold on to the doggy, and his eyes were wide and shiny as he watched her being taken away from him.

Peggy grabbed his shoulder to drag him off the chair and pulled him to the door. "Jimmy!" she admonished her elder son. "Put on your cap. Come on, now, or we're not going ice skating at all. Straight home it is then, and into your rooms."

Jimmy grabbed his knitted cap that he had put on the table and slipped off his chair with a sad expression.

Callie caught the same sadness in Falk's eyes as he watched the threesome leave the kitchen.

Callie said, "I'm really sorry that this whole thing disturbed your skating. They're nice kids."

Falk nodded slowly. "Thanks for looking after them."

"No problem. It took my mind of . . . you know what."

Falk studied her. "Yes, you look a little better now. Do you think you could answer some questions?"

Callie's stomach tightened as she thought of the unpleasantness ahead. Had Falk already seen the bloodstain on Sheila's dress? Had he talked to Brenda Brink?

Would the teacher tell him of her argument with Leadenby of her own accord? Probably not.

"Of course I can answer questions." *Better get it over with.* Callie wanted to follow Falk, but he said, "We can do it here." He gestured for her to sit down at the table again.

Callie seated herself with Daisy in her arms. The doggy seemed to miss the children, as she kept looking at the door through which they had vanished, her ears up as if she were listening for their voices coming back.

"So you organized the tea party here?" Falk said. "For Book Tea on Main Street? I already talked to your great aunt."

Callie nodded. "I'm spending some time here until the new year. Normally I live in Trenton. I can write down the full address for you."

"You great aunt already gave it to me." Falk had pulled out a notebook and was scribbling. "How was the atmosphere before the tea party started? When you were setting everything up?"

"Uh, quite normal, I'd say. Sheila was busy with all the preparations, wanting everything to be perfect." She didn't think she needed to mention Sheila's insistence that Leadenby change out of his stained shirt. It had been a small domestic matter. Normal tension when you were gearing up to receive guests. "I briefly talked to Amber and to Ben, her . . . friend."

"I thought he was her boyfriend? Someone mentioned something about them getting engaged today? During the tea party? But the ring went missing?"

Falk looked up at her. "Mrs. Moore seemed to think it was highly significant, but she couldn't give me any details. Not what kind of ring it was or where it had disappeared to."

"There was a big diamond in the center, surrounded by smaller ones. I'd guess it's valuable. But I only saw it briefly, before I had to put it in the cake."

"*In* the cake?"

"Ben was supposed to cut it and find the ring and then propose to Amber."

"I see." Falk grimaced as if he didn't appreciate such romantic gestures. He shrugged out of his leather jacket. "Too hot in here," he declared, placing it over the back of his chair.

Callie wasn't sure if she should offer him something to drink. Maybe it was inappropriate, since he was on duty?

Falk had opened his mouth to ask another question when the door opened and Sheila appeared on the threshold. "I'd really like to make my statement, Deputy, so I can go take off this dress. I feel quite uncomfortable wearing it with this stain."

Falk seemed to notice the bloodstain for the first time. His eyes narrowed, and he looked as if he was suddenly onto something. "Yes, of course." He rose and nodded at Callie. "We're not done yet. I'll be back here as soon as I've taken Mrs. Du Bouvrais's statement."

"Take your time." Callie leaned back, patting Daisy. "I'm not going anywhere."

Falk left in a rush after Sheila, who strode regally from the room.

Callie wondered why on earth Sheila was drawing attention to the stain on her dress. But maybe she thought Callie would mention it to the police and she'd rather bring it up herself to avoid the impression she had something to hide?

Callie hugged Daisy against her. "What a mess," she whispered. "The ring missing, the party ruined, the will not read and Leadenby . . ."

A knock on the window made her stiffen. She turned her head slowly to see someone standing outside in the snowdrift, gesturing at her.

# Chapter Six

"Amber?" Callie put Daisy on the floor and went to the back door to go out. She looked at the girl, who was shivering in her dress. "What are you doing here? I thought you'd be in bed by now. Your mother's insisting you can't be questioned. Are you sure you're all right?"

"I climbed out of my window and down here to talk to you. I have to talk to you before the police . . ." Amber's face contorted.

Callie looked at the kitchen windows. It was much warmer in there, but there was the risk of Deputy Falk returning and catching them. Where could they go?

Her gaze fell on a shedlike structure nearby, and she gestured for Amber to come with her. Fortunately, Amber had put on sturdy shoes to climb out the window and could walk in the snow. They ducked into the shed and stood side by side in the dimness. It was still chilly in there, but the cold bite of the wind was gone, at least.

Callie listened to Amber's ragged breathing. For a

moment, she wondered what she'd do if Amber confessed to having killed Leadenby. She felt an instinctive liking for this girl, a need to protect her and see her happy. She had already sensed it when they first met on the trip to Vienna. Amber had this . . . hunger for life, this wide-eyed wonder about the world. She deserved to be happy.

Amber said, "The ring. It was so stupid of me. It will look really weird now. The police will never believe me."

"The ring?" Callie echoed. "You want to talk to me about the engagement ring? Not about the murder?"

"No, I have no idea who did that." Amber's voice sounded breathless. Callie couldn't see the girl's expression in the dim light.

Amber said, "I took the ring out of the ring box when I was in the room alone. You had all left for a few moments, and . . . I came in from the outside, through the French doors. I opened the cake again and took the ring out of the box. I didn't want this stupid engagement to take place."

She reached up and pressed a hand against her face. "Dumb, I know. Mom would press for Ben to cut the cake and he'd find the empty box and . . . what a mess. But I only wanted to prevent . . . He doesn't love me. At least I hope he doesn't."

"Do you love him?" Callie asked softly.

"I don't know. I thought for a while that I did. He's kind, you know, considerate and funny. I can talk to him. But . . . I'm not in love with him like . . ." She fell silent.

Callie waited a moment for her to go on, but Amber just stood, clenching her hands together.

Callie said, "So because you aren't sure that you love Ben or that he loves you, you didn't want to get engaged today?"

"Mom just decided it would be perfect. She thought up this whole idea with the cake and the . . . witnesses. That's how it feels, like she invited these people to be witnesses. To make it official so we couldn't take it back."

Amber pressed her hand to her face again. "I don't want to wake up tomorrow and be engaged to Ben . . . I don't want to live a lie."

"You don't have to. Just admit you took the ring and why."

"But I don't have it."

"What?" Callie leaned closer to hear Amber better.

"I don't have it," the girl said with a desperate edge to her voice. "It's gone."

"How is that possible?"

"I took it from the ring box and slipped it into my pocket. I couldn't fit the whole box in my pocket or someone would definitely have noticed, so I put the box back inside the cake. After I talked to you, I went to my room to change for the tea party. Mom was very specific about what I had to wear and . . . I just wanted to please her. I left the ring in the pocket of my jeans, on the bed. When Ben found the empty box and he got so upset, and Mom too, and they started talking about the police, I . . . I went upstairs when there was a pause before Dorothea was going to make the announcement about her will, and I wanted to get the ring to prove it hadn't been stolen. But it wasn't there. I looked on the bed and under it, all over the floor, but it wasn't anywhere."

Amber swallowed audibly. "I wanted to ask Leadenby if he had taken it."

"Because . . ." Callie held her breath.

"Because I thought he needed money and might have taken it. I didn't want to think he was a thief, honestly I didn't, but . . . I couldn't imagine anyone else taking it. Dad and Dorothea knew nothing about the whole engagement plan. Besides, the ring is theirs. Why would they take their own property? But Leadenby . . . I thought sometimes he was jealous of how Dorothea lived here, that she owned the house and he was only a lodger. He said several times that he deserved more than he was getting. I just figured he had taken the ring because he felt entitled to it somehow. When I came into the conservatory to ask him, I saw him on the floor. Dead!" Amber broke into spasmodic crying again.

Callie put a hand on her shoulder. "It'll be all right. Just calm down now. You have to tell the police the truth. About the ring and why you went to see Leadenby. Just be honest about it all. Then it will be fine."

"But where's the ring? Who has it? What if they find it in Leadenby's pocket?"

"Then he took it. What else could they conclude?"

Callie waited for Amber to say something, but the girl was just sniffling and swallowing. She squeezed her shoulder. "You'll be fine. Just tell the deputy everything. He looks like a nice enough person to me."

Amber took a deep breath. "The police will try to hang it on Cole. But he has nothing to do with it."

"Who's Cole?" Callie asked, confused.

"The handyman who was working here this afternoon. You said yourself that you had seen his van leave when you were setting everything up for the tea party. You think he took the ring." Amber suddenly sounded accusing.

"Not at all," Callie said quickly. "I only said what I saw. His van did drive off right after I reentered the room. I never meant to incriminate him. I don't even know him."

"He has nothing to do with it." Amber pulled back, suddenly rigid. "You understand?" Then she turned away and ran out of the shed, fleeing across the snowy terrace to get back to her room.

Callie stared after her. It seemed Amber knew a little more about this Cole the handyman than she wanted to admit. Falk would also sense that and be suspicious.

And what had happened to Amber's faintness after discovering the body? She wasn't in bed resting, but climbing out of windows and running through the snow. Had she merely pretended to be shocked? Had her tears over Leadenby's death been an act?

Callie could hardly believe that. But still she knew Amber wasn't telling the full truth.

Amber wasn't, and Sheila wasn't. And Stephen had acted peculiar as well, saying Dorothea had been about to decide all of their lives. As if, for him, everything was riding on this new will.

It was like everybody had something they were desperate to hide from Falk.

Callie took a deep breath. Speaking of Falk, she had to get back into the kitchen before he returned and found her gone. He would then come after her, while she was the only one present on the scene who genuinely didn't know a thing. Who had landed headfirst in a puzzle with too many pieces.

She left the shed and carefully closed the door.

Looking up at the house, she thought for a moment she saw something moving behind the curtains on the second floor. Someone watching? Someone who had seen her and Amber having a little one-on-one in the shed?

Who? Would he or she tell the police?

Her heart pounding, Callie rushed back to the kitchen. She half expected Falk to be waiting for her there, where he would give her an accusing look and grill her about her disappearance.

But there was nobody but Daisy snuggling in front of the stove.

Callie gave her a cuddle before seating herself at the table again, leaning her hands on the edge and forcing a calm expression so she could face Falk upon his return.

\* \* \*

A few minutes later, Falk breezed in. He halted two steps away from the table and looked at the doormat. "You stepped out?"

Callie looked at the mat and immediately realized her mistake. On the rough surface were several clumps of telltale melting snow. She could have kicked herself for not having thought of that. "It's hot in here. I, uh, I needed some air."

Falk sat down and opened his notebook again. He didn't comment further, even though she had the distinct impression he didn't quite believe her casual lie.

Tapping his pen on the table's edge, he said, "Where were we? Oh, yes, how you experienced the atmosphere before the tea party began. No special tension, hmm?" He gave her a probing stare. "Didn't you notice any tension between Sheila Du Bouvrais and the victim?"

Callie sensed that he already knew something about Sheila's strained relationship with Leadenby—perhaps from Stephen or Sheila herself—and rushed to say, "I'm not sure. I mean, she did tell him off because he was wearing a shirt with stains on it and asked him to change it before the guests arrived, but that seems pretty normal to me. Nothing worth killing over."

"I see." Falk made a few notes.

Callie felt like he was taking too long, not really needing to write down all that much.

Then he looked up at her again. "Do you think Sheila Du Bouvrais is capable of killing someone?"

Not ready for this direct question, Callie took a deep breath. "I don't tend to think most people are capable of killing. Maybe in self-defense?"

"You mean, when cornered? Grabbing the weapon merely to ward someone off?"

Callie nodded.

Falk *hmm*ed. Without looking at her, he asked, "What was Leadenby wearing when you last saw him?"

"The dirty shirt Sheila objected to."

"I see. So he did change." Falk scribbled again. "And you didn't see him at all while the tea party was going on? I understand he didn't show up there?"

"No." Callie took another deep breath as she prepared herself to reveal what she had overheard earlier. "Right before the party began, Sheila noticed that Brenda Brink was missing. She asked me to look for her and send her in so all would be present when Dorothea came down. I went to the conservatory and heard voices. I overheard a snippet of a conversation between Brenda Brink and Leadenby. I left them to it, as . . . it seemed to be private."

"Private? In what way? He lived here at the Hall, and she was the schoolteacher in town. I can't see them having anything to do with each other. Leadenby didn't have kids or grandkids in her class. And I don't think he was the type who wanted to donate to the playground fund. You?"

"Not really, no." Callie twisted her bracelet. Despite her careful consideration of how to handle this tactfully, she really had no idea how to word this in a way that would not immediately incriminate the teacher. "She asked him not to reveal something about her."

Falk sucked in breath. "You're kidding me."

"I wish I was. But I did hear her say something along

the lines of 'You will ruin my entire life.' She sounded really hurt and upset. That's why I didn't go in to tell her the others were waiting for her."

"So Brenda Brink might have stabbed Leadenby," Falk said slowly. "And then she came to the tea party and pretended everything was all right."

Callie couldn't deny Brenda had looked upset when she came into the room. But she didn't say that. "I thought Leadenby was stabbed during the break in the tea party proceedings? After the ring was found to be missing."

"The exact time of death needs to be determined. It can't have been that long ago, because the body was still warm." Falk turned a page in his notebook. "Did you hear anything specific that might tell us what this conversation between the victim and Brenda Brink was about?"

"No. I just know for sure that Leadenby said that if Brenda didn't tell, he would. I think he said, 'Tell her,' so apparently there was a her who needed to know something."

"No names were mentioned? You have no idea to what person they referred?"

"No. Brenda did say she had never wanted it in the first place. That she had told Leadenby before."

"Hmmm." Falk made more notes. "That suggests they had been in touch before. That he had dropped by her place or called her, maybe? Very cryptic, all of it. I suppose if I grill her about it, she won't budge. She can make up any quick lie to explain what she said. After all, Leadenby is dead now and can't tell us the truth anymore."

"That doesn't prove *she* killed him. Maybe Leadenby knew something incriminating about somebody else as well. He lived here all his life and he loved stories."

Falk glanced at her. "Usually there aren't a ton of people who all hate the same person."

Such general statements irked Callie, and she sat up. "On exactly how many murder cases are you basing that observation?"

Falk leaned back, narrowing his eyes. His jaw tightened. "Are you questioning my competence, Miss Aspen?"

Oh, all of a sudden it was Miss Aspen, while earlier he had been so nice to her because she had taken care of his nephews.

Falk leaned on the table's edge. "Well?"

Callie realized she wasn't building any bridges by making the deputy her enemy. "I'm sorry if that came out wrong. I mean to say . . . how much do we really know about real-life murder cases, I mean, either you or I? I fully admit I know nothing beyond the murder mysteries I read."

"Agatha Christie and all that." Falk grimaced. "I must admit this is along those lines. A will to be read and somebody dies. But it isn't the testator and it doesn't seem to have anything to do with the will. Mrs. Du Bouvrais even insisted it must have been a burglar. Word about the will reading had been out around town, and she thinks someone took advantage of the moment when everybody was gathered to hear the will."

Callie didn't even listen to the burglar theory Sheila had

already acquainted her with but pounced on Falk's earlier conclusion. "How do you know Leadenby's death has nothing to do with the will? Maybe Leadenby stood to inherit a lot, and now that he's dead, all that money goes to somebody else. You have to look into that."

"And I will." Falk reached up and rubbed his forehead. "Look, I admit that it's not the most professional approach to come to a crime scene without your uniform and with two little boys in tow, but things are a little informal in the run-up to the Christmas holidays. The sheriff is out of town and . . . well, I hadn't expected anything major to come up."

"I really don't mind your clothes. Or Jimmy and Tate. They're really sweet. I mean, authority isn't in a badge. It . . ."

He looked up with a probing stare. "What are you trying to say?"

Callie thought of Amber, the missing ring, the handyman she was so protective of, Ben and his hurt feelings, Sheila with the stain on her dress, Stephen who had mentioned he was afraid of the fragility of life. How you could lose people suddenly.

She swallowed. "I care for the people involved in this case. I'm worried that . . . they will be hurt by hasty conclusions. I . . . I just feel so helpless. Dorothea wanted this tea party to change things for the better, but . . . it's all so muddled now."

Falk studied her. "Do you know what's in the will?"

"No, not at all."

"But you say Dorothea wanted to change things for the better. How do you know?"

"That's just what I think. It's almost Christmas. I feel like she wanted a family reunion and . . . Didn't she tell you what's in the will? What her plan was with revealing it in front of this particular group of people?"

Falk shook his head. "She barely told me anything. That housekeeper of hers kept interfering, saying she was tired and her heart is weak and I shouldn't strain her. I don't want another casualty, so I treated her with the greatest care. Still, it makes me feel like the answers I need are out of reach. I can't prove the will has anything to do with the death . . . I'm not sure the lawyer who drew it up will want to tell me anything."

Callie opened her mouth to say it had been drawn up in Ben's office and that Ben was there, then realized she would just put Ben in an awkward situation. He wasn't supposed to give out client information. If Falk needed it, he'd have to go through official channels to get it.

Falk said encouragingly, "Yes?"

"No, I just wanted to say you do have a point there."

Falk held her gaze as if he didn't believe her. Then he sighed. "Well, thank you for the information you've given me. If you remember anything more, give me a call." He rose. "I have more people to question, and I want to see how they're doing in the conservatory."

Callie nodded. She rose too. She wanted to know if the missing ring had been found on Leadenby's person or near his body, but she didn't want to arouse his suspicion. Amber had to bring that up, not her.

She was already sorry she had annoyed Falk with her questions. She said hurriedly, "I hope you can have your ice skating session with the boys some other time. They're nice kids."

Falk nodded. "They are. They . . . miss their dad, you know."

He seemed to want to say more, but just then there was a knock at the door and a woman in white put her head around the corner. "We have partial prints on the weapon. An attempt was made to wipe them off, but I think you can still use them."

"Excellent work. I'm coming." Falk left in a rush.

Callie stood motionless in the empty kitchen. An attempt had been made to wipe the fingerprints off the weapon. By whom?

Had Sheila recognized the weapon? Was it a knife belonging to someone in the house?

A penknife, for instance? A letter opener?

Callie's heart beat fast as she continued her train of thought.

That would explain why Sheila had knelt beside the body and gotten blood on her dress. She hadn't been trying to find a pulse or wanting to help Leadenby. No, she had tried to clean the weapon of fingerprints to protect someone.

Someone she suspected of murder . . .

# Chapter Seven

Callie threw herself on her back with a sigh. The bed creaked in protest, and the soft mattress sagged to one side. If she kept tossing and turning like this, she'd roll off the edge and crash to the floor.

But she just couldn't sleep. Everything that had happened kept going through her head, and her heartbeat wouldn't calm down as she worried about the trouble Amber and Sheila might be in. Having given her statement to Falk, she hadn't had any reason to stay at Haywood Hall, and soon after, she and Iphy had left. Callie had kind of hoped Iphy would be informed by the jungle drum of town gossip about the results of Falk's initial investigation, but the phone hadn't rung all evening. Was that good news?

Or bad?

Callie swung her legs over the edge of the bed and sat up for a moment. The cold in the room tickled her bare feet. She shivered and stuck her feet into her slippers. Standing up, she stretched her arms. In the corner, Daisy moved in her basket, making a protesting sound as if she didn't want it to be morning yet.

Callie went over and gave her a cuddle. "Everything is OK, girl. You stay here and sleep. I'll be back."

She left the room and went downstairs softly. A glass of warm milk might help.

In the hallway, she saw there was still a light on in the kitchen. The bright stripe under the door made her heart skip a beat. Had Iphy forgotten to turn off the light when they went to bed? She was sure her great aunt had come upstairs. She had heard the familiar creaking and then the door of her bedroom closing.

Taking a deep breath, Callie tiptoed over and opened the kitchen door.

At the sink, Iphy stood, fully dressed, leaning over a plate, carefully placing fresh raspberries on top of a chocolate square. The sink was full of bowls, spoons, and plates, and on the stove was a frying pan with something roasting in it.

Callie inhaled the spicy scent. Nuts of some kind.

Iphy turned to her. "Sit down. You can be the first to try my new creation."

Callie went to the table and sat down. She had always loved that Iphy never blinked when something out of the ordinary occurred. Her mother, for instance, would ask right away what she was doing out of bed in the dead of night, but Iphy seemed to find it perfectly normal.

Iphy picked up a small paper contraption she had put

together so she could get a very thin line of liquid chocolate onto her creations. White chocolate, Callie noticed, to put on the raspberries.

Now she caught sight of the other sweet treat on the plate: a light-brown base with a beige mousse and then a chocolate-chip cookie. Iphy topped that one off with the nuts she had been roasting in the pan.

She carried the plate to the table. "Voilà. I call it The Duel, as it is two pastries vying to be the tastiest."

"The one with the raspberries wins for me for presentation. I love dark chocolate and raspberries and . . ."

"Ah, but the other one has my secret weapon in it." Iphy lowered her voice. "Salted caramel."

Callie's eyes went wide. "Honestly?" She grabbed the fork Iphy handed her and took a bite of that one first. "Hmmm. It's soft and crispy and the mousse is just . . . Hmmm. Oh, now I taste the salted caramel. Fab."

She then dug the fork into the other one, with the raspberries. "They're so fresh and the white chocolate gives that bit of sweetness to . . . Wait! How did you make that dark chocolate base? It's superb!"

Taking alternating bites of the two treats, Callie *ooh*ed and *aah*ed about all the ingredients.

"This duel will be undecided," she mumbled with her mouth full.

Iphy laughed. "I guess that means I can put it on the menu in the tearoom?"

Callie nodded heartily. Around a raspberry she said,

"Are you up just to create this masterpiece or also pondering the murder?"

Iphy sighed. She turned on the hot water and held a dirty bowl under the stream. "It would be odd if I wasn't pondering the murder. I've known Leadenby all my life. He's part of our community. Yes, he was an odd man and he could be hard to deal with, but . . . I can't see why anybody would want to kill him. Murder is so drastic."

Callie threw her weight back against the chair, suddenly too full to eat more. "Do you think Deputy Falk can handle this case? I have no idea how good the sheriff is, but at least I know he has a lot more experience."

Iphy leaned against the sink and studied her. "What do *you* think of Falk?"

Callie blew a lock of hair from her face. "I don't think I endeared myself to him by asking questions about how he intended to handle the case. I should have known better. On my trips, I so dislike the people who interrupt my stories to give details they've read or, even worse, correct me, saying they know I'm wrong about something. Usually I'm not wrong, but they make me look like a fool in front of the entire group. I guess my behavior must have felt like that to Falk. An armchair detective telling the man with the badge how to handle the case. But I'm just so sorry for them all. Dorothea, Amber. Even Sheila. First that engagement ring debacle and then the murder. She must feel totally humiliated."

"She was lying." Iphy's voice was not cold or condemning, merely matter-of-fact. "She was holding something back or . . . I can't quite put my finger on it. I stood here making The Duel, just asking myself, is Sheila a killer? I don't think that she is, instinctively, but then again, I can't just exclude her. I mean, Sheila knows so well what she wants. What if something threatened that? Or someone. Would she really not react when everything she had worked for was at stake? The happiness of her only daughter?"

"Leadenby did seem to doubt Ben and Amber were more than friends. That could endanger the engagement. But . . . to kill someone for that? Sheila wasn't even sure Ben would propose to Amber. She merely relied on the ring in the box to do the trick."

Iphy took a deep breath. "Public opinion is an important thing. Could Ben *not* have proposed with all of us present?"

Her wrinkled face was worried. "However, contrary to what Sheila might have thought, there's more endangering this engagement than just Leadenby's opinion."

"The handyman," Callie said at once.

Iphy nodded. "Got it in one. Yes, the handyman. Cole Merton." She rinsed more bowls and put them on a tea towel to dry.

Callie pulled her feet onto the edge of the chair so she could rub them. Despite the warmth in the kitchen, they were ice-cold. "It was a no-brainer, really. Amber was so defensive of him. She had to know him somehow. Care for him. Did they meet at the Hall when he started working there? Wait a minute. Sheila said Amber had come into town this morning."

"Yes, but she was here before. I think she flew out for two days to see a cousin who had a baby and then came back this morning. She said something to me about giving the cousin a stuffed bear. She must have seen Cole at the Hall before she left for that little trip. Maybe Sheila even sent her on that little trip to get her away from Cole?"

"And arranged for the engagement as soon as she got back?"

"Possibly." Iphy gestured at Callie with a whisk she was about to clean. "You called Amber's attitude about Cole defensive. But no defense will help Cole now that the murder weapon turns out to be a screwdriver. I'm pretty certain it belonged to him."

"A screwdriver?" Callie echoed. "But . . . I simply assumed, since Leadenby was stabbed, that the weapon was a knife. I did consider a penknife, you know, or a letter opener. Something from the house that . . ." *That Sheila might have recognized and wiped clean . . .*

Iphy nodded. "So did I, initially. But I overheard a little conversation between Falk and the people who came out to collect all the evidence. It was a screwdriver. Now, the handyman was there to do some work, right? Wouldn't it be logical there were tools lying around? *His* tools?"

"Yes, probably," Callie acknowledged, "but . . . I thought Cole cleaned chimneys?"

"That also, but he was apparently doing some repairs on the conservatory. A cracked window and all that."

"So he actually worked there, inside Leadenby's sanctuary?"

"Exactly." Iphy nodded at her. "When you know the screwdriver was the murder weapon, you can't help but think in his direction."

"You don't know yet if the screwdriver in question was Cole's tool." Callie leaned her elbows on the table. "It might have belonged to Leadenby himself or someone else in the house. I suppose a handyman takes his toolkit with him when he leaves?"

"Not if he intends to come back to finish the job."

"He did drive off in an awful rush," Callie said pensively, remembering the scene. "Was he leaving for the day, or did he have another job to do somewhere else?"

She sat up. "That might even give him an alibi. If he was someplace else working when Leadenby was killed . . . Falk mentioned the body being warm and the murder not taking place long before. If it happened during the break in the tea party proceedings, Cole was long gone."

"He could have come back."

"For his forgotten screwdriver?" Callie hitched a brow in disbelief.

"That is for Falk to find out." Iphy nodded at her. "But he will have no qualms about going after Cole."

"Why is that? Amber also said something about the police wanting to hang it all on Cole." Her mind was racing to make sense of it all. If Cole had used the tool and his prints were on it, why on earth would Sheila have wanted to wipe those away? She was likely to want to protect her husband or daughter, but a local handyman?

Wouldn't she prefer that an outsider be accused instead of a family member?

Did that mean Sheila hadn't tried to wipe the prints away?

But someone had.

Amber?

Did that make sense?

Amber had claimed to have never been near the body. There also hadn't been any visible blood on her dress, just on Sheila's.

If Sheila hadn't been leaning over to wipe prints away from the murder weapon, what had she been doing at the body that had gotten the blood on her dress?

To focus on something concrete, Callie repeated, "Why will Falk go after Cole?"

Iphy shrugged as if it didn't matter. "Let's wait and see what happens."

"You know something about this Cole Merton. Do you also know why Amber is so keen on thinking the best of him?" That might help clear up the question of why Amber would risk something for Cole.

Iphy shook her head. "That isn't for me to tell you. I'm careful not to meddle in affairs of the heart."

Callie had to laugh. "Oh, that's why you agreed to bake

an engagement cake for Sheila and then went and hid a secret message in it for Amber. You wouldn't dream of meddling in affairs of the heart, right?"

Iphy didn't smile at Callie's mocking tone. "It's terrible how unhappy people are because they aren't listening to their hearts. They know deep down inside what the right thing to do is, but they don't do it, because they're trying to manipulate things. Dorothea with her will . . ."

"Do you know what's in it?" Callie held her great aunt's gaze. "Does Ben know?" She took a deep breath. "If he knows and he didn't want Leadenby to get a share in the estate . . ."

"Ben could be the killer?" Iphy asked with disbelief in her voice.

"He was out of the room during the break when Leadenby was murdered. I saw him wandering outside, but who says he didn't go into the conservatory, kill Leadenby, and then go outside to have an excuse for where he was and what he'd done in the time he was away? I saw his face when he came up to the front door. He was incredibly angry. Hurt too, I think, but angry most of all. Indignant."

"About the ring box being empty." Iphy nodded. "But that wasn't Leadenby's fault, was it?"

"It might have been if Leadenby took the ring. What if Ben saw him with it and confronted him? He might have stabbed him in blind rage."

Callie clenched her hands together. "I liked Ben at first sight, so I'm not eager to suspect him. However, I realize I don't really know him at all. And we have no idea if Leadenby said something to him that made him furious."

"Something like 'Amber doesn't love you'?" Iphy asked quietly.

"For instance. Leadenby acted like he knew about Ben and Amber, their friendship. He denied there was any romance in it. What did he know? Had he watched them, listened in on them? Or was it just speculation on his part?"

Iphy shrugged. "Your guess is as good as mine. All I can tell you is this: with news of the murder getting around, people will start talking. You have to keep your ears open, and you might learn a lot more than the police will. People don't want to come forward and point a finger at their neighbors. But a little gossip over tea . . ."

Callie narrowed her eyes. "You mean . . ."

Iphy pointed up at the ceiling. "Get some sleep and then dive into Book Tea as soon as we open. Walk around, serve customers, and you'll soon see exactly what I mean."

\* \* \*

"Three Miss Lemons and two Daily Surprises." Callie put down the tray with dirty cups and plates and stretched her shoulders for a second. "Is it always this busy? How do you keep up?"

Iphy opened the fridge to get out the fresh lemon topping for the cupcakes and shrugged. "Preparation, my dear. But this morning's busload was unforeseen. They're going to see the exhibition at Craig's Point and decided to stop off here. Help me with these, will you?"

Callie lent Iphy a hand as she quickly squeezed the topping onto the cupcakes, forming a profile of a lady with a bun like a little cameo. Miss Lemon, ready to tackle a case for the great Hercule Poirot.

The Daily Surprise was a carrot cake with a little marzipan book on top. Callie had already seen a woman wrap one of the tiny books carefully in a napkin to take home and show her husband. Several people had also taken photos with their phones to share on social media. Callie had told Iphy that in fancy restaurants, you weren't allowed to photograph and share the creations, as they were afraid of other places copying them, but Iphy had said that she was honored when people shared and that she'd probably be making something else again next month. Thinking up new things was the best part about running Book Tea, she had confided.

The bell rang to indicate new customers were coming in, and Callie rushed out to take their orders. These were locals, it seemed, for as she got closer, she just caught one woman saying to the other, "It's a good thing for Dorothea."

"How can you say that?" the other responded with exaggerated disapproval. Her cheeks were red, suggesting that, despite her indignant tone, she was rather enjoying this exchange.

The first woman said, "She never wanted him there. He

forced her to let him stay. They had a terrible fight about it not long ago. She wanted him to leave, but he wouldn't go. I'm almost certain he was making threats against her, intimidating her, so she kept him on."

"She knows exactly what she wants. Why put up with that behavior?"

The women took seats at the only free table, shrugging out of their coats and putting them over the backs of their chairs. Folding up her colorful knitted scarf, the first woman said, "She must have been afraid of him. At her age, one little push from a sturdy man like him could have broken her neck and killed her."

"But *she* didn't die. Do you think she might have . . . in self-defense or something?"

"I'm not sure. I think it takes some strength to club someone over the head. Skull was smashed, they say."

The second woman tutted.

Callie came up to them. "Can I help you? What would you like? Tea, coffee, hot chocolate? We have snowy chocolate too; that's made of white chocolate. You can have extra cream on top and marshmallows."

The first woman looked up at her. "It does sound lovely but rather heavy on the calories. I only have a week left to try and fit into my Christmas Eve dress. Tea for me. And nothing to go with it."

The other said, "I've given up and ordered a new dress in another size. Let's have the snowy chocolate, then, and, um . . . Caribbean Mystery? Is that with fruit?"

"It's a brownie with coconut flakes and fresh pineapple."

"Sounds delicious. Let's have that one."

Callie wrote it down and raced to the kitchen. "A tea, plain, and the snowy chocolate with a Caribbean Mystery. Look, they were saying something about the murder. Leadenby maybe having intimidated Dorothea into letting him stay there? Do you know anything about that?"

Iphy sighed. "I do know that Sheila didn't want him there. Maybe she pushed for him to leave and Dorothea had to break the bad news to him? I can imagine he wasn't happy about it, since he's lived there for many years. He considers the estate his home."

Grimacing, she corrected herself, "Considered. I still have to get used to the fact he's no longer there."

"There also seem to be rumors about how the murder took place, and they got it all wrong. They say he was clubbed over the head. Smashed skull and all. That can't be right."

"We never saw the body, so what do we know? But Falk might not think it a bad idea if they're talking about the wrong details so he can conduct his investigation in peace. Here are two tea specials and two cappuccinos for table four."

"On my way." Callie rushed out again with the order. She was glad that her great aunt's regular helpers were also on the scene to ensure speedy service to all customers.

Outside, it had started snowing again, and every few

minutes the doorbell jangled as shoppers with snow on their shoulders poured in to enjoy the warmth inside and the sweet treats on offer.

Pointing a few people to where they could hang up their snowy coats to dry, Callie heard a man say, "Yes, for forging documents. I have no idea what kind of documents. I think he might have been an accountant then? You sometimes hear how they fudge the books for their clients."

"It seems more likely to me that he ran some sort of scheme to get money out of people," the other said. "I mean, he had a safe-deposit box at the bank. What does a gardener need that for?"

Callie perked up. A safe-deposit box? That was interesting. What could be in there? Did Falk know about it? Would he go have a look?

She handed out menus and returned to the kitchen to ask Iphy if it was all right if she left for a while and took the car. "I've heard the oddest things about Leadenby this morning. Even that he forged documents, which means he was a criminal. Caught or not, but . . . It might just be rumors, but I want to talk to Dorothea and ask her what she knows about all of this."

Iphy held her gaze. "You want to make sure they're all right after the shock yesterday."

"Yes," Callie admitted, sheepishly, "I do want to see them and . . ."

Iphy gestured with both hands. "Go, go. We'll be fine. When people see how full it is, they'll realize they'll have to wait a little longer to be served. That's not a problem. I also want to know how everybody's doing at the Hall. Take Daisy. She can break the ice."

Callie picked up the leash, and Daisy, who had been sitting in the kitchen corner, came to her at once, wagging her tail. She was excited to get out and about. Callie also felt nerves in her stomach, but they were more the anxious kind. With the town alive with gossip about the murder and Leadenby's less pleasant sides looming large, it seemed more likely than before that people had disliked him and might even have decided he had to die. That was good news for the most likely suspects to come to mind: Cole because of the screwdriver and Brenda because of the argument.

But a bigger pool of suspects might also mean it would be even harder to narrow it down and get to the bottom of it.

# Chapter Eight

D riving up to Haywood Hall, Callie was struck by the similarities to her arrival just the day before. The house looked the same, with the Christmas decorations and the beauty of the frozen world all around. But one thing was certain: Leadenby would not come down the icy steps to help her with boxes or with anything else. Most of all, he would not provide any answers as to his own untimely death.

Standing there in the chilly wind, remembering his facial expression as he had come to help her and her own joy upon seeing him, she wondered if he had really been such a terrible man. Intimidating an old lady so he could live on her land? Hiding the proof of a criminal past in a safe-deposit box at a bank nearby?

Or were those just rumors, like the idea that he had been hit on the head? Did they have nothing to do with the case, and were they only hampering her insights into the real motive for murder?

She pulled Daisy up the steps and rang the bell. It took a long time before anybody came to the door. She had almost accepted that she would have to walk around to find another way in when the door swung open at last.

Stephen looked at her with weary eyes. There was stubble on his chin, and the sweater he wore was too large, so loose around his body that it almost seemed he had lost weight since she had last seen him. He forced a smile. "Callie! Come in."

"I just wanted to see how you're doing after . . ."

"Yes, yes, come in. It's cold. Sorry I kept you waiting." He stepped back and gestured. "Dorothea is in bed. She didn't want to get up at all this morning. I'm worried the shock is too much for her and her heart will just give out."

"No, that can't be." Callie was surprised at how much the idea of Dorothea dying hurt her. "She wanted to change things around here for the better. She must have that chance."

"Well, if you can talk to her and get anything out of her, you're welcome to it, but she's not giving me anything." Stephen shaded his eyes a moment. "This morning when I woke up, I almost felt like packing my bags and leaving."

"But you can't. I mean, the police need everyone involved to stay put, right?"

"Ever-practical Callie." Stephen's tone was mocking. "I suppose you've never had this urge to just run and not come back. No, you're too responsible for that. You finish what you start."

Callie tilted her head. "I thought you were responsible too."

Stephen scoffed. "That's my image, right? The responsible bookish type, the diplomat, the man who can talk himself out of any situation. But I feel stumped here. This house . . ."

He gestured around him. "It has been my legacy ever since I can remember. People liked me for it, even loved me for it." His voice faltered a moment. He looked at the stairs.

Callie wondered if he was thinking of Sheila. Could it be true that she had only been after Haywood Hall? At the time, Callie had honestly believed Sheila was really in love with Stephen. She had accepted their engagement, their marriage, without ever even asking either of them about it because she had believed genuine feelings were involved. But could she have been wrong? Had Stephen found out later that Sheila had chosen him for selfish reasons? For the Hall, or to be able to travel and see the world? Had Sheila freely admitted it even, perhaps in some ill-timed fight?

Stephen said, "We shouldn't have come here, Callie. It was a bad idea. I knew when Sheila suggested it."

"Sheila? But I thought Dorothea wanted you to come, because of the will?"

"Yes, yes, of course, but . . . Sheila had this other plan. Amber's engagement. I should have talked her out of it. It was a bad idea."

"Because of the ring? It's very valuable, I heard."

"I couldn't care less about the ring!" Stephen cried. His

voice echoed in the empty hallway. Then he lowered it. "I'm sorry. It's not your fault. I just can't believe that Sheila manipulated Dorothea into this. She's an old, lonely woman, not a pawn." He clenched his hands into fists by his side.

Callie wanted to say something, but she wasn't sure what. She couldn't deny that Stephen had always leaned on Sheila's judgment and that her take-charge attitude had made life easy for him. Wasn't it a little unfair to blame Sheila now for something he had never objected to before, something that had indeed been quite comfortable for him?

She said softly, "I thought you also wanted the engagement. You mentioned to me yesterday how the death of your friend on the golf course got you thinking . . ."

"Death, yes." Stephen looked at her with feverish eyes. "He died, all of a sudden, and now Leadenby died and . . . Death seems to be following us around wherever we go. I needed to get away from the grim reality for a while, just celebrate Christmas in the place I've always called home, but now . . . this is tainted as well. That's why I want to leave. Can't you see?"

He held her gaze. "Nothing makes sense anymore. Even Sheila hasn't been herself since it happened. I woke up last night and she was crying. Not a little; no, she was sobbing her heart out. I've never heard her like that. Sheila doesn't cry, except for a few quick tears, maybe, in frustration. Not like . . . the world just came to an end."

Callie's stomach filled with ice at this revelation. Did

Sheila's despair stem from her knowledge that she had taken a life and could never undo that? "Did you talk to her, ask her what was wrong?"

"No. I pretended to be asleep." Stephen's voice was bitter. "I was afraid to ask her. I was afraid to hear . . ."

"That she killed Leadenby?" Callie herself was afraid of that now as she stood here listening to the silence in the house. But she had to ask Stephen. He was Sheila's husband. He knew her best. "Do you really believe that she could do something like that?"

Stephen covered his face with both hands. "I don't know. I just know that Sheila's always the one who solves the problems. And when she can't . . ."

He dropped his hands to his sides and looked at Callie. "What are we going to do then?"

Callie took a deep breath. She supposed it meant that Stephen would have to play a part he wasn't used to playing: that of Sheila's support. She had to admit her former friend was a strong personality who never seemed to need anyone. Next to her, you had the urge to fade away a little and let her take the limelight. It was comfortable and safe. Sure, from time to time you also envied her and wanted to be like her, but then again, it was a sheltered life where another braved the storms for you.

The bell rang. Daisy, who had kept perfectly still during the conversation with Stephen, now lifted her head and barked.

Stephen froze. He looked at Callie. "Are you expecting someone?"

"No. This isn't my home. How . . ."

Stephen went to the door and looked through the peephole. "It's the deputy," he whispered. "Falk, looking like he's about to arrest someone."

"He probably wants to ask more questions. Yesterday he could only cover the essentials, since he also had to keep an eye on the people collecting fingerprints and looking at the body. There's so much to do. Just be honest. And . . ." Callie touched his arm. "Try not to look so tense. It's suspicious."

Stephen glared at her as if he was about to respond with some cynical comment, then shrugged and opened the door.

Falk made eye contact with him and wanted to speak, until he spotted Callie out of the corner of his eye. His brows drew together a moment as if he was forming some kind of conclusion. She felt the need to explain her presence, but decided to go with a brief, "Hello, Deputy."

Daisy stepped forward to greet Falk, but since she was on her leash, she couldn't reach him. Falk also ignored her and said to Stephen, "I had expected Mrs. Keats to open the door."

"She's looking after Dorothea. I'm afraid the shock of the murder has taken a toll on her, and she's not well at all."

"I'm sorry to hear that." Falk sounded distracted, as if

he wasn't fully focused on this little introduction but gearing up for sharing why he was really there.

He was in uniform now, making him look very official and stern. His badge gleamed like it had been polished that morning. Callie had said authority wasn't in someone's badge, meaning that she respected him regardless of whether he was wearing it or not, but right now she did see how wearing it made a difference. This man could take you away and put you in a cell. She wanted to break the ice by asking something innocent about Jimmy and Tate, but nothing came to mind. Her heartbeat sped up, and she unconsciously held her breath.

Falk asked, "Is Amber at home?"

"Yes," Stephen said. "But as you can imagine, she's very upset after the whole ordeal. I'd appreciate it if you don't disturb her. If you have more questions, perhaps we can do that at some other time, when . . ."

"She'll have to come to the station right now. I'm sorry, but she'll have to come with me. Of course, you're welcome to come along, if you want. You can also call a lawyer to be present as we question her."

"What's wrong?" Callie came to stand beside Stephen, blocking Falk's entrance into the house.

Falk looked at her. "You can only delay it, not prevent it." He seemed to tense a little before he added, "And if Amber's climbing out of her bedroom window right now to avoid this questioning, she'll end up in the arms of the other deputy. I sent him around back to catch her."

"My daughter is not climbing out of windows!" Stephen burst out. "She's not a rabid dog that needs to be caught." His cheeks turned red, and he seemed ready to shove Falk away from the front door. "She's not a criminal either. She's just a girl enjoying a vacation that has taken a terrible turn. Can't you understand that?"

"I'm sure," Falk said with steel in his voice, "that Miss Aspen knows exactly what I'm referring to."

Callie's heartbeat droned in her ears. The movement behind the upstairs window when she had come from the shed after her talk with Amber. Someone had seen them go into the shed together. While Amber was supposed to have been in bed, too shaken to make a statement.

Whoever had seen them together had told the police, believing it was somehow highly significant, and Falk now thought Callie was in on some terrible secret about Leadenby's death and trying to keep Amber out of the hands of the police.

She took a deep breath to carefully phrase her explanation, but Stephen spoke first. "This is ridiculous. Callie did nothing wrong. She's certainly not here to help Amber run away or something. She's here to support my family in these hard times. We were friends long before you became deputy here."

Ignoring this stab, Falk held Callie's gaze. "Do you know what I'm referring to, Miss Aspen?"

"Yes, I do know, Deputy, but you have the wrong view of the entire situation."

"Do I? Well, that must be because it's my first murder investigation."

Callie felt like dragging Falk into a room so they could speak one-on-one, where she could tell him that she was really sorry about having offended him the night before but had just been concerned for her friends. That she even wanted to apologize for her remark and for whatever else he was angry about, but that he shouldn't take out his anger on Amber.

Falk said, "I would like to see your daughter, Mr. Du Bouvrais. Right away."

Stephen looked from the deputy to Callie and back. "I don't understand," he said in a small voice.

Callie's heart hurt for him.

Falk pressed, "Please bring her here."

Stephen looked at Callie one more time as if he didn't know what to do, then turned away and went up the stairs. Daisy tried to follow him, but when the leash stopped her, she sank to the floor with a low whine.

Falk stood stiffly in the doorway.

"Better come in," Callie said. "All the heat is escaping, and it's so expensive to heat a large old house."

Falk stepped in, and she closed the door. Daisy started to sniff around his shoes, but Falk didn't bend down to pat her. His face seemed cut out of marble. Cold and emotionless.

Moments ago, Callie had wanted to be alone with him to explain; now she had no idea what to say without making things even worse. His uniform made him look so formal and imposing, his badge daring her to make another mistake and create even bigger problems for those she wanted to help.

"Amber climbed out the window yesterday," Falk said, "to talk to you. I thought you were in the kitchen waiting for me to come back while . . ."

"She knocked on the window. I couldn't let her just stand there in the cold. I only went out to hear what she had to say. It was about the missing engagement ring. She must have told you about the ring." Callie gave Falk a hopeful look, wishing fervently that Amber had indeed told him and she would not be obliged to explain that as well.

"How she took it from the ring box and hid it in her pocket? Yes, she did tell me that. She didn't mention, however, that she had already discussed her confession with you."

The word *confession* carried a mocking tone, as if he didn't believe Amber had told the truth. It was more like he suspected Amber of having made up a story. Together with Callie?

Callie straightened up. "Amber was very upset about the whole engagement thing. Her mother wanted to force Ben, who is just a friend to Amber, into asking for her hand in marriage, with all these people from town present. It was a complete setup. And after something like that, you can't just break off the engagement again. She had to do something, make an impromptu plan. It might not have been the best idea, I admit, but Amber only wanted to protect her friendship with Ben. Friendship is all it is."

Falk shook his head. He walked over to one of the Christmas trees and pretended to be studying a shiny ornament. "That's not what Ben told me. He loves her, and he claims she loves him too. That they had made concrete plans for their future."

"What? Amber told me about lots of plans, but none of them had to do with Ben."

Falk continued as if he hadn't heard her. "If she loved him too and they planned a future together, why would she take the ring? This would have been her moment of glory. A proposal in front of her parents, Dorothea . . ."

"It wasn't like that at all." Callie clearly remembered Amber's expression as she watched the scene unfold. She had known that the ring box would be empty, and to spare Ben the humiliation, she had even whispered to him not to open it.

Falk said, "Most importantly, where's the ring now? Amber can't produce it."

He walked back to Callie and held her gaze. "If she really took it, for whatever far-fetched reason, she would have it, don't you think? She would give it back to her mother with an apology and be done with it. But the ring is nowhere in sight. No, I don't buy her story at all. I think someone else stole the ring and she's taking the blame. Why? You tell me."

His stare became even more probing. "Women discuss

their love interests, right? Did she tell you about Cole Merton? Did you make up this 'I took the ring' tale together because you're a romantic at heart? You should have thought about what lying to the police might mean."

"I haven't lied to you," Callie protested.

"No," Falk scoffed. "You just omitted a few details."

Frustration washed through Callie at his tone, yes, but mostly at herself, that she had allowed this situation to unfold this way. Falk clearly thought she knew a lot more than she had admitted to him last night. That meant he didn't trust her and even believed she was a threat to his investigation.

Not only did she regret having lost his belief in her integrity, but she also realized that Falk was a police officer who could take steps against her for withholding information, obstructing his investigation or whatever. Unless she could convince him that she really hadn't known all that much, she could soon find herself at the police station as well.

But Amber hadn't revealed anything to her as to how well she knew Cole Merton or why she was so sure he had nothing to do with the missing ring. Callie had seen only a very upset girl needing a little encouragement to admit she had done a very stupid thing.

Callie said, "Amber told me she took the ring to make sure Ben wouldn't propose to her, and I believe her. Someone else must have taken the ring from her pocket after she put the jeans on her bed and changed into her party outfit.

The door to her bedroom wasn't locked, I suppose. Anybody could have gone in."

"Who? Why? And how would that person even have known the ring was in Amber's pocket? You just said it was an impromptu plan to take it out of the ring box. And she claims to have been alone in the room when she did it."

Falk shook his head. "No, no, I tell you that Cole Merton pinched the ring while you were briefly out of the room where the cake was placed. Amber's just protecting him because of his pretty face. But I'm not falling for it."

"You're taking her in to ascertain that? That she lied about the ring?" It put Amber in a spot, but at least it had nothing to do with Leadenby's murder.

Falk shook his head, dashing Callie's hopeful feeling.

"What then?" she asked, afraid of the answer.

Footsteps approached, and Stephen appeared with Amber by his side. She was wearing a long, thick knitted vest that seemed to swallow her whole. Her hair was pulled back in a ponytail, and without makeup she looked like a sixteen-year-old.

Stephen tried to put his arm around his daughter's shoulders, but Amber shrugged him off. She looked at Falk. "You want to talk to me? I told you all I know. Honestly."

"Amber Du Bouvrais, I'm arresting you on suspicion of murder. You don't have to say anything . . ."

"Murder?" Amber echoed, shrinking back from Falk. "Why?"

Stephen said, "This is ridiculous, and she's not coming with you if you take that accusing tone."

Ignoring his protests, Falk continued to Amber, "Your fingerprints were found on the murder weapon. You tried to wipe them off, but you didn't do a good enough job."

Amber stared at Falk. Her face lost all color. "No! I didn't wipe off any fingerprints."

"I did!" a voice cried, and Sheila came running down the stairs. Her hair hung loose around her mottled face, flying around her as she raced to them. "I killed Leadenby. I couldn't stand the prattling old fool anymore. I shoved the screwdriver into his chest."

She halted beside Stephen, not looking at him or Amber, just at the deputy. "I'm your killer. Take me in." She extended her hands, holding her wrists up for him to click the cuffs on.

Falk shook his head. "Your fingerprints aren't on the weapon, Mrs. Du Bouvrais. Your daughter's are."

"I wore gloves. There were gloves in the conservatory. Leadenby always used gloves when he handled his orchids. Something about the possibility of mold getting onto their roots."

"So your prints never got on the weapon. But how does that explain the presence of your daughter's prints?"

Sheila's eyes flashed from Falk to Amber and back as she seemed to scramble for answers.

Falk said, "When would Amber have handled the screwdriver if it wasn't at the time of the murder? She wasn't helping with the repairs to the conservatory, was she?" He shook his head again. "No, Mrs. Du Bouvrais. I appreciate that you're trying to take the blame for your daughter's actions, but I can't arrest you without proof."

"There was blood on my dress. That's proof!" Sheila held her arms out at him again, encouragingly. "Arrest me."

Falk said slowly, "I'm taking your daughter to the station. Not you."

"But I'm guilty. I killed Leadenby. I admitted as much. Why is that not enough?" Sheila was almost screaming now.

Stephen took her by the shoulders, saying she had to calm down, but she pulled free. "Not now, you fool." She looked at Falk with tears in her eyes. "I'll sign a full confession as soon as we're at the station. You'll have your murder case wrapped up in a day. Isn't that amazing? The whole town will be talking about it. You might even get a promotion."

Falk shook his head wearily. "I don't want to wrap it up in a hurry, make an arrest to satisfy public opinion. I want to arrest the real killer. And you aren't the killer."

"But Amber isn't it either, believe me." Sheila grabbed his arm. "Believe me." Tears ran down her face.

Daisy pressed her head against Sheila's leg as if to support her.

Falk gently shook off Sheila's grasp. He said to Amber, "Please come along without making a fuss. That will be best for everyone involved."

Amber nodded, her head down. "I understand. I'm sorry." She followed Falk outside.

Stephen looked at Callie, his eyes wide. "I'm sorry? What does she mean by that? Did she do it? No, it can't be!"

"Of course she didn't do it," Sheila barked at him. "How can you think that of your own child?"

Callie grabbed Sheila by the arm. "You're thinking it too, aren't you? Or else you wouldn't have needed to make a false confession. Taking the blame in Amber's stead."

Sheila looked at her. "What do you know? Maybe I did kill him. You weren't there when it happened. Nobody was."

Stephen seemed to wake from a state of half shock. "I have to go with them. I have to make sure she gets the best defense possible."

He walked out the door, into the snow, in his slippers and that much too large sweater.

Sheila stared after him, her eyes wide. "What's happened to my family?" she whispered.

Callie took her arm and squeezed it. "You have to be strong now, Sheila. That's the only way to help Amber. Why do you think she killed Leadenby? Because you do think that. You wanted to be arrested in her place to keep her safe."

Sheila held her gaze. For a moment, Callie was certain Sheila would just pull free and storm off, back to her room upstairs.

Callie pressed, "I want to help you, Sheila. I want to

help Amber. You must know by now that we met earlier, in Vienna on one of the trips where I was her tour guide. I realized when she told me a few things about her life that she was your daughter. I befriended her because . . . I care for her and for the things that bound us as children. Our summers here at the Hall."

"The Hall?" Sheila's voice was a whisper. "It brought us nothing but heartache. My entire family will be torn apart over this pile of bricks."

She gestured around her. "I loved the Hall. I wanted the Hall. Was that so bad? It probably was, because now I'm being punished for it. I'm losing everything that I love."

Callie thought of Stephen's story that he had heard Sheila sobbing her heart out, and now she could understand why. If Sheila really believed that she was losing everything she loved, or rather, the people she loved—her daughter and her husband—of course she would be in a state of terrible despair. Eager to do anything to prevent the worst.

Callie took Sheila into the sitting room and forced her into a chair. She pulled up a stool and sat close to her, holding her hand. Daisy sat beside them, looking up as if she also wanted to know the truth.

"Now tell me why you think Amber killed Leadenby."

Sheila looked at her. "I won't have to testify, right? They can't make me testify against my own daughter. There must be some law that says it can't be done. It's not human."

Callie urged, "Tell me what happened."

"Will you tell the police?"

"Falk basically just told me he doesn't trust me anymore because somebody told him that Amber and I spoke yesterday. She snuck out of her bedroom and told me about the ring. How she took it out of the cake and then lost it. Now that she can't produce it, Falk doesn't believe anything either of us has to say."

"It's all my fault!" Sheila's face crinkled. "I did everything wrong, didn't I? I wanted her to be happy with Ben. But now she's at the police station, accused of murder."

Callie squeezed her hand. "What did you see? Why do you assume Amber is involved in Leadenby's death?"

Sheila swallowed hard. "After what happened with the cake, I wanted to talk to Ben and explain I had never meant for him to look silly in front of our guests. I didn't see him anywhere, so I decided to go to the conservatory and tell Leadenby to stop being so stubborn and join us. I didn't personally care whether or not he was there, but I thought Dorothea would like him present. She seemed to value him. At least she never wanted to hear a bad word about him."

Because Leadenby had been pressuring her to keep him around? Callie wondered. The gossip at the Book Tea still intrigued her, and she wished she had told Falk about it. Maybe there was a valuable lead in there somewhere.

Sheila continued, "I only wanted everything to be . . . perfect." She laughed hollowly. "I came in and I saw . . . Amber on her knees next to something on the floor. I was so stunned I couldn't say anything at first. I wanted to ask what the matter was with Leadenby, if I could help, when I realized that Amber was trying to pull something from his chest. A screwdriver that was plunged into it. She had attacked him, hurt him, and she was trying to . . ."

Sheila gasped for breath. She had to struggle to continue. "I stood behind a palm watching her as she tried to get the thing out but couldn't. Then she stood and left. I heard her scream. I realized she was acting like she had just found the body. I didn't know what to think or do. But I did remember fingerprints. So I took gloves from the workbench and put them on, and then I used a cloth to wipe the screwdriver's grip clean. It wasn't even terrible to do; I just knew I had to do it. I put away the cloth and the gloves and then I went out to meet you in the hallway. I hadn't checked my dress for . . ."

She made a scoffing noise. "Sheila, who always thinks she's so clever. A bloodstain on my dress. And you saw it right away."

She looked Callie in the eye. "Maybe I should thank you for it. I had time to rehearse my story before Falk arrived to take our statements. The mayor called him right away. He had already wanted the police here for the missing ring, and now with the dead body . . ."

She rubbed her face. "I didn't do a good job wiping off the prints either. I was in a rush because Amber had already screamed and people might come in to look at the body. I didn't want to be seen. I did half the job and only made everything worse. How can this be happening to us? I can't understand it."

Ignoring her anguished question, Callie tried to focus on the facts. "So you saw Amber trying to pull the weapon from Leadenby's chest? But you never actually saw her attack him?"

"No." Sheila shook her head. "In fact, when I came in and saw her leaned over him, I thought she was . . . checking his chest for a heartbeat or something. I think I saw her hand on his chest . . . It sounds a bit silly, but it was almost like she was pulling his jacket over his chest. But I must have been mistaken. It doesn't make sense."

Callie's mind raced. "Maybe it does. Amber thought Leadenby might have taken the ring. Maybe she was looking for it?"

"But why? If you see a dead body, you run away, right?"

"Maybe Amber was certain someone would be implicated and she wanted to prevent that from happening?"

"Ben." Sheila sat up, raising a hand to her mouth. "Of course. Amber was worried Ben had gone to Leadenby and killed him in anger over the marriage proposal gone wrong."

Callie thought it was more likely Amber had wanted to protect Cole, the handyman, but now didn't seem like the best time to say this to Sheila.

She patted Sheila's hand. "You only saw her bent over the body. You didn't see her actually kill Leadenby. That's great."

"What will that matter to Falk? He thinks she's guilty."

"Well, what else could he think? He has her prints on the weapon. And your attempt to wipe them away makes it even worse in his mind. He has to act. The sheriff is out of town for the holidays, and as his replacement, Falk wants to handle this right. I can't blame him."

"So you think it's right that he arrested my baby?" Sheila huffed.

"No, of course not, but . . . try to see it from his point of view. None of us was honest with him last night. We all lied. We had reasons, good reasons, we believed, but Falk must feel like we all have something to hide, some guilty secret. He took an oath to uphold the law, to bring killers to justice. He can't just accept lies and . . ."

Callie bit her lip. "I feel like I'm to blame as well. I wasn't honest either. And I was critical of him, like I think he can't do a good job. I think I really hurt his feelings."

"Only his ego, I bet." Sheila sniffed. "Men are like that."

Callie stood up. "I have to go to the station. I have to tell Falk everything I know. I want him to know why I didn't say that . . . I thought I was protecting Amber and helping her, but I only made it worse. Falk deserves our full cooperation. It's the only way to solve the case without even more people getting hurt by suspicions and accusations."

Sheila sat motionless. "Now Amber believes I think she's a killer. How can I ever face her again?"

"She'll also realize you made a false confession to save her. You did it because you love her. So maybe it wasn't smart, but . . ." Callie patted Sheila's shoulder. "Why don't you take a shower, get dressed into something more formal, and put on some makeup and then join us at the station? You'll feel better when you look good. People know you around these parts, and . . ."

She felt a genuine smile come up. "After all, you will be lady of Haywood Hall one day. You have a reputation to live up to."

Sheila grabbed her hand. "Callie . . ." Her voice was hoarse. "Are you mad about . . . Stephen and . . ."

Callie shook her head. "No. I avoided you for a little bit because I thought it would hurt somehow, but yesterday I realized that it doesn't. We were friends, and I want us to be friends again. To help each other get through this."

Sheila held Callie's gaze a moment as if trying to determine if she meant it. Then she nodded. "I'll get myself into shape to show a brave face to the world. You go on and I'll be there soon."

Callie walked to the door, Daisy in tow. With her hand on the doorknob, she paused and turned back to Sheila. "Does Dorothea know about . . ."

"I don't think so. She's probably asleep. I'll tell Mrs. Keats though. She can take care of her. She's always protected this family. Like a lioness."

"OK. See you later." Callie was out the door already, her mind racing ahead to the inevitable confrontation at the police station. Would Deputy Falk believe anything either of them had to say?

# Chapter Nine

At the police station, Callie took Daisy in her arms, determined to use every little advantage she had. Walking up to the double glass doors that formed the entrance, she saw one swing open as a familiar figure exited.

Frank Smith, the president of the chamber of commerce.

He glanced at her, and then recognition seemed to dawn on him too. "Ah, Miss . . . uh . . ."

A flush rose in his face as he couldn't instantly produce her name. "We met at the will reading, right? Terrible business. I was just here to make a statement. I suppose I should have done it yesterday, but you don't like to turn on your own neighbors, right?"

He studied her. "I was just waiting for the statement to be printed off, for me to sign, when I saw Deputy Falk come in with Amber Du Bouvrais. Is she somehow . . . under suspicion?"

"I'm sure that Deputy Falk will talk about that with

Amber." Callie tried to smile pleasantly. She didn't want to
show worry to Frank Smith—or let him know how annoyed
she was at his blatant curiosity.

But Smith leaned over with a confidential look. "Well,
if she's under suspicion somehow, I can reassure you that
she'll soon be cleared. You see, my statement made it all so
obvious who the killer is."

He looked around as if to ascertain no one was near to
overhear what he had to say. "As a friend of the family,
you're naturally worried how this will pan out for the Hall
and the Du Bouvraises. But they have nothing to do with
it, and that was clear to me from the start. I should have
told the police right away, but like I said, nobody wants to
be a snitch. I thought all night about what I should do. But
there's something like civic duty, and I decided I had to
come here and speak up."

He took a deep breath. "I actually feel quite sorry for
her, you know. I mean, she came here with practically
nothing, unable to find a job anywhere, and we gave her a
chance. But I guess we shouldn't have."

He frowned. "I have no idea what could be so serious
you'd want to kill for it, but . . . anyway . . ." He shook his
head as if to refocus. "Leadenby knew something about
Brenda Brink. He mentioned it to me casually when I was
complaining about her needs for the school playground. I
said I was worried that Mrs. Finster would cave and give
her money. But Leadenby said I didn't need to worry, as

Brenda would soon have no favor with anybody around this town. He knew something explosive about her and he was about to tell it."

*To Dorothea Finster?*

Callie could still hear those charged voices talking: *If you don't tell her, I will.*

Yes, Leadenby had put pressure on Brenda to admit something, possibly to Dorothea Finster, and Brenda hadn't wanted to, even saying that Leadenby was ruining her entire life. That had sounded pretty serious.

She didn't bother telling Smith that Falk already knew about Leadenby's squeeze on Brenda because she had overheard a snippet of an argument between them. Smith could believe all he wanted that he had helped solve the case.

Callie did feel a twinge of pity for the young teacher. How desperate had she been, going to such lengths to protect her secret? What could it be?

"I'm sure the police will now focus all of their attention on Brenda Brink," Smith said. "A quick arrest, a confession, and then this whole nasty affair can be put to bed. We all want to celebrate Christmas, right?" He leaned over and said to Daisy, "Good little doggy."

Daisy bared her teeth at him, and Smith pulled back. "Yes, well. Happy holidays, then, Miss . . . Yes, good-bye."

Callie watched as he walked to his sedan, unlocking the doors from a distance. The car was as big and conspicuous as he himself was.

She shrugged and went inside. Daisy made a satisfied

sound when she felt the interior warmth on her fur. Behind the reception desk, a deputy sat typing away at a keyboard. To her left were some seats, where she spotted Stephen. He saw her too and came over at once. "Callie! Falk is getting together some paperwork while we wait for the lawyer to arrive. I can come in to watch the interrogation. Do you want to come as well?"

Callie looked doubtful. "I'm not sure whether the deputy will appreciate . . ."

"Nonsense, you can come." Stephen looked past her. "Ah, there's our lawyer." He shook hands with a stocky man with a head full of snow-white hair. "This is Callie Aspen, a friend of mine and Sheila's." He focused on Callie again. "How is Sheila?"

"Better. She wanted to freshen up and then she'll be here."

Before Callie could say more, Falk appeared. He was carrying a file folder and looking pensive. Perhaps because of what Smith had just told him about Brenda Brink? Did Falk now also believe he was looking in the wrong direction for his killer?

Falk came over to them.

Stephen said, "I'd appreciate it if Callie could sit in on the interrogation."

Falk looked at her. "Why would I allow that? You're the suspect's father, but what is she?"

Daisy tilted her head at his grim tone and barked.

Unperturbed, Falk said to Callie, "Who says *you* didn't kill Leadenby?"

Stephen protested, "She didn't have the time for it. She was serving tea. She did step out a moment, but then Ben saw her as he came back from a little walk outside. And while they were still together in the hallway, Amber screamed."

Falk stood up straight with an incredulous expression. "Why would I believe any of you?"

Callie said, "It will be hard if you distrust everything we say."

"Well, you could just have been honest to begin with. But nobody has been telling the full truth." Falk slapped the file folder against his thigh. "How do I know you'll suddenly tell me what really happened? I mean, everything you know, instead of bits and pieces?"

Callie remembered how nervous Stephen had been about the new will and wondered what he was holding back. Falk might not be getting his "full truth" anytime soon.

The lawyer suggested they go in and not let Amber wait any longer. "She must be nervous about this, and that's not conducive to a constructive statement, Deputy."

Falk nodded and gestured for the other deputy to take Stephen and the lawyer to the interrogation room. He himself stayed put and studied Callie with a frown. "What were you doing at Haywood Hall this morning? I thought you had to help your great aunt at the Book Tea. Or if you want to claim you're on vacation, you should be at the ice skating rink. You do skate, don't you?"

"Yes, and I intend to go to the rink soon. But the town is full of speculation about Leadenby's death. Some say he was pressuring Dorothea to let him stay at Haywood Hall. I wanted to ask Dorothea if that's true. Imagine an old woman being afraid in her own house. I sensed yesterday that she wasn't happy at all and wanted to change things with this new will. But we never got to reading it and . . . I don't quite see what she tried to accomplish with it."

"You think the will pertains to the case?"

"Well, whether it does or doesn't, I care about how Dorothea feels."

Falk sighed. "Emotions are just making a total mess of this case. Remember, Sheila Du Bouvrais just begged me to arrest her, all because she's protecting her daughter." He gestured over his shoulder. "Do you think I enjoy going in there and trying to get a nineteen-year-old to admit to murder? She could be going to jail for a long, long time."

"But . . . didn't you hear what Smith had to say about Brenda Brink? It fits with what I overheard. Brenda has some big secret that she doesn't want anyone to learn. Why didn't you rush out to bring her in for questioning?"

Falk stiffened at the mention of Smith's statement and Brenda's secret. "I'm going to question Amber first. Besides, who told you about Smith's statement?"

"Smith himself. I met him as he was leaving the station. He was gloating that he had about solved the case by handing you this vital piece of information."

Falk groaned. "So he's going to spread what he just told

me all over town. There should be a law against it. How can I work when everybody is throwing the evidence into the street?"

Daisy barked again, and Falk looked down on her. "No," he said in a semi-stern tone, "not even your cute face is going to persuade me to let your owner into the interrogation. There are rules I have to stick to."

He turned away from them and motioned to the deputy who had just returned. "Give Miss Aspen some coffee while she waits for the Du Bouvraises. And some water for the dog."

"Her name is Daisy," Callie called after him.

He waved the file folder and disappeared.

\* \* \*

Sheila had arrived and was waiting with Callie when Amber, Stephen, and the lawyer came out. Amber looked relieved and ran to hug her mother. Sheila held her tightly, then released her and studied her face, wiping her hair away from it like Amber was a little girl again. They smiled at each other.

Stephen stood beside them, awkwardly patting his daughter's shoulder. He didn't touch Sheila, Callie noticed. Was their marriage in trouble? Just because Sheila was so pushy? Or also because Stephen was hiding financial problems that might ruin Sheila's secure little life?

Amber said, "I was such an idiot for not explaining everything right away. I just didn't want to get anybody in trouble."

She continued to Sheila, "When I saw Leadenby dead on the floor, I was convinced the ring had something to do with it. I knelt down and searched his pockets for it, but it wasn't there. Then I realized that a screwdriver belonging to Cole Merton had been used to kill him. I didn't want him to be blamed, and on impulse, I grabbed it to pull it out. But the sight of the blood made me faint, and I got up and ran. I don't know how the prints got wiped away."

Sheila said, "I did that. I'm here to tell the deputy all about it."

"Let the lawyer go in with you," Stephen suggested.

Sheila nodded and turned to Falk, who had appeared and was giving the other deputy instructions. They could just overhear him saying, "Bring him in quietly. But make sure he doesn't get a chance to get away."

Amber asked in a high-pitched voice, "Are you arresting Cole now?"

Falk said, "I'm bringing him in for questioning. I just want to know how his screwdriver ended up in the chest of the victim. Left behind? Forgotten?" He sounded cynical.

"I know you don't trust him, but he's changed."

Falk scoffed. "I'll determine that."

Amber seemed ready to start a fight with the deputy, so Callie intervened quickly. "I'll take you back to the Hall. Your father can wait here for your mother. Come on." She pushed Daisy into Amber's arms and ushered her outside.

As she was being led out, Amber called to Falk, "Yes, Cole has been in trouble with the police in the past. But he's changed his ways, I'm sure. He's serious now; he has his business. He wouldn't risk that."

The glass doors snapped shut behind them, and Amber exhaled. "Falk is prejudiced."

"Falk has a lot on his plate, and all of our half statements yesterday mean he has double the work to do. Can you blame him for not being happy about that?"

"Of course not, but he can't take it out on Cole."

Callie remembered how Iphy had said that Falk wouldn't have qualms about going after Cole, and she winced inwardly. Stephen and Sheila would want Amber to stay out of this completely now that there was an explanation for her prints being on the weapon, but if Amber sensed that Falk was indeed intent on blaming Cole, she'd throw herself into it again. Somehow.

Callie directed the girl into the car and instructed her to buckle up. She got in on the driver's side, pulled the seat belt into place, and turned on the ignition. Glancing at Amber, she said, "Seems you know a lot about Cole."

"We went out once or twice. But that was when he was still a bad boy, you know. Skipping classes, doing damage on campus. He was convinced one of our teachers had it in for him, and after a bad grade, he took the mirror off the guy's car. It was a sports car, a really expensive one, so the owner filed charges. The police couldn't prove who had done it, but friends who had been with Cole when he did it, to sort of show off to them, turned him in."

Amber took the elastic band out of her hair and shook

it loose. "Cole always wanted to prove a point. He did stupid things, dangerous things. I didn't want anything to do with that. So I didn't want to see him anymore. A month after I told him so, he was kicked out of college, and I had no idea where he had gone. Imagine my surprise when I got here for the holidays, and there he was doing repairs on Dorothea's conservatory."

Amber played with the elastic band. "When I recognized him, I wanted to run, but I thought it might look like I was still hurt over ending our relationship. So I offered to make him coffee, and we talked."

She smiled to herself as she stared into the snowy world ahead of them. "He told me about his business and all, about being a volunteer at the shelter. He works with the toughest dogs there, the ones who have anxiety or aggression who no one can control. But he told me he knows how they feel because he used to feel like that. He's a completely different person now. Well, inside the same good looks, that is."

Callie couldn't help laughing at that addition. "So you're . . . falling for him again?"

Amber plucked at the elastic band. "I'm scared."

Callie kept her eyes on the road. "Why?"

"Because I thought I loved Ben. At least . . . he's stable, you know. He has a good job and prospects and Mom and Dad like him and . . . he's just right. Then Cole steps back into my life and . . . I feel things for him I never felt for Ben. But now I just think I let Ben down, and I never meant to, because he's the best friend I ever had. That whole scene yesterday. I could just crawl into a hole in the ground."

She sighed. "And now Cole is suspected of murder."

"You must care a lot for him if you even tried to hide his possible involvement in Leadenby's death."

"I was just looking for the ring, really, to make sure Ben wasn't involved, when I saw the handle of the screwdriver. I knew it was Cole's because he had been playing with it when we were talking. I took him coffee a couple of times. He had promised me he'd take me to the shelter sometime so I could see the dogs he works with. I was really looking forward to that. To . . . spending time with him also, you know."

Amber sighed. "What a mess. I don't want Ben to be involved in the murder, but I don't want Cole involved either. But somebody killed Leadenby. It was no accident."

She looked at Callie. "It wasn't Mom, was it? She only confessed to help me." Amber's eyes were wide, begging Callie for confirmation.

"Yes. I think so." Callie nodded slowly. "Sheila panicked when she saw you with the body and tried to wipe the prints off to keep you out of the case. I keep thinking about Frank Smith's sudden statement."

"Yeah, I saw him at the station. He looked at me like he couldn't wait to rush into town and tell everybody I had been arrested. Pompous idiot."

"I don't think he wanted to talk about your arrest at all. He told me that his statement changed everything for the case. That it pointed at another suspect. I can imagine he even wants to protect you, so he can claim to Dorothea that he helped her family. He's probably still hoping for money from the will."

Callie clenched the wheel. "It's very odd. I mean, why didn't he speak up yesterday? He claims that he felt sorry for Brenda, but I didn't have the impression he liked her at all. So why keep something back and then show up within twenty-four hours to tell it anyway?"

"No idea." Amber patted Daisy, who snuggled against her. "She's super cute. Like she can read people's minds and knows what they need."

"I'm trying to find her a home. Maybe you could take her."

"I'd love to, but I'm going back to college after the holidays. I can't have a dog there."

Callie put on the windshield wipers to clear some snow dust off the glass. Although it wasn't snowing at the moment, there was a constant drift of flakes coming down from trees and ledges. "How about Falk's sister, Peggy? Do you know her? I mean, you've been around here longer than I have."

"Yeah, I know her. I know of her, I mean. She has two kids. Two boys, I think."

"Yes, I saw them. Cute. Perfect playmates for Daisy."

"Are you joking? Daisy's too girly for them. They want a dog to play out in the woods with. A bigger one, I think. You're not giving her to them, are you? I mean, Peggy's seeing this really uptight guy, and I think he doesn't like dogs. He might just kick Daisy."

"What uptight guy?" Callie wanted to know.

Amber shrugged. "I've only seen them once on Main Street. He wore a suit and all, like he was selling insurance."

"I see." Callie didn't see how this would automatically brand the man as "uptight" and not a lover of dogs, but she supposed Amber had a different idea of the ideal man, especially with Cole Merton back in her life now. "But how about the boys' father?"

"Dead." Amber rebalanced the dog in her lap. "He was in the Coast Guard. They have to go out on risky missions, you know, when people get into trouble with their yachts or their sailboats. One time, he saved three teens, but he died himself. Don't think Peggy ever forgave him for that."

"For what?" Callie asked, frowning. She didn't quite see what there was to forgive about circumstances beyond someone's control.

"That he just left her with the boys. That he took a risk and that he died for it. I think this new guy she's seeing is a no-risk option." Amber nodded weightily. "I mean, his file folders won't kill him."

Callie glanced at her. "You can deduce all that from seeing her and a guy on Main Street once?"

"Well, I guess I understand about the no-risk option." Amber rubbed her face with her free hand. "When I get home, I bet Ben will fall all over me to hear how I'm doing. He's worried for me. He really cares. How can I tell him I lied to the police and almost went to jail for a guy I was once in love with?"

"Well, he might just think . . ." Callie glanced at her. "That you're still in love with this guy."

Amber exhaled. "That's what I thought." She banged her head back against the headrest and repeated, "What a mess."

Callie clutched the wheel, not speaking her thoughts out loud. How much had Ben known about Amber's old flame being back in her life? How much had he sensed of her reluctance to get close to him and seal the deal with an engagement? Had he been eager for it and determined to make sure Cole couldn't come between them?

Had Ben killed Leadenby with Cole's tool to get the handyman into trouble? To remove a rival from the scene?

It seemed cold and calculating, but people did the strangest things when they believed they were safeguarding what they couldn't stand to lose.

And Ben had been away from the party, out walking, he claimed, alone. So he would have had time to go into the conservatory and kill Leadenby.

A fine mess indeed.

# Chapter Ten

Having dropped Amber off at the Hall, Callie decided she needed to know more about the whereabouts of all the people present during the time the murder had been committed. She recalled that Mrs. Moore had shown an interest in everybody, moving to the door as soon as she heard Amber's scream and pushing her husband to call the police.

Would the inquisitive lady be able to tell her something worthwhile?

Callie drove to the house of Mr. and Mrs. Moore, a cute, comfortable villa on the outskirts of town with a giant lit reindeer in the garden, welcoming visitors. Along the path to the house front, box hedges were also bathed in colored Christmas lights—red, green, and golden.

At the door, two battery-operated Santas sang a Christmas medley, the first just one beat ahead of the other. They swung their paunches, the red velvet of their clothes riding up to reveal some precariously thin wires.

When Callie pressed the doorbell, violent barking started deep inside the house, coming closer and closer to the door.

Callie heard a dull thud as a body collided with the door and nails scratched the wood as if the dog was trying to dig a way out.

She reached down instinctively to pick up Daisy and hold her out of reach of the big guard dog that was about to appear as soon as the door was opened.

However, when the door swung back, Callie spied Mrs. Moore smiling at her. Behind her legs, peeking carefully at the intruders, was an apricot toy poodle.

"I thought you had a Rottweiler here," Callie said with a sigh of relief.

Mrs. Moore laughed. "You're not the first to be surprised at Butterfly's voice. Yes, you have a big bark, huh, girl. But a soft touch. Do come in."

In the hallway, on a sideboard beside the coat rack, was a towering piece of three wooden layers with a train track and a steam engine working its way up in circles to the highest tier, past tiny houses and snow-dusted pines. On the top, mounted on a turning metal hook, Santa flew in his sleigh, drawn by fluffy felt reindeer. Their red harnesses even had tiny golden bells. Mrs. Moore looked on as Callie put Daisy down to greet Butterfly and hung her coat on the rack. The two dogs approached each other carefully, stretching their noses and sniffing. Then they circled each other, tails starting to wag.

Callie complimented her hostess on the Christmas train, but realized she was in for more when she entered the living room. The space in front of the three large windows was filled by a table decked with a white cloth and fake snow holding a complete village of houses, a church, shops, an ice skating rink, horse-drawn carriages, and small animals. Tiny human figures went about their business, shopping, baking, building snowmen. Everything was lit with the light from miniature lampposts and lights from the houses' tiny windows.

"What a fairy-tale sight," Callie said.

Mrs. Moore beamed. "My husband made all of those. It's his hobby. He works on it year-round to be able to add more at Christmastime. People travel here especially to see the display."

"I can imagine."

"He used to have it up at the community center. But he isn't allowed anymore." She sounded piqued.

"By whom?"

"Frank Smith said it was unprofessional." Mrs. Moore huffed. "As if he gets to decide that."

"Well, apparently he does, if your husband has his display here now," Callie pointed out gently.

"Yes, Smith got other councilmembers to vote in his favor. He said that if the community center has a Christmas display, it should be a rented one, via some company he recommended. I bet it's a friend of his and he'll get a fat commission out of it. Shameful! It was a blow to my husband, I can tell you. He served this town all his life, first in the council, now as mayor. And you get no respect and appreciation for it. None at all."

"Well, I wouldn't put it quite like that. Mrs. Finster did invite you to her will reading yesterday."

"Yes, she did, didn't she?" Mrs. Moore sat down on the sofa that held Christmas-themed pillows covered in robins and deer. She gestured to Callie to choose a chair nearby. She continued, "That was a bit of a surprise, to be honest. Mrs. Finster isn't much into the town community anymore, it seems. I tend to think it's her health. I mean, she is over ninety. It must have been such a shock to her to have the police in her house. I wonder how she is, poor dear."

This was accompanied by questioning looks suggesting Mrs. Moore assumed Callie had more knowledge of this.

"I think she spent most of today in bed." Callie felt sorry for revealing information about Dorothea, but she had to give something to get this woman talking.

The mayor's wife clicked her tongue. "Poor dear. And to have everybody talking about her. I bet she hates it. But it can't be avoided. Not with a murder occurring at your house."

Mrs. Moore's almost gleeful tone suggested she had found the experience exciting rather than frightening.

Callie quickly sprang on the opportunity. "Did you leave the room at all, during the break in the proceedings when tea was served?"

"No, I was there the whole time. I watched all the

comings and goings. That young man rushed off and Sheila went after him like a flash. Amber left the room as well, looking quite upset, I bet about this engagement business. Imagine a priceless ring going missing like that. I wonder who took it. Or if it was never there to begin with. They do whisper in town that the family fortune isn't as large as it used to be."

Callie filed away this information for later. "You were left with Dorothea and Mrs. Keats? And your husband?" Her heart beat fast as she realized she needed to find another suspect other than the people she cared for, and the mayor could just be it.

But he was married to the woman sitting opposite her. Could she actually expect Mrs. Moore to say anything that might incriminate her own husband?

Mrs. Moore said, "Iphy was there, of course, handing out all the sweet treats. I dare say she did a good job with them. The little wills on the cupcakes were so clever. Then you left the room. Stephen kept a close eye on you. He stood at the door, watching you while you were in the hallway."

Callie flushed at this revelation but tried to look untouched. "So you were in the room all of the time with Dorothea, Mrs. Keats, and Iphy. But your husband did leave. He had to make a phone call?" She knew it had been Frank Smith who had made the call, but she hoped Mrs. Moore would say something interesting.

"No. He was there all the time. He sat beside me." Mrs. Moore reached out to a small table where scented candles in holders were spreading a sweet vanilla scent. She rearranged them as she added, "He was upset we never got to reading that will. I mean, the town could do with some money for renovations. When you walk in the street and step into a hole in the pavement, well, that's not good advertising for our town."

She picked up small scissors and cut a bit off the wick of one of the candles. Immediately it burned more brightly. Mrs. Moore gave a satisfied grunt. "Frank Smith has all of these grand plans for Heart's Harbor, but no money to spend. But there's a fund. I know it."

"A fund?" Callie repeated, puzzled.

"Yes. Twenty years ago, Dorothea's husband gave the chamber of commerce a fund. With substantial money in it. Frank should use that."

Callie narrowed her eyes. "But he wants more money from Mrs. Finster?"

"Yes. I heard him say that since she has no children, she should leave her fortune to the town. I find that a bit drastic, don't you? I mean, we all know Stephen Du Bouvrais was groomed to be her heir. You can't deny him something he expected to get all his life. Although I daresay he earns enough, now that he's a diplomat and all. He doesn't really need money, I suppose. But once a thing is promised to you, you depend on it. And Dorothea is a woman of her word. She'll give him something, I imagine. The Hall at least, I suppose."

There was a lot of supposing here, but Callie decided to

let it go on. Mrs. Moore said cheerfully, "That pile of bricks wouldn't serve us anyway. We need hard cash. That's what my husband said to me when we got the invitation to the tea party with mention of the new will."

"Yes, and did your husband ever have anything to do with Leadenby? The victim?"

"I wouldn't call him a victim." Mrs. Moore waved with the scissors she had just used to trim the wick. "Oh, yes, Leadenby might have been killed, but he always was a nasty little man. He liked to make people feel uncomfortable."

"What do you mean?"

Mrs. Moore leaned toward Callie and took a confidential tone. "He hinted at things he knew about them. All nonsense, if you ask me. How could he know such things? He never was in any position of trust where he might have learned secrets. I mean, if you work in the police station or at a lawyer's office, you might know things, but he was just a gardener. Always making himself important and making people feel bad. I disliked him, I won't lie. Now that he's dead, we should of course say nothing but nice things about him, but I don't feel obliged."

Remembering all the gossip about Leadenby at the Book Tea that morning, Callie supposed Mrs. Moore wasn't the only local who didn't feel obliged to speak well of the dead. "But did he really know things? I mean, if he was just pretending, that's hardly a reason to kill someone."

Mrs. Moore sighed. "You'd think not. Butterfly! Come here." The poodle and Daisy had ambled through the room together during the interview but were now chasing each other under the table holding the Christmas village. Mrs. Moore called her dog again, snapping her fingers. As Butterfly hurried to her, Mrs. Moore cooed, "Yes, good girl."

Callie tried to attract Daisy's attention, but she was curling up under the pipes of the central heating, apparently convinced she had found the warmest place in the house.

Mrs. Moore tickled the poodle's side. "But maybe Leadenby was a case of . . . what do you call it?" Her face scrunched up in deep concentration. "I read a very interesting article about it in a magazine. That sometimes people pretend they're important and make up all kinds of fantastical things, but one day they get it right. Maybe Leadenby got something right for once? Maybe he knew a real secret this time."

Or someone had misinterpreted his malicious hinting and merely *thought* he knew a secret. A secret worth killing for.

Had Leadenby actually died because of his big mouth?

"As the mayor's wife, you must feel so close to all the people in this town. The mayor is called the town father, right? Well, then you must be the town mother. You must feel for those involved now. Such a thing to happen when you all know each other."

"Yes, but I don't mind some people getting into trouble. They deserve it. Take that boy Cole Merton. He starts a business that lets him get into people's houses. Now he can just take their wallets or their phones or their cutlery. He could have done something else to earn money. Deliver newspapers or something."

"That's more of a small job. If he needs to support himself . . ."

"Why here of all places? I'm glad people told him off. They didn't want him to work for them. Frankly, I was surprised that Mrs. Finster invited him into her home. I think someone should have told her not to do it. Maybe someone did. She was very stubborn. Probably thought she knew better. Oh well, now she can see what he did. Murdered someone under her roof."

"You think Cole Merton did it?" Callie tried to assume a sort of sensationalist gossipy tone.

Mrs. Moore nodded. "Of course. Leadenby must have hinted to him that he knew about his past and . . ."

"But wait. You just said people knew Cole had done bad things before and already refused to let him work for them. If that wasn't a big secret, then why would he have had to kill Leadenby?"

"Well, you never know what Leadenby knew about him. Cole might have done more than just take things. He might have been in a fight and hurt someone. Killed him. Young people are violent these days when they've had too much to drink. Or when they take drugs."

Callie remembered Amber's story about the broken car mirror after the bad grade. Back then, Cole had obviously been vindictive when he felt someone had wronged him.

Amber had also said he had done stupid or dangerous things. Had Cole's temper gotten the better of him?

"I just wish he hadn't started a business here. We have quite a nice little town and we don't need troublemakers. In fact, I think someone wrote him a note like that. Or sprayed it on his van. Or something."

Callie sat up. "But spraying incriminating words on a van is violating someone's property. Did Cole Merton report the incident to the police?"

"Like they're going to listen to him." Mrs. Moore crossed her arms over her chest and nodded, as if she had personally ensured that the police didn't listen to people like Cole Merton.

Callie's heart clenched at the idea that Falk wouldn't take a complaint about somebody's van being ruined seriously just because that somebody had done something wrong years before. Judging by Amber's story, Cole had turned his life around, building his business and volunteering at the shelter rehoming the toughest dogs. If that was true, he didn't deserve new trouble, a bill for getting his van cleaned, financial losses because locals didn't want to hire him.

Mrs. Moore interrupted her thoughts, "You have such a cute little dog. Usually Butterfly doesn't like other dogs, but they seem to get along really nicely."

Callie smiled as she watched the toy poodle walk up to Daisy and give her a playful push with her nose. Daisy got to her feet and they ran after each other again, circling the legs of a chair. "Has Frank Smith ever said anything negative to you about Brenda Brink?" Callie asked.

"Brenda? No, not that I can remember. But I wouldn't have been surprised if he had. He doesn't like her at all. In fact, he seems to hate her. He couldn't stand her asking for funds for the playground. He wanted to have the money all to himself. When he heard she was also invited to come to the Hall, well, he about exploded."

"So you think he would badmouth her if he got a chance?"

"Oh yes."

That was interesting. But . . . Frank's testimony had been true. He had said Brenda had been threatened by Leadenby, and that was in line with what Callie herself had overheard. So the president hadn't told lies.

Maybe Mrs. Moore had only thought that Smith was maligning Brenda when in reality Brenda did have some deep, dark secret? Deep and dark enough to kill for? Would Falk have questioned her yet? And did he know about the threats against Cole Merton?

*Time to find out.*

Callie got up and admired the Christmas village up close and then thanked her hostess and excused herself, saying she had to pick up some things for dinner. Mrs. Moore told her to give her regards to Iphy and remind her that she needed the quote for the crochet club's annual tea party at the Book Tea. "She's never so late with it, but then I suppose she was busy for Dorothea. Dorothea has this way of . . . commanding people's time and efforts."

Callie assured her she'd bring it up with Iphy first thing and left, not heading for the supermarket or the Book Tea at all. She wanted to talk to Falk. A call to the police station told her he was off for the day and had gone home. Of course his address wasn't listed, but Callie had access to a source more knowledgeable than the Internet.

Iphy answered on the third ring, told Callie she was making stew, and asked if she would be home for dinner. Callie said she wasn't sure yet and asked for Deputy Falk's address.

"If you think you're going to get a free meal at Falk's, forget it."

Callie flushed. "I'm not after a free meal, just some information."

Iphy sighed. "I doubt you'll get that either. But you can always try. He lives in a log cabin a little off the beaten path. It doesn't even have a street address. But I'll give you some directions. As a tour guide, you should be able to find your way."

# Chapter Eleven

As her car gingerly crossed the thickly iced dirt road, Callie wondered if she even wanted to find her way. There was no light other than from her headlights, and Daisy was restless beside her, lifting up her head as if to look out the front window and determine where on earth they were going.

At last Callie saw the cabin and light streaming from the windows.

She parked the car and climbed out, then slithered around it to let Daisy out on the other side. Glancing up, she saw there were stars in the clear sky. Temps were dropping fast, and Callie shivered as she walked up to the cabin and climbed the bare wooden steps. No Christmas lights here, no Santas, no music.

Not even a bell.

Callie formed her hand into a fist and banged it on the door. She knew better than to try with her knuckles and risk losing all of her skin on the rough surface.

It took only a moment for Falk to come to the door. He

was dressed in a checkered shirt and jeans again, walking around in his socks. His expression registered surprise, then suspicion.

"I won't be staying long," Callie assured him. "But I do want to come in. It's freezing out here already."

He nodded and stepped aside. She noticed at least four pairs of boots by the door, all kinds of jackets and coats tossed into a twined basket. The scent of freshly cut wood was heavy in the air. A log fire burned, and Daisy immediately stretched her nose in that direction as if to say, *I want to sit right there.*

Falk gestured to it. "Make yourselves at home."

It sounded a little sarcastic, but Callie went over and sat on the sheepskin in front of the fireplace, depositing Daisy beside her. "It's really getting very cold." She rubbed her hands and even blew on them to get some feeling back into her numb fingers.

Falk shrugged. "It's December." He studied her. "Have you been investigating all day long?"

Callie flushed and studied her surroundings. Leather couch, low table with a few dirty coffee mugs, newspapers piled up. Not a computer in sight.

"Seen it all?" Falk asked.

She blushed even deeper. "It's just the contrast. Mrs. Moore's house is Christmas from top to toe, from pillows to candles and a ton of fake snow, and here there isn't a sign of the festive season. It could be January for all I know."

"I'm not a big fan of the holidays." Falk said it as if the mere words left a bad taste in his mouth.

"Why? I mean, everybody seems to love this time of year."

She studied Falk's tight posture as he moved through the room. It seemed like he wanted to get into the darkest corner so she couldn't see his expression well when he answered.

"I don't like things that are forced onto me." Falk stood, looping his thumbs into his belt. "Like people muscling in on my investigation. You weren't at Mrs. Moore's to admire her husband's Christmas village."

"Well, it's very pretty." Seeing his dark stare, Callie added quickly, "But no, you're right. I wanted to know her thoughts on what happened yesterday. She mentioned a couple of very interesting things."

Falk rolled his eyes. "Everything is a revelation to her. What people earn, what people spend, what they name their children. Why they use pink stationery. I don't want to hear what Mrs. Moore had to say."

Callie dug her heels into the sheepskin rug as if to brace herself for impact. "You'll have to, because I think there are crimes being committed around town that you know nothing about."

"Crimes? Plural?" Falk hitched a brow at her. "You're really trying to outdo me."

"No. This is not a competition. I'm trying to help. Not you, obviously. Amber and other people involved. Even Cole Merton."

"Cole Merton?" Falk laughed softly. "He took a swing at my deputy to escape questioning. He could be charged with assaulting a police officer. And that's the least of his worries with his screwdriver being found buried in Leadenby's chest."

"Come on, we all know he might have left it at the house while he was working there. Anyone could have picked it up and used it."

"Admittedly. But if Cole Merton is as pure as the driven snow . . ." Falk gestured to the windows. "How come he's so eager to avoid my questions?"

"Did you know his van was vandalized? That someone sprayed threats on it, suggesting he should leave town?"

Falk held her gaze. A moment ago, she'd been sure he was going to throw her out because he'd had enough of her meddling, but he said slowly, "No. I didn't know that. He didn't press charges. When people don't press charges, we can't know, can we?"

"Mrs. Moore knew. I bet others know. Maybe you heard a rumor and didn't want to know? After all, Cole Merton's just a small-time crook. Better if he left town, right?"

Falk exhaled audibly. "You've got a nerve."

Callie combed through the rug. "I'm just trying to figure out where you stand. Mrs. Moore told me about these threats against Cole Merton quite gleefully. She seems to think he deserves it. Now I'm trying to establish if more people feel that way. Because that could mean someone consciously used Cole Merton's screwdriver to make sure he leaves town. For good."

Falk held her gaze. "You're pretty worried about someone you don't even know. Or did you happen to bump into Mr. Charming?"

"Never met him. Don't even have any idea what he looks like. But I do know that spraying threats on someone's van can be the start of something nasty. And now with a dead body . . ."

Falk took a deep breath. She was sure he was going to tell her to stop playing cop and go back to the Book Tea to make marzipan books or something.

But instead he said, "Want a beer?"

Callie wasn't a big fan of beer, but if it could buy her time in his presence, time to figure out more about the death and about him, she was fine with it. "Sure."

Falk vanished from sight, and she heard a fridge opening and closing, then caps popping. He came back and handed her the bottle. He clinked the neck of his bottle against hers. "Cheers. Not that there's anything to celebrate." He dropped himself in a rocking chair and moved it with one foot on the floor as he drank deeply from his beer.

Callie took a sip and rested the beer bottle on the sheepskin.

Daisy came over and sniffed. She sneezed and pulled back.

Falk had to laugh. "She seems to like it just as much as you do."

"I hardly ever drink," Callie admitted to him. "I work as a tour guide, and it's my responsibility to look after the people in my group. I taught myself not to drink or do anything else that might keep me from having a clear head. The guests are in a strange country and they depend on me. I take that very seriously."

Falk nodded. "I see."

The creaking of the rocking chair was the only sound in the room.

Callie played with the cold beer bottle. "It seems like Cole Merton was harassed to make sure he left town again. Do you have any idea why?"

"Probably just people not liking a guy with a bad reputation setting up shop here."

"Did Cole tell you anything about Leadenby after you brought him in?"

Falk shook his head. "He didn't talk at all. He sat there and we asked him questions and he just stared back at us. He reminded me a little of a tiger in the zoo. There's glass between you and him, but if there weren't, he'd grab you."

"He knows he's suspected of murder. Did you call a lawyer for him?"

"He didn't want one. He explicitly said so. I have it on the record."

Callie exhaled in a huff.

"Look," Falk said, "if he wants to be stupid, I'm not going to argue with him. But since you seem so certain he didn't do it, maybe you can give me another suspect?" He held her gaze. "But since it can't be Sheila or Amber or Stephen—and Dorothea and her housekeeper and Mr. and

Mrs. Moore can all alibi each other—I don't see that you have many options left. Aside from Brenda Brink, maybe."

He stopped rocking as if a sudden thought struck him. "How about Ben? Are you going to protect him too? Or can he be sacrificed for the rest of the family?"

Callie clutched the beer bottle. Falk's challenging tone was getting to her, but she supposed that he must be frustrated after a long, hard day of work that had run him in circles. He had lost Amber as a suspect; now he had Cole, who wasn't giving him anything. He could have scooped up Sheila, but he hadn't believed her story.

And Ben? What would his motive have been, really? Anger, jealousy, the need to pin it all on Cole so a rival for Amber's affections would be removed from the scene?

It felt far-fetched, untrue. "Do you know anything about a fund Dorothea's husband established years ago for the town?"

"Oh, yes, I heard about it. It seems that the town pays a lot of things out of that fund." Falk stretched his legs. "I suppose it has to do with investments, stocks, that sort of thing."

"Any idea who handles it for them? I mean, a lawyer, or a banker, or . . ."

"No idea, but I could find out. How come?"

"I don't know. People were eager to get Dorothea's money. Do they really need it? Bad enough to kill for it?"

"Leadenby wasn't the one who made the will," Falk

reminded her. He leaned his head back and stared at the ceiling. "Can you cook?"

"Cook?" Callie echoed, overtaken by the sudden question.

"You could cook us dinner."

"Why would I do that?"

"Because in the meantime I could dig into this fund."

"And you'll share your findings with me?"

"You have no idea what a good meal does for a man's mood."

Callie had to laugh. "Do I have access to a stove? Or would it be marshmallows over an open fire?"

"Marshmallows are not dinner. I teach that to Tate and Jimmy, so I better stick to my own rules."

She noticed the tight look on his face. She wanted to ask if he felt responsible for his nephews after their father died, but it would be a very personal question between virtual strangers.

"Stove is in the kitchen." He gestured to where he had disappeared to get the beers. "You can raid the cupboards for a winning combination."

"You don't mind me going through your things?"

"Canned beans and ketchup?" He hitched a brow at her. "That's about all there is in there."

Callie pushed herself up. "Deal. But I don't see how you're going to do research without a computer."

Falk pointed at a writing desk in the far corner. "It hides

a laptop. I even have an Internet connection here. Hush, don't tell anyone."

Callie had to laugh again. She walked into the kitchen and looked at the sink. It was empty and shiny as if it had been cleaned an hour ago. Somehow she had expected a busy bachelor's household to be a little disorganized. She had pictured Falk eating his breakfast standing at the sink, then leaving the dirty bowl until he felt like doing some dishes. She herself had been guilty of that on the rare occasions when she had been at home. Spoiled, probably, by too many hotel breakfasts where the staff cleaned up after her. "No dirty dishes?" she called to him in a light tone. "I'm impressed."

"Oh, I forgot to tell you," Falk responded in the same joking vein. "Don't look in the lower cupboards. Just the ones along the far wall."

Still laughing, Callie shook her head and started to hunt for dinner. Reaching out to open the fridge, she noticed the many sheets of paper stuck to it. Kids' drawings. In one of them, she recognized Falk's cabin and figures playing outside with a kite. A tall figure and two small ones.

\* \* \*

As Callie carried two steaming plates into the living room, Falk was seated behind the desk and typing away at the keyboard. He barely looked up as she came to stand beside him.

"What are you caught up in?"

"Something not too pretty. I found photos online of the threats sprayed on Cole Merton's van. Someone apparently thought his creativity should be preserved for posterity. Then I looked at sites where you can rate businesses. Let's say Cole's rating isn't the best. And guess what?"

"All anonymous complaints?" Callie suggested.

"Exactly. No wonder he's acting so hostile. He really has nowhere to turn." Falk looked up at her. "Thanks for bringing this to my attention."

"Don't mention it. Amber seems to like Cole, so . . . I'm just doing a little research to see how good or bad he is. I don't want her to hook up with the wrong guy, you know. On the other hand, I'm not going to malign him just because he made mistakes in the past."

Falk sniffed. "What did you make?"

"Hash browns and fish. A sauce from mayonnaise and pickles. Nothing fancy."

"You don't call that fancy? More work than I usually bother with." Falk rose and stretched his shoulders. "Let's eat, then."

Callie seated herself in front of the fireplace again and patted Daisy, who wanted a bite. "You have to wait until we get home, girl. I don't have dog food for you here."

Daisy whined a moment, looking at Falk to see if he was going to feed her.

He shook his head. "Dogs are just like kids, huh? You have to send a single message."

"Something like that." Callie picked up her fork. "I appreciate that you dug into Cole Merton's problems, and I do think that if you show him you care, he might open up and be more responsive in the murder case, but, uh . . . how about that business fund?"

"I stepped out while you were so busy cooking"—Falk gestured with his fork to the plate in his lap—"and made a few calls. Let's say the news is . . . pretty surprising. At least to me."

He held her gaze, stretching the suspense.

Callie felt like throwing something at him, but there was nothing within reach.

Falk said, "The financial manager at the investment firm I talked to didn't want to give any information at first, claiming it was confidential and I needed to go through official channels. Things like that can take forever, so I gave him a little inducement by suggesting that any official investigation would also draw publicity to his firm and might harm their reputation. Those people are scared to death of any whisper that something might be wrong on their end. So he huffed and puffed a little and then said he might as well tell me. The fund is nonexistent. It was all spent."

"Spent?" Callie echoed. "By whom?"

"Well, Moore signed for the transactions. He did invest some money in the town initially, but the last couple of years he also gave orders to make dubious investments in funds that would create big returns and never did. The financial manager said he warned him about the risks, but Moore insisted he wanted the investments made."

"The mayor gambled away the town's money?"

"If you want to put it like that, yes. Of course, I've just heard this over the phone, and I'd need paperwork to prove it. Also to ensure that the financial manager himself hasn't made mistakes and tried to blame Moore for it. You know how these things go sometimes. They give you only half the picture, and, eager for a fast return, you invest. Then, poof, the money is gone and you're left with nothing." Falk took a big bite and chewed. "Delicious."

Callie stared ahead, deep in thought. "So Moore had every reason to hope for a big donation from Dorothea so he'd never have to admit he was out of funds. Who knew about this? Leadenby? If he did, it would have been explosive. He could have blackmailed Moore with it." She frowned. "But how would Leadenby have found out about it? You just said the financial manager was reluctant to tell you anything. I assume he wouldn't have given information at all if it hadn't been for the murder case."

Falk nodded. "Exactly. And I understood from both Mrs. Moore and Dorothea Finster that our good mayor was in the room the entire time. When would he have had the time to go out and kill Leadenby?"

Callie considered this. "So we're back to Cole Merton or Brenda Brink?"

Falk gestured with his fork. "Of course I'll grill Moore

over the missing funds. Maybe he'll tell me something revealing."

Callie wondered if the smart mayor would say anything at all. As Falk had just suggested, he could always claim that he had been misinformed about the risks of the investments and had only had the town's future at heart when he had tried for a big return on the money. It wasn't like he had put the money in his own bank account or something.

Her cell phone buzzed. She put the plate down and reached into her pocket. Pulling out the phone, she looked at the screen. Unknown number. She pushed accept. "Hello?"

A muffled voice said, "Stop poking around or you'll regret it." Then the line went dead.

Callie wasn't quite sure she had heard right. "Hello? Hello? Who's there?"

Falk looked at her. "Wrong number?"

Callie put down the phone and looked at the screen again. Of course the caller had made sure his or her number was withheld. To make the threat anonymous.

"What?" Falk pressed.

"Some crank caller." Her heart beating fast, she put the phone back in her pocket. If she told Falk it was some kind of threat, he would also urge her to leave the investigation alone. And she wasn't about to do that now that she had already come this far. The threat itself had to mean that someone felt like she was getting too close to some truth. Something significant she wasn't supposed to discover. *Stop poking around.*

Who knew she was poking around?

Mrs. Moore with her friendly face and her cute toy poodle.

Frank Smith, who had seen her at the police station.

Ben, who was staying with the family and had to have heard of her involvement today.

Cole Merton, who was feeling more and more cornered?

"Is Cole Merton still at the station?" Callie asked Falk.

"Yes. I didn't think it could hurt to keep him overnight. How come? Do you think he was calling you?" Falk looked probing now. "What did that caller say?"

"Nothing important."

"Come on."

"That reminds me. Frank Smith got a call during the tea party and he went out to answer it. Did you check who it came from?"

"No, of course not. What good would that do us? Besides, contrary to popular belief, we can't just check everybody's phone records. We have to be sure it's related to the case. He told us during questioning it was his secretary calling about something to do with a business meeting."

"Yes, he also said that to us when he came back after the call. But when he pulled his phone from his pocket and looked at the screen, his expression was pretty surprised. I don't know. Like he hadn't expected that particular call."

"He might have told his secretary not to call him, and when she did anyway, he wondered what could be so important. I could ask her, but I don't think it's really worth a lot of fuss."

"Oh, fine." After the threatening call, Callie didn't feel much like eating. "Look, I'd love to sit and chat, but it's getting late, and I did promise Iphy I'd help out with some cake making. Besides, the road isn't getting any better."

"I can drive you back," Falk offered at once, putting aside his own plate.

Callie looked at him. "What about my car? I mean, Iphy's car actually." She got to her feet. "Nah, it's better if I drive back myself. I'll just drive slowly. I took a course once, brake training and all, so I should be good."

"You sure?" Falk rose as well, looking hesitant to just let her leave. He walked with her to the front door. "You'll be fine?"

"Perfectly." She picked up Daisy. The dog licked her neck, and Callie held her tighter against her. "I'll be extra careful."

Falk held her gaze a moment with a probing look, as if he sensed her insecurity. "You do that," he said slowly. "You do that."

# Chapter Twelve

The road ahead was dark, and the only thing she could see clearly was the white snow drifting from on high. The flakes formed a dense curtain, obstructing her view of the surroundings. Suddenly something shone at her, blinding her. A big diamond was in the road, blocking it completely. It reflected bright white light that hurt her eyes.

A phone rang in the distance, an irritating repetitive beeping, and a hushed voice said, *Stop poking, stop poking.*

Then it changed to *Stop cooking, stop cooking.*

The diamond was a pan full of pasta, boiling over, creating a river of hot water flowing toward her while two little boys pulled at her legs, screaming that they wanted cocoa and cookies.

Callie woke up with a start, staring into the space overhead. There was the familiar ceiling and oak beams that she remembered so well from her childhood summers. Beneath her, she heard the sounds of someone in the kitchen, putting the kettle on.

What time was it?

Turning her head to the left, she checked the red figures of her alarm clock. Eight. It felt like she had slept only an hour or so. Those terrible dreams. The road, the snow, the cooking.

No more cooking.

No, that wasn't right. No more poking.

She cringed when she thought about Falk finding out she had been threatened and hadn't listened. But hey, he had said they couldn't just check phone records, so telling him she had been threatened wouldn't have helped either. He couldn't look into who the caller was anyway.

Wincing as her stiff muscles locked, Callie got up and showered, dressed in a pale-pink sweater and gray pants, and put on a little makeup. Her head was heavy, as it always was when snow was in the air. She loved the winter season, but it played havoc with her body.

Iphy served her breakfast without asking any questions about her trip to see Falk the night before. In fact, her great aunt's innocent silence bothered Callie more than if Iphy had asked a dozen questions. She knew her great aunt too well. Iphy was cooking up something.

Trouble, probably.

"I have to go out and talk to Amber about the missing ring," Callie announced as they finished breakfast. "I want to know if she has any idea who saw her put it in her pocket. I mean, someone must have known where it was or they couldn't have removed it later on. I hope to be back here and help out at the Book Tea when you open around ten."

"That's fine, dear. You do what you have to."

See. That smile, that sweet tone. Iphy was up to something.

Callie groaned inwardly and left with Daisy for the Hall. At the general store, people gathered to buy the special Christmas doughnuts the general store owner's wife baked each year, and in front of the community center a group of kids were building a large snowman.

When Callie cruised by them, she cast a loving look at their rosy faces and listened to their excited cries with fond memories of her own winter adventures. It was great to be a kid.

Or was it?

A few yards down the street, she caught a glimpse of a small figure walking with his head down, his shoulders slumped. A second look told her it was Tate, Falk's youngest nephew. He seemed totally dejected. What had happened?

She hit the brakes and stopped the car, got out, and went over to him.

"Hello there."

As Tate looked up at her, Callie's heart clenched to see the tears on his cheeks. There were patches of snow on his coat, the white smudges already melting and the cold water seeping into the fabric.

"What's wrong?" she asked, squatting in front of him.

He looked at her, blinking away more tears. He struggled to get the words out. "I wanted to help build the snowman. But there are bigger kids I don't know."

"They're probably here for the holidays. You can just ask them if you can join in. We can go see together."

He shook his head. "They're mean. They threw ice balls at me."

So that was how the snowy smudges had gotten onto his clothes.

Callie bristled at the idea that a couple of kids from out of town were doing this in the heart of their little village and stood up. "They probably think they can do whatever they want. But they also have to play by the rules. Let the younger kids join in. I'll go over and tell them not to throw ice balls at anybody anymore."

Before Tate could protest her intervention, she marched off.

Closing in on the kids, she noticed that two boys were considerably older than the others and that they were completely in charge. They ordered the smaller kids around, and when one of them wasn't quick enough to do the older ones' bidding, he got a shove and fell in the snow. He didn't protest though, but scrambled to his feet again, apparently not risking his chance to play with the older kids. If he had just witnessed Tate's departure, he was probably forewarned.

Anger now pumped in Callie's veins, and she stood with her shoulders pulled back and her hands clenched into fists by her side. "Boys," her voice was trembling. "Can you please play in such a way that all the kids can participate? Let the little ones have some fun too, huh? It's almost Christmas."

One of the older boys, in a black coat with a red hat,

looked at her. "Who are you, our teacher?" His tone was rude and his eyes flashed at her.

"A little boy is crying because you threw ice balls at him. What do you think of that?"

"Did Tate run to you to cry? Tate is a crybaby. Tate is a crybaby."

His mean chant was soon copied by all the kids, and they screamed their loudest.

Callie cringed and retreated two paces. It had not been her intention to make it even worse for Tate. She didn't dare look back to where he was waiting for her. Or maybe he had walked on, afraid of what was about to happen?

The boy with the red hat leaned down. Fast like lightning, he formed the snow into a hard ball and threw it at her. It hit her in the chest. Pain shot through her.

His comrade had also picked up snow, and another ball hit her in the head. The icy mass exploded against Callie's temple, and for a moment she saw stars. She stepped back again.

The smaller children had all grabbed snow and threw it at her, more or less formed into projectiles. The bits rained down around her, and she took flight.

Her temple hurt like crazy, and when she reached up, she actually felt something sticky against her hand. Her head spun, but she was looking out for Tate, determined to get him away from these kids. He still stood near her car, not looking at what was happening but quietly crying to himself.

Her heart broke for him as she closed the distance, sank

to her haunches, and wrapped her arms around him. Vaguely she heard the taunting chants, "Tate is a crybaby." The idea she had made it all worse for him hurt more than her chest and head.

"I'm sorry," she whispered as she held him tightly. "I'm sorry, Tate."

Tate moved in her arms, and she lifted her head to look at him.

His eyes were wide as he studied her. "You're bleeding."

"Yes, they threw ice balls at me too. You know why? Not because I'm a crybaby, but because they're mean. They want to be in charge. They want everybody to be scared of them and to do what they say. It's not about you, Tate. It's about them."

Tate looked at her. She wasn't sure he actually understood what she was trying to explain. "Where's your brother?" she asked.

He shrugged. "With them, I guess."

Callie straightened up and looked back at the children. They had resumed their play like nothing had happened. Their excited voices carried to where she stood. She couldn't see Jimmy among them. But there were a lot of kids, and some of them were running around to gather more snow from far corners. Was it possible he had been looking on and not helping his little brother?

And where was their mother? Why was Peggy not keeping an eye on her sons? Did she just believe that in a small town the kids would care for one another?

Callie reached out her hand to Tate. "Come on. We're going to get you a hot cocoa."

She brought him to Book Tea and delivered him to Iphy in the kitchen. Iphy took one glance at Tate's mottled face, the snow on his clothes, and then at Callie and shook her head. "I thought you'd be at the Hall by now."

"Can Tate stay here this morning? He'd like some cocoa and cookies."

"And a coloring book and pencils, I bet." Iphy winked at the little boy. She then asked Callie, "Does his mother know where he is?"

"I have no idea. I didn't see his older brother either. Maybe you can give her a call and tell her Tate is here?" Having noticed Peggy's hostility the other day when she had arrived at the Hall to get the children, Callie wasn't eager to get in touch with her again.

Iphy nodded. "Of course. Do you need to wash that cut?"

Callie winced at the idea of just looking at her temple. "I'll do it later."

"Is it the Moore boys again?"

Callie hitched a brow and wished she hadn't as pain seared her temple. "The Moore boys?"

"Mayor Moore's grandsons. They think they can run the town. They terrorized the skating rink the other day. Seems nobody did much about it. All afraid to cross our good town father."

So Moore had a lot of power in town. How much of that would be left if people found out he had been squandering the money from the fund started by Dorothea's husband?

Mayor Moore would have every reason to keep his mistakes under wraps. Was he the one who had threatened her last night? Informed by his wife that she had stopped by and asked questions?

"Sometimes it isn't smart to pick a fight," Iphy said. Of course she meant with the mean kids, but Callie felt like the warning also included the investigation. Did she really understand who she was up against?

To steady her nerves, she pulled her shoulders back and tried to sound firm. "Doing nothing isn't helping either."

Iphy seemed to want to say something in defense of her opinion, but Callie was already on the move. She didn't need her great aunt to tell her she wasn't handling this in the best way. She knew that already, but she didn't see what else she could have done. Maybe take Tate to the Book Tea without confronting the kids about their behavior? Probably.

With a sigh, she got into her car again, patted Daisy, and went on her way to Haywood Hall.

*　*　*

At the Hall, Mrs. Keats opened the door and let her in. The woman looked decidedly unhappy, and Callie asked quietly how Dorothea was doing. Mrs. Keats just shook her head and then asked for whom she was calling. Callie asked for Amber and was told to wait as Mrs. Keats fetched her.

In the sitting room, Callie tried to detect the source of a

delicious spicy scent and discovered a fresh arrangement of evergreen with dried orange slices, cinnamon, and star anise. The foot of its tall brass container was powdered with fake snow, and some small felt birds sat in snow strewn around it.

A creak in the doorway announced the arrival of Amber. She asked Mrs. Keats for some tea and smiled at Callie. "I made that. I just had to do something to take my mind off everything that happened."

"It looks great."

"Yeah, sometimes I think I want to be a florist. Decorate venues for weddings and all. That would be fun."

Callie wasn't quite sure how this fit with the graphic design plans or learning Spanish during a stay in Barcelona. She could imagine that single-minded Sheila found it hard to deal with her daughter's ever-changing plans and had thought it best to steer her in a focused direction.

Daisy greeted Amber by running for her and twirling around her legs, barking and whining until Amber leaned down and cuddled her. Daisy even threw herself on her back to have her tummy patted, something she rarely did. Maybe she sensed Amber was sad and hoped to cheer her up.

Amber laughed softly and stroked the dog's fur. "You're sweet. You're a doll." She looked up at Callie, her eyes turning indignant. "Falk kept Cole at the station overnight. He locked him up like a criminal."

"If Falk wants to charge Cole with the murder, he probably thought he better keep him there overnight so Cole couldn't leave town."

"He's not guilty and he's not running."

"No? I heard Cole lashed out at a police officer when he was asked to come in for questioning. Not exactly a smart move, if you ask me."

Amber huffed. "Cole realized they're just trying to pin everything on him. Mom even thinks I lied about taking the ring because I'm trying to cover for Cole. She thinks he stole the ring and I lied about taking it so he won't get in trouble."

Her cheeks turned fiery red. "I don't want Cole to be accused, of course, but I really did take the ring. Someone must have come into my room and taken it."

"But Amber . . ." Callie frowned. "That's only possible if someone knew you had taken the ring from the ring box and put it in your pocket. How could that be if you were alone in the room when you took it?"

Amber shrugged. "I don't know. But I did take it. When I moved the middle tier of the cake to get to the hole, some ice crystals fell off. I put them back in place."

"All but one. I noticed it had come loose. But I didn't figure out right away that someone had been messing with my cake."

Amber hung her head. "I'm sorry. This tea party should have been perfect, good advertising for the Book Tea."

"How long was the ring in your pocket? I mean, how much time passed after you left the room until you changed?"

"Uh . . . not a lot of time. You came back into the room, and I talked to you. Then I went up to change. I took off my jeans and tossed them on the bed. I meant to put them in the closet before I left the room, but . . . I don't think I did. I was in a rush to get my hair done and put on the necklace Mom had asked me to wear."

Callie remembered the gold chain with the coinlike pendant. "Your mother asked you to wear that? It struck me as a little too . . . casual for her taste. Shouldn't it have been a diamond of some kind?"

Amber shook her head. "Mom gave it to me to wear. She said it was special. It had to do with Dad and her."

Callie was surprised that Sheila would be so sentimental, wanting her daughter, upon her engagement, to wear a necklace that had featured in her own relationship. Maybe Callie would have a chance sometime to ask her about it?

Amber said, "I left the jeans on my bed. I never gave it a second thought. People don't usually go into my bedroom and through my things." Her eyes were angry. "I have no idea who did that, but I'd like to know."

She knotted her fingers. "I was sure only Leadenby could have taken the ring because he needed money. Who else would take the ring, and why? It couldn't have been to stop the engagement. I had already removed the ring from the cake. That prevented Ben's proposal."

Callie nodded. "It seems so. Your mother had no idea you had removed the ring, so she couldn't have taken it. Your father didn't know about any of it. None of the guests would have just gone up to your bedroom. How would they even know which room it was? Ben knew, of course . . ."

Amber bit her lip. "I've been wondering if it was him. I mean, after my mother denied putting in an empty box to put him in place, he must have thought about other options. Maybe he realized I . . . didn't want us to get engaged and . . ." She looked at the floor.

"But was there enough time for him to get it while we were all still downstairs?" Callie looked doubtful. "Does Ben know about Cole?"

"No. He wasn't here when I talked to Cole. Ben only flew in for the tea party."

"With the new will? I heard his office was involved in it. Did he work on it? Does he know what's in it?"

"I have no idea. I don't think so. It would be something a senior partner would handle. Dorothea's been a client there for all of her life. And they know Ben's a friend of mine. They might think it was unprofessional."

Callie nodded. That made perfect sense. "Still, I'd like to talk to Ben. He's dropped into the background of this whole thing somehow, and . . ."

"He's not here. I think he said something about needing some file information and going to an Internet cafe."

Callie hitched a brow. "But you have an Internet connection here, I presume?"

Amber shook her head. "The Hall doesn't have Internet. Dorothea never wanted anything modern to invade her home. No television either. We're lucky we have cell phone service here."

Callie nodded. "I see."

Her mind was processing the information Amber had just provided. She tried to see the jeans on the bed and Amber quickly putting the last touches to her looks. The necklace, maybe a touch more lip gloss. Then she left the room and the door closed. The jeans lay on the bed. The door opened again and . . . who came in?

Someone who knew their way around the house. Someone who would go into one of the family bedrooms. Someone who would . . . feel entitled to interfere in the family situation?

Suddenly words came back to her. A remark Sheila had made the other day:

*She has always protected this family. Like a lioness.*

Mrs. Keats.

The housekeeper. Someone who could walk about and barely be noticed. Someone who would feel at ease entering rooms, even bedrooms. Someone who would not even get a suspicious glance if she was seen coming out of a bedroom. She worked here; she took care of things.

Had she taken the ring? Trying to prevent an engagement she thought all wrong? For Amber, for Ben? Had she witnessed Amber getting closer to Cole again? Had she drawn her own conclusions?

"I think I'd like to talk to Mrs. Keats, alone. I'll catch up with Ben later."

Amber didn't seem to draw any conclusions from this sudden announcement. "Sure. She'll be here with the tea any minute now."

There was something of relief in Amber's voice. Satisfaction that she could get away from the questions and the embarrassment of having lost the family heirloom?

Or from the confusion about her own feelings? Torn between two men who were important to her, each in his own way?

Mrs. Keats entered quietly and put the tray with the tea things on the table. Amber said, "I'll be back later. Come on, Daisy. Want to play?" She left the room with the dog in tow.

Mrs. Keats's blue eyes searched Callie's expression. "I thought you wanted to speak with Amber."

"Yes, I did. But . . ." Callie wondered for a moment what the best tactic would be in this case. Beat about the bush? Put it bluntly? "The police are holding Cole Merton. In connection with the murder, but also because of the missing engagement ring. I think it would really help Cole's case if the ring turned up again."

Mrs. Keats looked at her, not blinking. Nothing in her expression betrayed whether she knew what Callie was driving at.

Callie continued, "There won't be any harm done if whoever took the engagement ring can explain that he or she just took it for safekeeping. I'm sure that charges of theft can be avoided altogether."

"Maybe charges are not what the . . . person who took it is worried about." Mrs. Keats spoke calmly, as if hypothesizing about a fictional case. Just a nice little chat to kill time.

"I can't imagine what else this person could be worried about."

Mrs. Keats poured the tea. She took her time to fill the cup, place it exactly in the center of the saucer, and put a spoon beside it. At last she spoke. "Perhaps it would be better for the object in question not to be studied too closely."

Callie was stunned. She stared at the housekeeper, trying to give meaning to these cryptic words.

Mrs. Keats handed her the tea. "There are cookies here. Not as good as your great aunt makes them, no doubt, but . . ."

"I don't need a cookie, thank you." Callie stirred her tea, although there was no sugar in it.

"Contrary to what Mrs. Du Bouvrais seems to believe, the ring doesn't belong to her," Mrs. Keats said. "It belongs to Mrs. Finster's family. Mrs. Du Bouvrais had no right to get it out of the safe and simply try to pass it off to her daughter. To wear."

The latter especially seemed to horrify Mrs. Keats.

Still mystified, Callie said, "But I understood that Sheila wore it on many occasions. When she was engaged to Stephen and later in life, at diplomatic parties and all that. But that a few years ago the ring was suddenly locked away."

Mrs. Keats nodded. "Yes, that's right. It was locked away for a reason." She straightened her dress. "Do you think Cole Merton will be accused of having stolen the ring? I mean, there's no real evidence to implicate him, is there?"

"No. I suppose not." Callie blew on the hot tea. "Still, he's in a tight spot."

Mrs. Keats sighed as if she wasn't happy to hear that.

"I assume that the person who took the ring acted out of loyalty to the family."

"To Mrs. Finster." Mrs. Keats's eyes flashed. "Not the Du Bouvraises. They're all here to get something out of her. But she should be protected. At all costs."

Callie nodded slowly. She began to understand a little of what Mrs. Keats had done. She believed she was acting in the best interests of her employer. A fragile old woman who had known so little happiness in her life. Softly she asked, "At all costs, you say. Even at the cost of an innocent person being accused?"

"You just said there's no real evidence against Cole Merton."

"It would be helpful if the ring turned up. Here in the house. If we can say it was simply . . . mislaid, perhaps?"

Mrs. Keats shook her head with determination. "That won't fix it. It should have stayed hidden away in the safe."

Callie frowned. It should have stayed hidden away, Amber shouldn't wear it, nobody should take a closer look at it . . . "What's wrong with the ring?" she asked softly. "I only saw it for a few moments, but it looked amazing."

Mrs. Keats laughed. "Yes, I suppose . . ." She hesitated, apparently weighing her options. Then she met Callie's gaze. "I suppose it does look amazing when you're not an expert and can't distinguish between real stones and very good copies."

Callie gasped. "The stones in the ring aren't real? The precious family heirloom isn't precious at all?"

"It used to be. But Mrs. Finster had to sell some things. She didn't want Stephen to know. She had this copy made. And not just of the ring."

Callie stared at her. Her mind raced, trying to make sense of this. "I don't understand. We were all gathered here to find out about her new will. The disposition of her substantial fortune. Why would she need to sell off some jewelry if she has so much?"

"You'd have to ask Mrs. Finster about that. I can't speak for her." The housekeeper bowed her head. "She'll already be angry enough at me when she finds out I made the ring disappear. I never meant to cause anybody any harm. I just didn't want the truth about the ring to come to light. Mrs. Finster was certain that, with the ring in the safe, the secret would never get out. When I discovered Mrs. Du Bouvrais had taken it to put it in that cake and have it shown off to everybody as Amber's engagement ring . . ."

"You must have panicked. You acted to protect the family. I can understand that. How did you know that Amber had the ring?"

"I saw her come from the room. She had her hand in her pocket. She looked furtive. Worried, half afraid. I went up after her, and when she came out of her bedroom in her dress, I slipped in and checked what was in her pocket. I found the ring and . . . took it. I just wanted it to stay out of sight." Mrs. Keats straightened. "I'll take you to

Mrs. Finster. I'll tell her exactly what I did and that you know about it now. She has to decide about the rest. That's not for me to do."

Callie put her teacup down and followed Mrs. Keats out of the room and up the stairs.

\* \* \*

In a room where hesitant December sunshine crept through the window, Dorothea Finster sat in a chair, a plaid shawl wrapped around her. Her hands resting on the shawl seemed so breakable, thin and full of green veins.

Callie swallowed as she came closer. How would the old lady take this revelation from her loyal housekeeper? Could she deal with all of the shocks she'd had to face these past few days? Not exactly the festive Christmastime she'd been hoping for.

"Miss Aspen is here to see you," Mrs. Keats said. "I need to . . . She found out that . . ." She took a deep breath and continued, more firmly, "On the day of the tea party, I took the engagement ring from Amber's pocket. She had left her jeans in her bedroom after changing. I took the ring because of the stones."

Despite this rather meager explanation, Dorothea understood at once. She looked at Mrs. Keats with her sharp eyes and shook her head. "Meddling. Everybody was meddling. And nobody got what they wanted."

"You didn't either," Callie said. "You wanted to read your new will to us. But you never got the chance."

Dorothea looked at her. "What happened to you? There's a bruise on your face, and is that blood?"

"Just a silly little accident. Some kids were having a snowball fight, and one of their ice balls hit me." Callie shrugged. No need to burden Dorothea with a story of a little boy crying because the Moore grandsons tried to rule the town.

"Sit down." Dorothea pointed at a nearby chair. She gestured to Mrs. Keats to leave them. The housekeeper retreated and quietly closed the door.

Dorothea said, "When I first saw you, that very first summer you came to spend here in Heart's Harbor, I thought you were a very intelligent girl. Had to be, since you're related to Iphy, and she's one of the most perceptive people I know. That summer seems a hundred years ago. But not so long that you couldn't come back here. And I should have understood right away that you would be onto us in a heartbeat. After all, you share part of our past."

She smiled. "You could have been part of our future as well. If Stephen had married you."

The warmth in her voice touched Callie, but she knew for certain that a match between her and Stephen wouldn't have worked. Without averting her eyes, she said, "Stephen never loved me."

"But did he ever love Sheila? Did she ever love him? I wonder." There was sadness in her face. "I want Amber to be happy. She's young, and that's when you have the best chances of enjoying your life. She can travel and . . . Sheila thinks she needs money, more than she has now. A fund with money from this estate and then a man by her side who values her because of that money. I understood what she was after with that impromptu engagement. Ben had to be part of my will as well. But he can't be."

Callie studied Dorothea's expression, trying to understand the reasons behind her frank statement. "He can't be because you don't think he's the right man for Amber? How well do you know him? Have you taken the time to talk to him? I know it appears they're just friends, but . . . Amber may be in love with Cole Merton, but will that feeling last? Do we know he's the right man for her?" In asking this, she was also phrasing her own thoughts and questions aloud.

Dorothea smiled softly. She stared into the distance, her hands patting the shawl covering her legs. "It's not because I know Ben isn't the right man for Amber. I don't know any such thing. It's because . . . there's nothing to divide."

The words lingered in the room, hovering in the sunshine. Callie tried to process them.

"Nothing?" She repeated that rather final word.

"They all came out here for the will reading, hoping I had left the majority to them. Moore wants it for the town; Smith does too, in his own way. Lampposts on Main Street, I think? Miss Brink wants a playground with a climbing wall. Even though she said she wanted nothing from me. Almost like I had done her harm. Like she disliked me. But I don't even know her."

Dorothea focused on Callie, her fine brows drawn together. "Isn't that odd?"

"Yes, I noticed it too." Callie didn't want to say that Brenda had been hiding a secret that Leadenby had known about. A secret that he had wanted Brenda to reveal to someone. To Dorothea perhaps? What could it be? Could it explain Brenda's dislike of the elderly lady? Had she seen her as a threat to her future in Heart's Harbor?

"Sheila wants it all for Amber. I don't think she wants it for herself. I think she has quite enough off what Stephen makes. But Amber is her only child." Dorothea's hands clasped together in a painful intensity. "I think when you have a child, you must love them and want the best for them and . . ." Her voice died away.

Callie wasn't quite sure what Dorothea was thinking of now, perhaps times in her life when she had hoped for children, only to have that hope dashed? Still single herself and uncertain whether she'd ever have a family, Callie could relate to the feeling. At times she felt perfectly happy with her life, and then suddenly she felt something missing and wanted to change everything.

Confused by the emotions bubbling inside her, she tried to lead the conversation back to the will. "Everybody wanted money once they heard you were going to reveal the contents of your new will," she said, paraphrasing what Dorothea had just told her. "But your new will wasn't about money?"

"No. It's about a legacy and keeping it. It's not about getting something, but putting something in. Money, time, effort. To keep something you love alive." Dorothea's eyes sparkled. "I didn't want to hand out something, but to ask people to step up to an enormous task. I knew it would be hard. And now I never even got around to it."

"But the murder didn't change . . ." Callie looked for words to express it right. "Your will can still be read."

Dorothea looked at her. "What if someone killed for the money? The *supposed* money. What if somebody wanted it so badly he or she took a human life for it?"

Her voice rose. "There never was any money. Leadenby died for nothing!"

"But . . ." Callie reached out and touched the old woman's hand. "We don't know what Leadenby died for. Maybe it had nothing to do with the will."

Dorothea looked at her, hope shimmering in her tearful eyes. "Do you really believe that?"

"I heard enough about him. That he was . . . rather persuasive when he wanted to have things his way. Maybe he made an enemy?"

Dorothea looked down at her hands. At Callie's hand on hers.

Callie wasn't sure if she was overstepping and should remove her hand.

But Dorothea said, "The engagement ring that Amber was supposed to wear is full of fake stones, Miss Aspen. This house is burdened by debt. I've been offered a chance to sell it so it can become a hotel or a wellness resort. I don't want to sell. So I made a plan. I made a new will in which I'm leaving this place to people who will fight for its survival. Please . . ."

She gestured to a small table in a corner of the room. "Fetch that envelope for me."

With her heart pounding, Callie got up, picked up the envelope, and carried it to Dorothea.

The elderly lady took it and opened it, pulling out some sheets of paper. She handed them to Callie. "Read it."

"Are you sure? Don't you think that others are more entitled to know . . ." Despite her reluctance, her eyes glanced down at the first sheet. Dorothea declaring she was of sound mind . . .

Her eyes fell on something familiar, and her heart skipped a beat. She read, barely knowing if she was seeing it right. If it could be.

Dorothea Finster was leaving Haywood Hall to Iphy. And to her. Calliope Aspen. "To care for and conserve, as a venue for parties, a place where history will be retold, a museum perhaps, where old times are kept alive and the library so carefully built over the years will always have pride of place."

Callie looked up at Dorothea with a start. "You can't do this."

"You've loved Haywood Hall ever since you were a girl. You came here every day to read and to walk the grounds and to play until the sun went down. You loved it and . . ."

"But Stephen loves it too. And Sheila. You can't just exclude them to . . . How can I face them?" Callie's voice rose in panic. "How can I tell them I'm taking their family legacy away from them?"

Dorothea shook her head. "You're not taking it away

from them. They can join in to keep it up. I just didn't want to burden them with the debts and . . . Stephen is a diplomat. He lives abroad. He needs to travel. He needs change. He doesn't want to sit around here and . . ."

"But I have a life too. I'm a travel guide. I can't just . . . stick around here and . . ."

Callie's head spun. She thought of Daisy and how the dog had attached herself to her and how hard it would be to leave her behind as January rolled around. About Iphy and Book Tea and how at home she felt there. About Falk, who had told her she was a great cook.

She shook her head to refocus. "You can't just change somebody's life completely. How is this different than what Sheila did, trying to marry Amber off to Ben? Not even asking her if she agreed. You could at least have gauged our interest in taking care of Haywood Hall before you put our names into your will just like that."

"Sheila's plan failed," Dorothea said with a sad half smile. "And so did mine. The will was never read. You're holding it. You can destroy it, and no one will ever know what was in it."

Callie took a deep breath. She stood here in Haywood Hall, a place that had always been like home to her. A house she had loved and had never stopped loving. When she had returned to it, just two days ago, she had seen it and smiled, as if at an old friend.

She had realized she didn't care for Stephen anymore as she once had, but she still cared for Haywood Hall, for

Heart's Harbor, for what she had built here and what had remained, even during her years away.

Could she just tear up this will, burn it? Say no to the chance of a lifetime?

Dorothea gave her the envelope. "Put it back in there. Read it carefully. Discuss it with Iphy. Think about it. Then let me know. There's no rush. I'm not selling to the hotel chain."

Callie wanted to tell her that she should not, ever, but knew it would be hypocritical as she wasn't offering another solution for Haywood Hall's survival. Apparently the house was burdened with debts and . . .

She would be a fool to get into this.

And yet . . .

She held the envelope tightly. "I'll think about it. And the police will have to know that the engagement ring was never really missing. You don't need to tell them it was a fake. You can simply call them and tell them you found it."

"It's not that simple. If it was, Mrs. Keats would have told me sooner. But she realizes what I realize, and you will too, if you think it over. The police know that Amber took the ring from the cake. She testified that it vanished from her bedroom, from the pocket of her jeans. The police will wonder who took the ring from Amber's bedroom. Leadenby is dead. This is not about theft, but about murder. We should not forget that."

"I haven't forgotten that." Callie held Dorothea's gaze. "They say that Leadenby had argued with you. That he wanted to stay here but you weren't that happy about it."

Dorothea sighed. She twisted the simple silver ring on her finger. "Leadenby believed he was entitled to live here. I tried to persuade him to look for another place to stay. I knew that he wasn't getting along with Sheila and . . . I do want to see more of them before I die. More of Amber."

The elderly lady pursed her lips. "Leadenby had a strange effect on people. They seemed to . . . shy away from him. I don't know when that started. In the past, he was jovial and kind. He taught you all you know about plants."

Callie nodded. "I was glad to see him again. But I also noticed the tension. Do you have any idea how he made money?"

Dorothea shook her head. "He never asked me for any. But he lived here for free, so maybe he didn't need much?"

Still, Amber had thought Leadenby needed money, badly enough to steal the ring.

Callie smoothed the envelope containing the will. It seemed that instead of finding answers and unraveling the mystery, she was hitting on more and more complications that hampered her sight of what had truly happened in the conservatory. "We'll have to solve the murder somehow. We owe it to Leadenby. He might have had an unpleasant side, but . . ."

"You be very careful what you do." Dorothea looked at Callie's bruised temple. "Not everything that happens is an accident."

# Chapter Thirteen

Coming down the stairs with the envelope in her hand, Callie ran into Sheila, who was breezing in, wearing a black coat with a velvet scarf in wine red. Her hair was brushed back and her makeup impeccable. Her uncertainty of the other day seemed washed away.

"Callie! I was looking for you in town. I was at the Book Tea."

Before Callie could say anything in return, she saw that Sheila wasn't alone. Right behind her was Falk's sister Peggy, with a murderous look on her face. As soon as she spotted Callie, she came straight at her, screaming, "You can't take my children away from me!"

Callie raised both hands in a defensive gesture. The envelope with the will flapped in the air. "I only wanted . . ."

"You stay away from my children! You have nothing to do with them. I bet you think you can take better care of them. Because you have a job and all. That's what my brother has been after all along. To set up this perfect little home so he can have the boys. But I won't let him. Or you. I'll fight you every step of the way."

"Tate was being harassed by much bigger boys at the community center. Did you know that? His older brother was nowhere in sight. I only took him to Book Tea to get him away from them. He was crying."

Peggy's face was a mask. "You're lying. You're just making that up so I'll look bad. But I won't let you take them."

"Here." Callie pointed at her bloody temple. "I got this bruise when the older kids threw snowballs at me. I tried to protect Tate. It wasn't about you at all; it was about him."

"Just stay away from him. I won't tell you again." The blonde woman turned and marched out the front door, pulling it shut behind her with a resounding bang.

Sheila shook her head. "It's never smart to interfere with other people's children. I did say something sometimes, you know, at parties where kids were misbehaving? Parents turn into predators then, tearing you apart." She looked Callie over. "I had no idea you were involved with the deputy."

"I'm not. I only saw Tate in the street, crying because Mayor Moore's grandsons had been throwing ice balls at him and . . . never mind. I'll try and explain it to Falk later. He should know that Moore's grandsons are misbehaving and take it up with Moore or the boys' parents."

Sheila tilted her head. "Did you really get that bruise from a snowball? It looks nasty. Shouldn't it be cleaned? Or dressed?"

"I'll be fine." Now that the adrenaline from the sudden confrontation with Peggy was fading, Callie felt like the envelope was burning in her hand. It contained a will that didn't leave Haywood Hall to Stephen and thereby to Sheila. How would her former friend take that news?

As if Sheila could sense her uncertainty, her eyes narrowed as she studied Callie. "What is that envelope? Is that the logo of Dorothea's lawyer?"

"Yes, she asked me to read through these . . . papers." Callie didn't dare mention the word *will*. She wished fervently she hadn't run into Sheila just then.

"You, read through legal papers?" Sheila's face was full of disbelief. "What on earth for? You have nothing to do with Dorry's affairs. Or . . ." She turned pale. Her whole posture went rigid.

Her voice was a whisper when she said, "Does she want to . . . leave Haywood Hall to you?"

Before Callie could say anything to explain the awkward situation, Sheila continued, "She always liked you better. She never wanted me to marry Stephen. She never . . ." Her voice was strangled.

"Sheila!" Callie wanted to catch her arm, but Sheila pulled away. Her nostrils flared as she visibly struggled not to burst into tears.

"It's not what you think. Dorothea only wants to protect you. The Hall is in trouble, and it will take a lot of effort to save it. You have your life abroad, your friends, your charitable activities, and . . ."

Sheila didn't seem to be listening. She walked to the stairs with stiff, mechanical movements.

"Maybe I just better pack and leave. If I'm not welcome here."

"You're not listening to me. The Hall isn't what you think it is. Why don't you read what the will says?"

Sheila hurried up the stairs.

"Why don't you ask Dorothea what she intended?" Callie pressed, rushing after her. "Then you'll understand better what she's trying to do. Also for you, Stephen, and Amber."

But Sheila was faster. She disappeared into her bedroom and shut the door. Callie heard the key turn in the lock.

She knocked on the door. "Sheila! Listen to me. You're misunderstanding all of this. Please. I want to explain it to you. Open the door."

But there was no reply.

Callie rested her forehead against the door a moment. Her painful temple burned. She stared at the envelope in her hands. A legacy she cared for deeply but that other people didn't want her to have. Could she just take the will and discuss it with Iphy, ignoring how hurt Sheila was about these developments?

No.

She sat on the floor and shoved the envelope under the door.

Sheila should read it and talk to Dorothea about it. They were family. Callie was an outsider. Someone who now fervently wished she hadn't decided to spend the Christmas holidays at home.

Home?

So Heart's Harbor was her home? A home where kids threw ice balls at her and her former friends hated her for getting between them and their expected inheritance?

Some home.

With tears burning behind her eyes, Callie rose to her feet and walked quickly away.

* * *

Shrugging off Amber's questions of what was wrong, Callie collected Daisy and went to her car. Diving behind the wheel, she wasn't quite sure where to go or what to do. She had promised to go back to Book Tea to help out, but having just discovered that Falk's sister Peggy had made a big scene there about Tate's presence, she felt awkward about it. And her head was full of thoughts about the implications of Dorothea's will. She needed to do something different, for distraction. Since the schools were closed for the holidays, Brenda Brink had to be free as well, and Callie decided to drive by her house to ask how she was doing after the shock of the murder. Maybe she could somehow steer the conversation to what she had overheard of the argument between Brenda and Leadenby shortly before he died.

She hardly believed that Brenda would just pour out her heart to her, but maybe there was an explanation for the whole thing and it didn't have to do with the murder. After all, Mrs. Keats's taking the ring had also caused confusion, even though she had simply done it to prevent people from finding out about the fake stones in it.

In a small town, it was easy enough to find out where somebody lived by simply asking the mailman, who was delivering stacks of colorful envelopes with Christmas cards to every home. He gave her directions that she could easily follow, sending her past houses with reindeer on the roof, shooting stars attached to porch pillars, and wreaths of evergreen and golden bows on garage doors. Everybody seemed to have made an effort to sprinkle holiday cheer everywhere.

Brenda's home—made of brick with a roof that was completely covered with snow—also had a beautifully crafted wreath with small felted foxes, and Callie wondered if Brenda had made those herself. As a teacher, she might always be on the lookout for new crafts to try in class with her kids. That might be a nice way to start a conversation.

But nobody came to the door. Callie rang the bell again and knocked. Still no answer. Maybe Brenda was out shopping?

But wouldn't she have taken her car then? The red compact sat snugly in the icy drive. Surely it was too slippery and cold to go out on a bike? If Brenda even had one.

Daisy had ambled off the porch steps again and was sniffing at footprints leading around back. "What do you see, girl?" Callie asked. "Do you think we can go that way and see if we can find Brenda?"

Her voice sounded too loud in the quiet around her. It was like the snow had sucked away all other sounds.

Callie shivered. In her head, she again heard that sinister whisper telling her to stop poking around. Cold sweat formed on her back as she followed the footprints in the snow to the back of the house. In a lovely little garden, birds were busy pecking at the nuts and seeds left for them on a feeding table. They ignored her and Daisy completely as they made their way to the back door.

There was a large window beside the door, and Callie peeked in. It was the kitchen. On the sink sat some dirty dishes, probably from breakfast, judging by the egg yolk on one of them. On the stove, the kettle was boiling. Callie could see the steam forming in the air. So Brenda had to be home. Why hadn't she answered the door?

She knocked at the window and waited. The icy wind made her shiver again, and she turned up her collar. Another window sat a few feet away from her. It wasn't Callie's habit to peek into people's houses, but somehow the eerie quiet around Brenda's cottage was getting on her nerves. Why put the kettle on and then forget all about it?

Callie rubbed her hands a moment in indecision and then stepped forward. She didn't stand fully in front of the window but stayed beside it, just tilting her head at an angle to see inside. She didn't know what exactly she was expecting. To see Brenda with someone else? Caught up in an argument?

A fight, maybe?

Brenda being assaulted? By someone who didn't want her to tell the truth about Leadenby's death?

Brenda tied to a chair with a gag in her mouth while someone went through her things?

All those scenarios raced through Callie's mind as she peeked into the room, making sure she couldn't be seen from the inside. Her heart skipped a beat when she caught sight of the open cupboard doors and drawers, the pile of clothes on the bed. But there was a suitcase on the bed as well, and hands busily packed the skirts and blouses. Brenda Brink's face was red and her hands seemed to tremble as she fumbled to get things into the suitcase.

Callie held her breath. The schoolteacher was not tied up or arguing with someone. She was packing. She wanted to leave? For an innocent family visit for the holidays?

But didn't Brenda know that the police expected people involved in a murder case to stay in town? Just leaving might arouse suspicion. Christmas or no Christmas.

Callie raised her hand and knocked on the window.

Brenda jumped back. Clothes she had just picked up fell to the floor in front of her. She stared at the window, her eyes wide with shock.

Callie gestured at her, then at the back door.

Brenda seemed to want to disappear into the floorboards but realized she could not. She looked about her, slammed the suitcase shut, and made for the bedroom door.

Callie went to the back door and waited for Brenda to appear and let her in. Nothing happened.

Suddenly suspicious, she raced to the front of the house, Daisy following her, barking.

Brenda was at her car, throwing her suitcase into the back, then opening the driver's door to slip in herself.

"Stop!" Callie called. "Don't run. If you do, the police will come after you."

Brenda stood and stared at her.

The blank panic in the woman's eyes clawed at Callie's heart.

She raised both hands in a placating gesture. "I just want to talk to you."

Brenda swallowed. "What about?"

"Can you just come back here? Can we go in? It's very cold." Callie tried to sound innocent. "I also hurt my head this morning. I feel a bit faint."

Brenda frowned. "Who hit you?" Her tone was anxious, as if Callie's injured head confirmed her worst suspicions about her own position.

"Nobody," Callie rushed to assure her. "Some kids were throwing ice balls and getting a bit rough with the little ones. I told them to stop it and they threw some ice at me. Mayor Moore's grandsons. You must know them."

Brenda nodded. "They were here for the summer vacation as well. Apart they're not so bad, but together they're up to nothing but mischief."

She seemed to hesitate as to whether she should come back to the house.

Callie acted like she was teetering on her feet. "They

might not have meant to hurt me, but they did hit me in a sensitive spot. I do need to sit down now. Please?"

Brenda closed the car door and came over to her. "All right then." She unlocked the front door and let her in.

As Callie stepped into the warmth and the scent of even more Christmas greenery, like the wreath on the door, a little voice of warning was whispering in the back of her head. Brenda was acting suspiciously, perhaps attempting to flee, and Callie was now alone with her. Inside a house far away from its neighbors. If Brenda suddenly attacked her and she screamed, would anybody hear her?

What if Brenda was Leadenby's killer? What if she would kill again to be able to get away from town, stay out of the hands of the police?

But if that was the case, why had Brenda not left town right after the murder? The police had been busy looking elsewhere, going after Sheila first for the bloodstain on her dress, then Amber for the fingerprints on the murder weapon, then Cole Merton because it had been his screwdriver. Why wait until they had eliminated others and came knocking on her door?

"Sit down." Brenda pointed at the couch. "Your head does look nasty."

She was the second one to say so, and Callie now really did feel a bit faint. She sat down quickly. "Thank you so much. Those ice balls are harder than you'd think."

"Kids can be wild when they're on vacation. They sometimes don't understand the results of their own actions."

"I think they do understand when they call Tate a crybaby."

Brenda's expression tightened. She lowered herself into a chair and pushed a pillow behind her back. "Tate was really upset after his dad died. He started crying in the classroom. The other kids talked about it, and word got around." She shook her head. "Kids can be cruel. They have no idea what it means to lose your father. They just want to fit in with the group and chant along."

Callie looked Brenda over. Maybe she had lost her father too and felt for little Tate?

Brenda said, "If you're here to talk to me about this incident, I'm afraid I can do very little about it. I notify the parents when their children misbehave, but sometimes they don't take it very seriously. They think kids just like to play and boys can be rough. That sort of thing. They don't understand the impact of name-calling or pushing and shoving. And Mayor Moore's grandsons don't even live here. They're not in my class."

"And what can you do about it even when they are in your class? I mean, in the classroom or the schoolyard?"

Brenda sighed. She huddled in her chair like a cold little bird. "Not much, really. Maybe I'm not cut out to be a teacher."

Callie studied her. "How did you end up here?"

Brenda shrugged. "Just got lucky, I guess. I had been applying everywhere, and got turned down everywhere. Then they hired me here."

"Still, you were about to go away." Callie held her gaze.

"Just a family visit for the holidays."

"You're aware that you're still part of a murder case? You can't just leave town. Does Deputy Falk know of your plans?"

Brenda sat up. "I told them everything I know."

"About Leadenby's threats to you?"

Brenda's eyes went wide. "Falk told you about that? Why? I thought information in a case was treated confidentially." Her indignation was evident, and Callie rushed to explain.

"Falk didn't have to tell me. I overheard something. I came looking for you when the tea party was about to start. I overheard Leadenby threatening you that if you didn't tell something, he would. You said he'd ruin your entire life."

Brenda was deathly pale now. She leaned forward with her elbows on her knees. "And?" she asked in a trembling voice.

"I told Falk what I overheard. I felt I had to. That was it. But he'll want to know what it's about."

"Yes, he asked me. I said that Leadenby had told me before that I was a bad teacher and I should resign. I didn't want to."

Callie narrowed her eyes. That didn't ring true. "How would Leadenby know if you're a bad teacher? He doesn't have kids at your school. I think it was about something else."

"You think, but you don't know. So stop interfering."

*Stop poking around . . .*

Callie sat up. "Did you call me last night and threaten me? Did you say I had to stop poking around or I would be sorry?"

Brenda now looked like she was about to faint. "No, of course not," she whispered.

"I was with Falk when the call came in," Callie pressed to gain ground now that Brenda was overtaken. "He'll look into it to find out who it was. The police can trace calls."

"It wasn't me. Honest." Brenda stared at Callie. "You think I would threaten you? Why? I had no idea you knew anything. Until now."

Callie sat motionless as the words lingered in the quiet room.

*Until now.*

What would Brenda do? Rise from that chair, grab a poker from the fireplace, and take a swing at her? If she believed Callie was already faint from her head wound, she might think she could easily disable her and make a run for it.

"I told Falk the truth." Brenda sounded as if she was also trying to convince herself. "I have nothing to worry about."

"Then why are you leaving?"

Brenda swallowed. "Because I'm scared of the killer on the loose. It is not me, that much I know. But I don't know who did do it. I just don't want to stay in town. I live alone. I don't feel safe."

"Why would the killer come after you?"

"I have no idea. I just feel that way." Brenda wrapped her arms around herself. "Let Falk check the anonymous call to your phone."

"How do you know it was an anonymous call?"

"Just guessing. Otherwise you'd know who it was, right?"

Brenda seemed to get a bit of her fighting spirit back. "You're just coming around, accusing me. You caught a snippet of a conversation that you were never meant to hear and you think you can just say anything to me. Without proof!"

Callie shook her head. "I'm not accusing you of anything. I just want to know what you know."

"Nothing. I told the police everything I do know and that's it. I want nothing else to do with it. It's bad enough. A dead body . . ." Brenda shivered. "I'm glad I never saw it."

"Leadenby threatened to reveal something about you. Whatever it was, it must make you glad he's dead."

"Not really. Nobody deserves to die. Not like that. He was a nasty character, yes, but . . ."

"He said you'd have to tell *her* the truth. Who was he talking about? I had the impression it was Mrs. Finster. But if it was just about the school and you not doing a good job there, why would you have to tell her, of all people?"

"Leadenby thought I would be getting money for the school from the new will. He wanted me to reveal that I was a bad teacher and didn't deserve the money. He wanted to have it."

Callie tilted her head. "And why would Mrs. Finster leave anything to him?"

"I don't know. But he said he was entitled to it."

Callie shook her head. "That doesn't make sense."

Her phone rang, and she pulled it out of her pocket. Keeping her eyes on Brenda, she answered. "Yes?"

"Callie? It's Amber. I'm so happy!" The girl's voice

danced across the line. "Cole is off the hook. The police established that he has an alibi for the time of the murder. He was at another job. Several people can vouch that he was there or that they saw him driving over there. He couldn't have killed Leadenby! I'm mad that Falk actually put him in a cell overnight, but now he's free to go. Cleared! I still can't believe it. I'm meeting him for coffee."

Amber sounded like a teen going on a first date with her crush. "I just wanted to tell you. Mom's not interested. She claims she has a headache and has to lie down, but I bet she's just mad because things didn't work out the way she wanted."

Callie's heart clenched as she thought of Sheila and the enormous disappointment the new will was to her. "Your mother has had a couple of shocks, Amber. Please be considerate to her."

"She can wallow in bed all she wants. I'm going out with Cole. Bye!" And Amber hung up.

Callie lowered the phone. "That was Amber," she explained to Brenda, "telling me that Cole Merton has been released by the police. He has an alibi for the time of the murder. They're now looking for other suspects again."

Brenda cringed. "I have to finish packing. My family is counting on me coming over. I told them nothing about the murder. They'd just be upset."

"Brenda . . ." Callie put force and conviction into her voice. "They will be coming after you. Do you want to be hunted down? You have to talk to them. You have to tell them what Leadenby was accusing you of."

"Then Falk will think I killed him!" Brenda's eyes were frantic. "Falk is running out of suspects fast." She covered her face. "I wish I had left town right away when I had the chance."

Daisy came to sit at her feet and pressed her head against Brenda's leg as if to offer her support. Callie asked softly, "Why didn't you leave?"

"I had hoped . . ." Brenda's voice faded.

"That Cole Merton would be accused? While he's innocent?"

"I didn't know if he was innocent. All I know is I didn't kill Leadenby." Brenda groaned. "Everything is just going to get even worse."

Callie rose and came to stand beside the teacher. She put a hand on her shoulder. "Brenda, listen to me. If you didn't kill Leadenby, you have nothing to worry about. You have to tell the truth about what happened, and then Falk will sort it all out."

Brenda scoffed, mumbling between her hands, "Sure. If I admit to Falk that Leadenby was blackmailing me, he'll believe right off the bat that I have nothing to do with the murder. It will give me the perfect motive for killing him!"

"Blackmail is a terrible thing. But it's over now."

"No, it's not." Brenda pulled her hands away and lifted her contorted face to Callie. "Leadenby may be dead, but I'll have to tell the police why he was blackmailing me. The story will get out anyway, and . . ." She took a deep breath. "I'm not worried about me so much as the others involved."

"What others involved?" Callie asked in surprise. She hadn't thought that Brenda's secret would touch more people than just Brenda herself.

Brenda took another deep breath. She held it, then released it in a long, low hiss. "Your friends. The Du Bouvraises. Mrs. Finster. Everybody at Haywood Hall."

Callie felt her legs go wobbly. What secret could Leadenby have known? He had lived there for so long. He could know painful secrets. She said slowly, "Still, you *will* have to tell. There's no other way."

"Leadenby is dead now. I can't prove he thought it all up. I'll be blamed for starting this story. They'll think I'm after money! But I never wanted anything from her. Honestly."

"Just tell me the story. I'll help you figure out what to do."

Brenda held her gaze a moment as if to determine if she should go along with this. Then she nodded and began, "I was desperate to find a job as a teacher. When this opportunity here in Heart's Harbor came up, I grabbed it with both hands. But Leadenby soon appeared at my door. He said that he had a proposition. He had forged some documents that could prove I was . . . Mrs. Finster's granddaughter."

"Granddaughter?" Callie echoed. "But Dorothea never had any children."

"I know. Leadenby said that he had forged paperwork to prove she had a child when she was very young, before she ever met her husband and got married. A child she abandoned because she couldn't take care of it at the time. I was supposedly that child's daughter. I had to ask the Du

Bouvraises for money to keep my past a secret. Leadenby said that they would be desperate to keep me away from Dorothea, so they could inherit everything. That they would pay me a large sum so I wouldn't talk. He said they had plenty of money, since Mr. Du Bouvrais is a rich diplomat. He said Mrs. Du Bouvrais hated scandal and would pay up just so the story would never get out. He said they'd never even check if it was true. And that if they did, he had it all covered with his fake paperwork. I refused to do it. But he kept harassing me about it. Even before the tea party started. He wanted to tell her if I didn't."

"Her being Sheila?" Callie asked. Her bet had been on Dorothea all this time, but why couldn't the "her" mentioned have been Sheila?

Brenda wrung her hands. "I was desperate. I didn't want to tell people lies for money. Let them inherit the Hall. It was never mine to begin with."

She brushed a strand of hair away from her face. "I couldn't get Leadenby to listen though. He was dead set on using the tea party to tell all. I walked out. I was completely devastated at the idea that he would go through with it. He had always emphasized to me that he couldn't blackmail the Du Bouvraises himself because they wouldn't believe him. That it would only work if I, the alleged granddaughter, contacted them myself. I think he was also afraid that word of it would get back to Mrs. Finster somehow and she'd turn him out of the Hall. He always seemed to genuinely love that house. When he threatened to reveal all at the tea party, I reminded him that he had said he couldn't reveal anything himself because Mrs. Finster would turn him out. But then he said that he didn't care anymore. That he would do it, at all costs."

Brenda swallowed hard. "I think he meant it. I ran off in a panic. But I left him alive. I didn't kill him. I just left the conservatory while he was still alive and well. When Dorothea began her speech, I was waiting for him to come in and speak up. I was so scared I can barely remember what she said."

Callie nodded. Brenda had indeed looked very frightened and emotional, struggling for control. "And have you ever seen those forged documents? I heard Leadenby had a safe-deposit box at a bank. He must have kept his blackmail material in there."

"The police are onto that? Then they'll find out anyway." Brenda exhaled, as if it was a relief that this decision had been made for her. "I'd better go see them."

"No. Not yet. You have to do something else first."

"What?" Brenda asked, perplexed.

"See Dorothea. Find out if there's any truth in Leadenby's claim."

Brenda's jaw dropped. "What? He told me he had *forged* the paperwork. That means it was a lie, right? I'm not her granddaughter."

"Maybe not." Callie looked her over. "But you deserve to know the truth, and so does Dorothea. I doubt Leadenby would just have made up some far-fetched story. He knew things. He might have known enough to be fairly confident he would get far with this story. Yes, he might have forged the paperwork, but what if there's some truth in it? What if there was a child in Dorothea's younger years that she parted with?"

Brenda stared at her. "You think she'd want to know?"

"She's old and close to death. I think that's a time in life when people want to set things right. Her new will was her way of trying to restore things. And now that you tell me this . . . We have to at least tell her before you go see Falk. So she knows what's going to be said about her. Word will get out and . . ."

Brenda wiped her eyes. "You're right. I have to tell her. I can't just let her find out via the jungle drum. I don't think it could be true at all, but anyway . . . I'll come with you."

"Good." Callie straightened. She didn't want to go back to the Hall where Sheila was lying in bed, heartbroken by Dorothea's decision about her new will.

She didn't even want to confront Dorothea with Leadenby's manipulations. But she had to do this to try to save something. To clear the air so Christmas could come and find them, not torn apart but united.

# Chapter Fourteen

Parked in front of the Hall's stately steps was a police car. This time, no curious boys' faces peeked out through the back-seat window. The blue lights weren't flashing either. Still, the car's solemn presence made Callie's stomach contract. Why was Falk here? Who had he come for?

Brenda nodded at the car, her eyes wide. "I can't go in now."

Callie took her arm and pulled her along. "We're going to talk to Dorothea. I'm sure Falk isn't going to arrest *her*. Come on."

Stephen opened the door and said in a low voice, "Falk is here to talk to Mrs. Keats about the ring. It seems he's suddenly quite eager to clear this Cole Merton of all charges. Amber rushed off to meet him for coffee." He rubbed his forehead. "But there's also bad news. When Falk is done with Mrs. Keats, he wants to take Ben to the station."

"Why?" Callie asked.

"Something about footprints outside the conservatory

door. And traces left inside. Snow, water, mud. I'm not sure."

Callie's heart skipped a beat. Had Ben entered the conservatory from the outside to kill Leadenby? The possibility had occurred to her earlier. But why would Ben have wanted to kill the old man? Just a flash of anger? Somehow it didn't seem to be enough. But then, Callie didn't know how hotheaded Ben might be.

A door slammed, and Falk appeared, walking fast. When he spotted Callie, he froze. His gaze scanned her face, then rested on the bruise on her temple. "Did Peggy do that?"

"No."

"I heard she made a major scene in the Book Tea."

"I wasn't there at the time."

"Wait a minute." Stephen stepped up to Falk. "You think someone hit Callie? What for?"

Falk gestured with his hands. "It's a private matter."

"Not when people get hurt. Just look at her."

"Nobody hit me," Callie said. "Some boys were throwing snowballs, and one hit me. I heard from Brenda that the mayor's grandsons have caused trouble before, during summer vacations. We should really do something about their behavior." She hoped this would explain Brenda's presence by her side and Falk's attention wouldn't fall on her in relation to the murder case.

Stephen looked like he didn't believe her story, but Falk

said he was taking Ben along and looked into the sitting room, calling, "We can go now."

Ben appeared, in a neat suit, his chin up as if to defy any of them to have an opinion about him. As the deputy and the young lawyer walked out of the house, Callie went after them quickly. "Can I talk to you for just a moment?"

Falk sent Ben ahead to the police car and asked curtly, "What is it?"

"Peggy seems to think you want to take Jimmy and Tate away from her. Is that true?"

"Of course not. I'm a bachelor; what would I do with two small kids? I just want to help her care for them."

"That's not how she sees it." Callie held Falk's gaze, trying to read the full story in his eyes. "There must be some reason for her to think you don't trust her." She had begun to suspect that Peggy was overreacting to things because she had the impression people didn't believe in her abilities as a mother. On top of the loss of her husband, that had to hurt bad.

Falk sighed. "Peggy is just . . . She's taking risks and I don't like it. Who is this guy she's seeing? What is she doing at night when I call her and she doesn't answer the phone?"

Aha. So Falk was keeping tabs on Peggy, and Peggy didn't like that. "Maybe she doesn't answer the phone because you're checking on her. She's a grown woman. She's the children's mother. Have a little faith in her."

Falk looked her over with a puzzled frown. "*You're*

telling me that? After the scene Peggy made? Why on earth would you defend her?"

"I'm trying to put myself in her position. She lost her husband. She must feel completely abandoned."

"Abandoned? Greg would have done anything for his family. The guy was selfless to the core. He even died saving others."

"Yes, saving others, and now Tate doesn't have a daddy anymore. Do you have any idea what it's like for Peggy to see her son upset all the time when she can't do anything about it? I held him this morning while he was crying. It broke my heart, and I'm not even his mother. I can't imagine how Peggy must feel. She doesn't need you or me or anybody to tell her to do better, Falk. She just needs you to be there for her."

Falk looked away. "I'm not good at this psychobabble stuff. I have a suspect to question." He walked away from her.

Callie blew hair out of her face. Her temple was burning, and she could just kick herself for getting involved with Falk's sister and the boys. For giving Falk advice he wasn't about to take.

Advice that might be presumptuous, too. What did she even know about it? She was just guessing how Peggy felt and how Falk's questions about whom she saw and what she did at night were making her feel even worse.

But hadn't she seen the drawings on Falk's fridge? Didn't she know he loved those boys? Why had she made him feel like he was handling it wrong?

But in drawing the boys closer to him, Falk was alienating Peggy. And Peggy might need him just as much as Jimmy and Tate did.

Callie shook her head and went inside, where Brenda was nervously waiting for her.

\* \* \*

Dorothea was no longer seated in her room but had gone into the library. She looked very frail standing in the middle of the large room, the ceiling-high rows of shelves towering over her, full of their leather-bound volumes with gold lettering on the spines. She turned to the door when it opened, surprise in her features as she recognized Brenda. "Miss Brink, what are you doing here? If you want to know how I am after the shock of the murder, I am fine."

Dorothea sounded a little agitated. She pulled the colorful silk scarf around her thin shoulders. "The new will doesn't benefit the schoolyard, I'm afraid. But then, you had already said you wanted nothing from me."

Brenda cringed when her own curt words at the tea party were flung back at her. She glanced at Callie and whispered in an agonized voice, "I can't do this."

Callie said, "Dorothea, I think you should listen to what Brenda has to say. It could be important. In any case, you should be the first to know."

"Very well then." Dorothea walked, with her back painfully stiff, to the large leather chair behind the desk in the center of the room. She sat down and leaned her hands on the desk. The position of power, the seat of the lord of the manor, gave her a regal bearing. She waved a bony hand to the hard-backed chairs in front of the desk. "Sit. I'm listening."

Brenda walked over and sat, just as upright as Dorothea. "I didn't want to come here and tell you. I'm certainly not after money. I refused to cooperate all this time *because* I didn't want the money. But the police will have to know now. So I'm telling you first. Leadenby was blackmailing me."

Dorothea's eyes flashed a moment, but Callie couldn't make out with what emotion. Surprise? Anger?

Fear?

"He came to my house when I had just moved here. He claimed to have paperwork that proved that . . . I'm related to you."

Again there was a response in Dorothea's face.

Callie held her breath. Did this mean it was somehow true? Had Dorothea had a child?

"He claimed to be able to prove, through paperwork he had forged, that you had a child in your younger years and that that child was my father. I don't know what exactly he had, as he never showed it to me. But as Miss Aspen here told me that the police have found out he had a safe-deposit box at a bank, I'm sure they'll gain access to the papers soon."

Dorothea's hands on the desk were very still.

"He wanted me to approach Mr. Du Bouvrais or his wife and ask them for a large sum of money to keep it a secret that Mr. Du Bouvrais isn't your only relative and therefore not your only heir. If they wanted to get Haywood Hall, they had to buy me off. I refused to do it. Leadenby approached me again and again, wanting me to send emails to them or call them. Then, when they came to stay here for Christmas, he said I had to do it now. We fought about it right before the tea party started. Miss Aspen overheard something and told the police. I lied and said that he was blackmailing me about something having to do with the school. But the truth is that he was holding these papers over my head. I refused to go along with his scheme, but I left him alive. I have no idea who killed him."

Brenda sat and waited, apparently done with her story.

"What is your father's name?" Dorothea asked.

Brenda looked up. "Brink, of course, like mine."

"I mean his first name."

"Oh. That's rather unusual." Brenda shifted her weight in her chair. "He told me it was because he was born in Switzerland when his parents were on vacation there."

"Gentian," Dorothea said.

Brenda blinked. "Yes. How do you know that?"

"Gentian, like those flowers that grow high up in the mountains and weather every storm. You need to be able to weather something when you're abandoned as a baby."

Brenda sat motionless.

"I never thought I'd hear anything about him again," Dorothea said in a whisper.

"You know my father?"

Callie's heart beat fast under her chest bone. She saw the old woman behind the desk and the younger one in front of it through a haze. Dorothea's knowledge could mean only one thing.

Dorothea said, looking at Brenda, "Gentian is my son."

Brenda sagged back against the chair. "That can't be. Leadenby said the paperwork was forged. He made it all up."

Dorothea shook her head. "He might have told you that because he wanted you to be afraid of the power he had. To create false leads. But it's true. When I was a girl, I was in love and I had a baby. I was still in boarding school, and my parents thought me too young to marry and raise a child. They wanted me to study and travel and see the world and . . . I let myself be talked into it. I gave up Gentian. He was such a pretty little boy. But his father had turned his back on me by then, and . . . Friends of my parents in Switzerland took care of everything. Because it happened abroad, they were confident nothing could ever be proven later on. My reputation would be safe."

She laughed softly. "How sorry I was later. I wanted to know what had happened to Gentian, but it was impossible to find out. Nobody wanted to talk about it and there was no paper trail, at least not via any official channel I could appeal to. I listened to all the people who said it was better this way. And who knows, perhaps it was better? I'm sure his adoptive parents loved him very much."

"I loved going to my grandparents'. They're no longer

alive, but . . . we were so close. I can't believe they knew this and never said . . . My father doesn't even know!"

"He's still alive?" Dorothea's eyes lit.

"Yes." Brenda's gaze wandered through the room. "I can't believe this. I thought Leadenby was lying. I was so sure it couldn't be true."

"He wasn't lying. I'm sorry he harassed you. If I had known . . ." Dorothea wrung her hands. "Two years ago I asked Leadenby to help me look for Gentian one more time. Leadenby had told me that he had friends who could ferret out information, even illegally. I wanted one more chance to find my son. Leadenby took a lot of money to conduct his search and then reported to me it had been fruitless. I had no idea he lied."

"You did know he could be nasty," Callie said. "He forced you to let him stay here."

"He could be persuasive. But I never hated him. Nor did I think he hated me. What you're telling me now is a low trick. I can't imagine why he did it. Lie to me that he hadn't been able to find Gentian, when he really had all along. I wish I could tell him off about it now. But he's dead."

Dorothea sighed. "You must forgive me, for you'll think I pity a man who deserves no pity, but I am sorry for my old friend. He was bitter about how life had turned out for him. He was jealous of people who had more than he did and who, to his mind, didn't deserve that. I try to imagine how afraid he must have been of having to leave Haywood

Hall. I can only guess that was the reason for his lie to me. Why else not tell me about Gentian and about you; why not reunite me with you? His fear must have changed him. He made mistakes, yes, but don't we all? I still cannot hate him."

"I didn't hate him either; I just wanted it to stop." Brenda hugged herself. "I just wanted him to let me live my life here. At last I had a job and kids to care for and . . ."

"I won't tell a soul about it if you wish." Dorothea smiled sadly. "You see, there is no big inheritance to give away here. I just revealed to Callie today that Haywood Hall is in debt. I'd have to sell it unless someone can turn it around. Organize parties here and make it a museum. To save it for the generations to come. I cannot make you my heir and leave you my house and my wealth."

"I never wanted any house and any wealth," Brenda cried. "I just wanted to be happy here in this nice little town. I just wanted to . . . feel like I belonged."

Dorothea winced. She lowered her head. "I'm sorry."

It was very quiet in the big library. Only the ticking of a clock broke the silence. Tick-tock. The relentless rhythm of time. Reminding them of all the years that had slipped away and all the time that had not been spent with people it could have been spent with.

Brenda rose to her feet. She rounded the desk and leaned down to put her arm around the small figure in the big chair. "I'm sorry for you. That you could not have the love of your life, marry him, have your baby, and have a family.

I'm sorry that we all make you feel like this house matters more to us than you do."

Dorothea lifted her head. "At the tea party you said you wanted nothing from me. I was insulted when you said it; I thought you wanted to hurt my feelings. But now I understand what you meant. You never wanted to take anything from me. You . . ."

Brenda smiled down on her. "Leadenby couldn't make me do it. He can't hurt us now."

Dorothea reached up and touched Brenda's cheek. "Welcome to Haywood Hall."

Brenda's face split into a wide smile, and she hugged Dorothea.

Looking at them, Callie felt warmth rush through her, a sense of having put at least a little bit in place. Made things better for just these two people. She slipped quietly to the door, leaving them to each other.

# Chapter Fifteen

At the Book Tea, prepared to make profuse apologies for her absence, Callie found Iphy happily engaged in conversation with a whole group of women who had come in for a themed tea. She whispered to Callie that she should take some time off and go skating. "You can rent skates at the rink," she said, patting Callie's arm. "I know you used to be so good at it. You never forget, you know. No, no objections. I'm sending you off. Here's a late lunch. I bet you didn't eat a bite running after all this murder business. You need to unwind. Daisy can stay here with me and enjoy a nap by the fire. Now shoo, shoo."

Outside, Callie opened the bag her aunt had thrust upon her and found some kaiser rolls with lettuce, salami and cheese, a boiled egg she could peel, and a banana. She ate it all in the car, feeling ravenous after her strenuous day, and then drove out to the ice skating rink.

Despite there still being a few hours of daylight left, the lanterns were already lit, and the scent of burning wood

226

was in the air, mixing with spicy soup, hot chocolate, and popcorn. Callie got her skates at the booth, paying a small fee for them, and sat on a bench to put them on.

Just as she was testing the laces to make sure they were tight and wouldn't become undone right away, a shadow fell over her.

Glancing up, she saw Falk, on skates, in dark-blue ski pants, a sweater, and a bright-red scarf. He reached out his gloved hands to her. "I don't doubt you can skate very well, but it's always a little wobbly at first, and I don't want you to pick up a matching bruise."

She put her gloved hands in his and let him pull her to her feet. It was indeed a bit wobbly, and she had to rebalance herself constantly as she took her first few insecure steps.

But then she figured out how to push her legs away and how to prevent herself from tipping over, and soon they were making speed, the wind in their faces and the ice perfectly smooth beneath their skates. "You're really good," Falk said.

Callie grinned. "I'm surprised to see you here. I thought you were grilling Ben."

"I let him think it over. He hasn't been forthcoming with information. I'm somehow sure he knows something."

"Maybe he also saw Amber beside the body? Maybe he doesn't want to incriminate her. I think he cares for her."

"But she's head over heels for Cole. Watch out." Falk steered her around a fallen child and his mother, who was trying to get him back on his feet again. The boy was wailing that he never, ever wanted to skate again.

"Where are Tate and Jimmy?" Callie asked.

"Peggy took them to some meeting. I have no idea where." Falk looked uptight. "I think she's planning something insane like moving away from town."

"Why would she? She knows everybody around here."

"She wants to prove something to me. I don't know what."

"Maybe that she's a good mother? When did you last tell her that?"

Falk didn't say anything.

Callie focused on her skating. The wind was less chilly, it seemed, and the sun had come out to play across their faces. Children laughed and a girl did a spin and got a round of applause.

Callie had skated on much bigger and better rinks all across the world as part of her traveling, but she had never had quite this feeling. Like she was flying. Like she was weightless. Like she was . . . just happy about everything that was right here around her.

"There'll be a drawing soon where you can win Christmas goodies," Falk said. "Did you buy a ticket?"

Callie shook her head. "I'm never lucky in drawings."

Falk nodded in the direction of a stall. "Nice prizes, though. Chocolate Santas, gingerbread houses."

"Did you get tickets?"

"Sure. Whatever I win can go to the boys. I don't have a sweet tooth."

After another trip around the rink, the announcement was made through a megaphone that the drawing was about to take place, and everybody gathered around the stall in question. Callie rushed back to the bench to take off her skates and put her boots back on. Sticking her left foot into the boot, she felt some resistance. What was that?

She pulled out her foot and reached in her hand. It was a ball of crinkled glossy paper. She smoothed it and saw it was a colorful advertisement for the Book Tea. The flyers were posted at the local library and in the community center. Someone had written across the photo of the shop in red felt-tip: *Love this? Then quit poking.*

Callie stared at it, not quite able to grasp what it meant. Then as the words began to sink in, her heartbeat sped up. This was a threat, possibly from the same person who had called her last night. The word choice seemed about the same.

Her stomach tightened. Whoever had done this had walked past her boots and dropped the ball of paper inside. He or she had walked right past the ice skating rink where Callie had been doing her rounds with Falk. With a police officer, and still the killer hadn't cared. And he or she had gotten away with it. Callie hadn't seen anything.

"Are you coming?" Falk stood beside her, a carefree smile on his face. Then his gaze dropped to the paper in her hands. "What's that?"

"Nothing."

"Give it to me." Falk took it out of her hands, his fingers brushing hers. He studied it with a frown. "Where did you get this?"

"It was inside my left boot. I noticed it when I tried to

put my foot in." Callie leaned down and put said boot on her foot so she didn't have to look at Falk. "We'd better hurry. The drawing is about to begin."

"This is a threat. I'll have to see if I can find any fingerprints on it."

"Not a chance. First of all, I smoothed it out to read it, so any prints must be smudged. And just look around you. Everyone is wearing gloves because of the cold. Whoever dropped this didn't look suspicious at all, handling it with gloves on."

Falk sighed. "I want to look closer anyway."

"Fine with me. Keep it. I don't want it." Callie walked away to the stall where the prizes for the drawing were on display. She now saw that there were also Christmas tree ornaments to win and a nativity scene made out of wood, plus some already wrapped presents with contents unknown.

Mayor Moore appeared to oversee the proceedings. Several ladies who had provided items for the drawing were going to turn the wheel on a round metal basket full of balls; one small ball would fall out and that number would be the winner.

"That's used for bingo nights, normally," Falk said at her ear. "Well, at least it's better than last year, when somebody dipped his hand into a bowl full of folded notes with the numbers on it, and I later heard that he could see the numbers right through the note paper and knew exactly what number he was drawing."

"Did anyone get charged for this fraudulent activity?" Callie asked with a wink.

"Not a chance."

The lady who handled the bingo machine cried, "And the first winning number is eighteen. Which one of you has eighteen? Ah, Mrs. Mulberry. Over here, please."

The proud winner carried off the first gingerbread house, and from there excited cries rang out as shiny baubles, felt hearts, bottles of homemade cider, and other mysterious parcels found their new owners.

Falk was studying his numbers with a grimace. So far he hadn't been able to scoop up a single prize.

"Ah," Mr. Moore cried, "I see that we have some visitors in our midst today. Can I ask Miss Aspen to come on over here and draw some numbers?"

A little embarrassed by the sudden attention but unable to get out of this friendly request, Callie went around the stall and stood behind the counter, turning the handle. "Number seventy," she shouted. "Who has seventy?"

A man with a black terrier on a leash came forward and accepted his prize: a woven basket full of cheese.

Callie called numbers forty-three, fifteen, and nine, each time holding her breath as the ball fell in place and each time releasing it with a disappointed huff. She had seen what numbers Falk had and was hoping he'd get something at least. She couldn't influence the draw, but still, while turning, she hoped the right ball would get scooped up.

With a plop, the next ball fell and she smiled to herself. *At last.* "Number thirty-two," she called.

Falk raised his hand. "That's mine."

"Ah, the deputy!" Moore cried. "Come on over, good man. We have a prize here for you."

Callie noticed that one of the ladies who assisted was holding up a mystery parcel, but Moore ignored her and reached behind the stall. He produced a small fir with snow on it. "As it has come to my attention you still haven't put up the Christmas tree at the station, this is for you." He handed the tree to Falk.

It looked ridiculously small compared to his tall, broad figure, and there were a few snickers in the audience. Falk said with a forced smile, "Thank you, Mayor, I'm sure we can find a perfect place for that."

He went back to stand among the crowd. Mayor Moore ignored the woman with the mystery parcel who wanted to say something to him, and they completed the drawing.

Callie went back to Falk, who was putting the lottery tickets into his pocket. "No littering allowed," he said with a sour face, "or I'd tear them up on the spot. That whole thing is rigged. Even with the bingo device, Moore knows exactly who's getting what. He enjoyed making me look silly with this pitiful excuse for a fir tree. I'll find a place for it, all right, but certainly not inside the police station. We don't put up a tree there because we're dealing with serious business." He added in a low voice, "Like that threat to you."

Ignoring this, Callie focused on the fir in his hand. "Take it home. You haven't got anything Christmassy now. It's small and you don't need to buy a ton of decorations for it. Keep it simple. The boys would love it."

"Deputy!" The woman with the mystery parcel appeared by their sides. "I don't know where the mayor got that tree . . ." She scanned it with disgust. "But we arranged for decent prizes to hand out. I'm sorry you bought so many tickets and didn't get anything but that."

Falk tried to say it didn't matter since it was for a good cause, but the woman pushed the mystery parcel into his hand. "You take this. It was allotted to your number." She cast a scorching look in the direction of Mayor Moore, who was talking to some other men. "He thinks he can determine everything!" And with a harrumph, she stormed off to join her friends for hot chocolate.

Falk looked at the mystery parcel. "I wonder what's in there," he said, considering the box. "It's sort of sturdy but not as solid as a book would be."

"Let me feel it," Callie said, but Falk pulled it back. "Uh, uh, no peeking. I'm saving this for Christmas Eve. And I'm not saying I'll open it myself."

Callie's heart skipped a beat. Of course, she told herself, he meant he was going to give it to Tate or Jimmy. Or maybe even to Peggy to mend relations?

He didn't mean he was going to give it to her. Why would he?

Falk's phone rang, and he pulled it up from his pocket and answered. His relaxed expression turned grim. "What? How did that happen? No, I don't want to hear any lame excuses. I'm coming right now. Put out an APB on him. He can't leave the state."

He disconnected and looked at Callie. "Seems the perfect son-in-law-to-be isn't so perfect after all. Ben Matthews escaped from the police station."

"Escaped?" Callie echoed. "Was he locked up, then?"

"No, he was waiting to be questioned again. But why would he take off? He didn't even have a car there. Someone must have come to pick him up. I'd like to know who that was. Maybe they're in it together." His face got a faraway look as if he was devising a whole new theory.

"There are some things you should know," Callie said quickly, thinking of Brenda and Dorothea and Leadenby's safe-deposit box. Maybe it held more material than just the supposedly forged papers about Dorothea's Swiss-born son?

Falk waved a hand. "Not now." He wanted to walk away, then leaned over. "You be careful what you do. Get back to the Book Tea and stay there. Don't go anywhere alone. And if something suspicious happens at the Book Tea, you call me at once. OK?"

Callie wasn't sure what he was expecting, but she nodded. He had enough on his mind with Ben Matthews on the run.

"Good." Carrying off his prizes, Falk made for the police car parked on the edge of the lot.

"Problems?" Moore appeared by Callie's side, his tone just a little too eager.

"Nothing special." Callie wasn't about to reveal that a suspect had slipped away from the police station while Falk wasn't around to prevent it. He and the mayor didn't seem to be the best of friends.

She focused on Moore. "I was at your house yesterday and saw your Christmas village. So lovely. You must put so much time and dedication into that."

"It's my little hobby, yes. A passion, so to speak. The eye for detail, making it as true to life as possible."

"Your wife mentioned to me that Dorothea's husband left a fund for the town. I was wondering, if I was going to stay around"—she was making this up as she went—"and wanted to start my own little business, if you could help me out with some initial investment. Money?"

"You're more than wanted at the Book Tea, I'd think." Moore rubbed his hands. "Iphy isn't getting any younger."

"But there is money for starting businesses, I suppose? The fund was quite substantial, I gather."

"My wife often talks about things she knows next to nothing about." Moore waved at someone. "Excuse me, I must go and say hello to a few people."

But a few minutes later, Callie saw the mayor standing alone, talking into his cell phone. He seemed angry and trying to make a point. Was he reprimanding his talkative wife?

Or warning an accomplice that their deceit was about to become public knowledge?

Thinking of the bright-red words written across her great aunt's beloved Book Tea, Callie pulled her coat tighter around herself but couldn't lock out the cold that seemed to seep into her very core.

# Chapter Sixteen

Callie lowered the last plate into the dishwasher and stood up straight. Her muscles were aching from the skating. She had to do it more often. Her gaze strayed to the kitchen clock—half past six—and she wondered how Falk was getting on with his search for Ben. Her stomach rumbled, and she tried to remember what was in Iphy's fridge that could be turned into a quick dinner. All this washing up after the guests left the Book Tea took longer than you'd think. Iphy had to be aching for a hot bite and a quiet evening as well.

The swinging doors burst open and Iphy ran in, holding her phone. "We have to get our coats," she called. "I'll drive."

"Where to?" Callie asked in bewilderment. Suddenly her quiet evening seemed to fly out the window.

"Dinner. My treat. The Golden Chef along the highway."

It sounded quite inviting, but Callie wasn't eager for a venture into the snowy world. "Uh, can't we just stay in and pop a pizza into the oven or something? I'm bushed."

"Nonsense. Wrap up warm. I'll ask a neighbor to look after Daisy. It'll be far too crowded for her there."

Callie sighed as her overactive great aunt scooped up the Boston terrier and carried her off, cooing to her. But *crowded* sounded good. At least Callie wouldn't be breaking her promise to Falk, as she wasn't going anywhere alone.

In the car, Iphy said in a confidential tone, "I'm sure that a public place is perfectly safe for it."

"For what?" Callie asked, not understanding. The word *safe* sent her heartbeat skittering. What was her great aunt up to? More than just dinner, it seemed.

"A meeting with an informant. He claims to have the skinny on the case."

Callie sat up. "Wait. What? Can you just speak plainly?"

Iphy pulled a face. "Can't I have fun at my age? Can't I go out and play detective for an hour or two? You've been at it all day, leaving me to serve muffins and cakes. I mean, they are my own muffins and cakes, so I don't hate them, but still . . . there are other priorities in life. You get all the excitement."

"Yes, like getting hit in the head by an ice ball," Callie said with a sour expression.

"That didn't happen because of the case," Iphy corrected her cheerfully. "You're just too kindhearted for your own good."

"No, I'm too interfering for my own good. I should never have started to dig into the case or . . ." Peggy's relationship with Falk, the boys, everything that was complicated.

And she hadn't told Iphy about the threat to the Book Tea yet. Her great aunt had a far too simple view of the whole situation. "I intend to change my ways and stay away from trouble from now on. And if you don't tell me right away what's up at the Golden Chef, I'm getting out of this car right now."

"How? We're doing fifty on solid asphalt."

Callie sighed. "I mean, what are we getting ourselves into? This so-called informant could be the killer wanting to . . ."

"Silence us for what we know?" Iphy glanced at her. "First of all, we know precious little. You've been busy clearing the suspects one by one until there's no one left."

The indignation in her great aunt's voice riled Callie. She countered, "I wouldn't say no one. Mayor Moore has been acting very secretive. I'm sure he's hiding something. And Frank Smith isn't even being considered a suspect. Falk refused to check on that call Smith received when he had to step out, away from the tea party guests."

"And second," Iphy continued, as if she hadn't heard Callie list the suspects that had been ignored so far, "I don't think anyone is going to kill us in the Golden Chef tonight. It's the trial run night for Christmas dinner."

"What do you mean, trial run for Christmas dinner?"

"Well, suppose you have no talent at all for cooking. Or you have in-laws coming who are super critical. Or you just don't want to spend all your time in the kitchen when you could be spending it with your grandkids playing some game or watching a cute movie. Then you can order everything you need ready-made from the Golden Chef. They deliver it the day before Christmas and you can simply keep it fresh in the fridge and heat it when you need it."

Callie clicked her tongue. "Sounds like a winner in the city, but I'd think in a small town your cranberry sauce would have to be homemade or they'd run you out of town."

Iphy laughed. "How old-fashioned. We have many young families here who love to use the Golden Chef services. And even some of my friends get the meringues because they're simply better than they can ever make them. It's an art to make good meringues."

"I suppose so," Callie said with a sigh. "So we're going to eat at this Golden Chef place while it's stuffed with diners trying out what dishes they're going to purchase for their Christmas guests? How are we even going to recognize this informant?"

"He said he'd recognize us." Iphy poked an elbow at her. "Isn't this exciting?"

"It would be if there wasn't a very real dead body involved."

Iphy looked at her. "I do realize that. And I would never have agreed to meet in a lonely place. I'd never put you in danger."

"Aw, I know that." Callie patted her great aunt's arm.

"You're just trying to get to the heart of the matter. We all are."

\* \* \*

The Golden Chef's parking lot was so full they had to drive through it a couple of times to find an empty space. From the warm car into the chilly air was quite a change, and Callie wrapped her scarf around her head and half of her face. She wasn't keen on this informant saying he'd recognize them. Who could it be?

Iphy strode ahead of her, waving at someone she knew who was just leaving. "Going already? Only had soup?"

"Only thing worth eating," the answer came back briskly.

Iphy shook her head. The entry doors had been decorated with lots of cotton ball snowflakes, and inside, Christmas music played. Not on a sound system but produced by a real man behind a piano.

Callie glanced around at the many booths where diners were sitting with tall red and gold candles lit between them, glasses full of bubbly liquid being raised to drink to the occasion and the happy days ahead.

Waitresses in stylish black dresses with silver sparkles carried plates full of roast beef with rosemary potatoes or turkey and gravy to the tables.

Iphy spied around. "There, in the back," she pointed.

Callie followed her gaze, not sure what she had spotted. She did see Moore and his wife with another couple, sampling the roast beef with a critical expression as if it wasn't up to par.

Fortunately, they didn't seem to see her. Callie almost slunk after Iphy, hoping they could sit down quickly and vanish into the background.

In a booth, a man was sitting on his own. He had a baseball cap on and wore dark glasses. He sat hunched over the table, a beer in his hands.

Iphy slipped into the booth opposite him. "Hello, Ben."

Callie's mouth fell open. "Ben?" she echoed.

The figure looked up. "Not so loud. Sit down and don't look conspicuous."

"You're not exactly blending in yourself," Callie whispered as she took her seat. "You're the only one here alone and you're not eating. And that outfit! Where did you learn how to disguise yourself?"

Ben pulled the glasses down his nose so he could look across. "I'm running from the police. That's not funny."

Callie held his gaze. "No. Are you running for a reason?"

"I don't know."

"What do you mean, you don't know?"

Ben sighed. He took off the glasses and put them on the table beside his beer. "I have nothing to hide. Honestly. I wanted to cooperate with the police. But someone called me while I was waiting at the station and said there's something in the safe-deposit box Leadenby had that incriminates Amber. That proves that she had every reason to kill

Leadenby. The only way to save her was if I ran away so the police would think I was the guilty party."

"And you believed that?" Callie asked, glancing at Iphy.

"I don't know what to believe. I also thought she loved me, and now it turns out she wants this guy Cole." Ben's shoulders slumped.

Iphy said, "You thought if you ran away and the police came after you, and Amber heard about the reason for it, she might care for you again. You want to win her back."

Ben nodded. "I just want to show her how much she means to me."

"I think she knows that, Ben, but she's just . . . in love with somebody else. You can't force feelings."

Ben sagged even more. "I know. What now? I'm on the run and the police will never believe this insane story. They won't even believe I got a call. And they can't trace it either, I bet."

Callie said, "I also got a call, threatening me if I didn't stop snooping around. Someone is trying to manipulate things."

"You never told me you got a call threatening you!" Iphy exclaimed.

Callie ignored her. Now didn't seem like the right time to discuss the call or the threat left in her boot at the ice skating rink. They had to help Ben first. "It must be the same person."

Ben looked at her expectantly. "Do you know who it was?"

"No. Did you see anything at the tea party, anything that might help us figure out who did it?"

Ben shook his head. "I was just so angry about that stupid empty ring box that I took off. First I ran up the stairs, then I realized I needed fresh air. I went down again and out the front door. I walked around the house."

"You must have come near the conservatory. It's all glass. Didn't you see anything?"

Ben shook his head. "I wasn't paying attention. Besides, if it's hot inside and cold out, the glass gets foggy. I don't think I could have seen anything, not even if I had wanted to."

"Good point," Callie acknowledged. "I hadn't thought about that." The killer must have realized that too and felt perfectly safe as he was about to deal the final blow.

Ben sighed. "I guess I'm in deep trouble now. How can I tell the police the truth without ending up in a cell?"

"We can ask the deputy to come out here and hear your story," Iphy suggested. "Then you can go back to Haywood Hall. If you promise not to run again, it will be fine."

"Why would he even believe me?" Ben lamented.

Iphy looked at Callie. "Call Falk, will you? I'm going to order dinner for four."

Callie raised a hand. "Wait a sec. Falk isn't going to have dinner here with us."

"Why not? I bet he isn't going to cook anything special for himself this Christmas. He could try out the food here and see if he wants to place an order." Iphy nodded and then stood up and walked off to one of the busy waitresses.

243

Ben stared after her. "She knows what she wants."

"And usually gets it. I'll call Falk."

As expected, Falk was still at the station. Callie suspected him of even sleeping there, as he was deep into recovery of his missing suspect. She said, "Could you come out to the Golden Chef? I have someone here who wants to talk to you. You'll be very interested to meet with him. Then I think you can cancel your ABP and spend the night in your bed at home."

"You've got Ben there?" Falk exclaimed.

"Not so loud." Callie already envisioned the other deputy believing he could score points with the sheriff and pop up too, to arrest Ben with a full show of force. "Come alone. Tell no one about this."

"What does Ben want from you? He could be the killer. You're being careful, aren't you? I told you not to—"

"It's super crowded here. Perfectly safe. Now hurry. Bye." And she disconnected before he could ask more questions or express more concerns.

As she came back to the booth, the waitress had already brought candles for them and glasses of white wine. Iphy raised hers to toast Callie. "I asked for mineral water. I need to drive you home safely tonight." She winked. "Unless you think someone else will want to do that."

Ben seemed to prick up his ears, and Callie said hurriedly, "I need to freshen up."

Making her way to the restrooms, her gaze passed over the people in the other booths. Suddenly her forward movement froze. In one of the booths sat Peggy, her blonde hair done up, her face flushed. She leaned over to the man opposite her, smiling. He was a serious-looking, suit-clad type, probably the same guy Amber had seen her with before. Someone who'd sell insurance, Amber had said.

Callie walked past them quickly, glad that Peggy hadn't looked up and recognized her. She might think she was being watched, on Falk's orders.

But wait a minute . . .

Callie's stomach clenched. Falk was coming here. She had to make sure he didn't see Peggy and start a scene about where the boys were.

She washed her hands quickly, holding her wrists under the cold water to calm down, then looked at her hair and makeup. Her temple looked nasty in the pale restroom light. Why oh why did all of this have to be so complicated all of the time?

Callie left the restroom and made sure she hung around the entrance until she saw Falk coming. His tall figure stood out, and the light from the restaurant sign over the entrance reflected off his badge.

He stepped in and spotted her right away. "Hello. Now what's up? Don't tell me Ben took off again?"

"No, he's right here. Come on. But keep a low profile, please."

That was kind of hard to do in that uniform, she supposed, but with the waitresses buzzing about and people milling around to say hi to friends, it might work.

She sighed with relief when they arrived at the table and Ben was still there.

Falk cast a suspicious look at the candles and the wine glasses.

Iphy said innocently, "Just a little cover, Deputy. We're innocently sampling Christmas dinner options. I hope you don't mind, I ordered roast beef for you."

"Not at all. I hate turkey."

"Me too," Iphy sympathized. "Often it's so dry."

Iphy gestured that he should sit beside Ben. Ben wasn't happy to now be locked into the booth by a policeman, and Callie felt a little uncomfortable taking her place opposite Falk. The table seemed to have gotten smaller, and the candlelight reflecting in his brown eyes made them look far too considerate for her liking. This was all business, she had to remind herself. Clearing up a difficult case.

"So what's the story?" Falk asked Ben. "We have an APB out for you. That's not good news for anybody involved. We use manpower to look for you. You're at the risk of being apprehended by force."

"I'm not dangerous. Why on earth did you put out that APB about me? Because I might resist arrest? I'm only trying to help Amber."

"Amber? Did she do something, then? Did you see her attack Leadenby?"

Ben shook his head. He told Falk about the call he'd gotten about evidence in the safe-deposit box Leadenby was supposed to have at the bank.

Falk laughed softly. "You've been had. I've been to that bank and I had a look inside that box. There was nothing worthwhile in it."

"What?" Callie said. "Not even paperwork about . . ." She gave him a significant look.

Falk nodded at her. "I talked to Dorothea and the other party involved. But whatever Leadenby claimed to have, it wasn't in that box."

"Did anybody else have access to it? Could that someone have emptied it right after Leadenby died?"

"I thought of that myself and asked the bank employees about it, but no one has been there for the box."

"Leadenby must have emptied it himself," Callie mused. "He wanted to use the tea party for some explosive revelations. But it never came to that. He was killed first."

Falk nodded. "Something like that."

A waitress brought their food, and they dug in. Callie had to admit that this was better than anything she had ever had abroad. A chef with a golden touch indeed.

Iphy said pensively, "If Leadenby planned to use the tea party for an exposé, where's the material he wanted to lay out? You found nothing in the conservatory, I assume. Otherwise you would have known it all by now."

Falk nodded, chewing. He swallowed and said, "We found nothing there. Not on his person, either."

"The killer must have taken it," Iphy mused. "So we have to assume it incriminated him or her."

Callie expected Falk to retort that "we" were not

assuming anything, as he was not investigating the case with *them*, but he lifted his fork for emphasis. "But if it was paperwork, as in several sheets of paper, or something substantial, where did the killer put it? Whoever it was couldn't have just kept it on their person. And burning it while in the conservatory would have taken too long. Besides, the smell of burned paper would have lingered and someone would have noticed."

Callie leaned over her plate with a frown, trying to picture the scene. The killer had stabbed Leadenby and had to leave with the incriminating paperwork. But there was indeed no place to put it. So what did the killer do then? "Didn't you say there were wet spots in the conservatory—snowy bits, water, mud?" Callie asked. "Didn't you think someone had come in from the outside? Isn't that why you suspected Ben of being involved?"

Falk nodded. "I still don't see how it got there," he mumbled around a bite. "If Ben never went in from the outside, who did?"

"Maybe the killer opened the door into the garden and hid the papers under the snow?" Callie looked at the faces of the other three. "It would be a perfect hiding place. The weather isn't about to turn, so the snow won't melt away. And when it eventually does, the paper will have become such a mess it's all illegible."

"Forensics have pretty good restoring tactics," Falk said. "They might still be able to recreate the writing on it."

Callie leaned back, resting her fork on her plate. "We could use it to set a trap for the killer."

Falk shook his head. "Oh, no, we aren't doing any such thing."

"What do you mean, Callie?" Iphy asked with a sparkle in her eyes.

"Falk could leak to the jungle drum that he believes evidence is hidden in or around the conservatory and he's going to look for it again. The killer will try to beat him to it and come back to remove the evidence."

Falk shook his head. "Not in a million years."

Callie continued, "It might be the only way to catch whoever it is. You don't know anything else that can seal the case."

Falk sat up indignantly. "I followed up on every lead I had. I even checked those phone records you asked for."

He pointed at her with his fork. "You asked who had called Frank Smith at the tea party. I first checked with his secretary, who he had said had called him, but it wasn't her. Then I looked at the number. And guess what number it was?"

Callie shrugged. "No idea."

"Haywood Hall."

"You mean . . ." Callie frowned. "Someone from inside Haywood Hall used the Haywood Hall phone to call Frank Smith? But that doesn't make any sense. We were all together for the party. Why would anyone . . ."

She fell silent.

Iphy, who was cutting up her roast beef, said to Falk, "Ah, now we're getting somewhere. Callie just got it."

Falk shook his head. "Callie can't get anything, because it makes no sense at all."

"But it does." Callie put down her cutlery and stared at Falk. "It makes perfect sense."

She shot to her feet. "I have to talk to you. Right now. We have to be quick if we want to get anywhere."

Falk protested that he didn't have a clue as to what she was driving at, but Callie marched off. Too late, she remembered Peggy and her date. She walked past their booth quickly, not even glancing at them, wishing fervently Falk wouldn't see . . .

"Peggy?" She heard his voice behind her back.

No.

She turned around and smiled. "Are you coming?"

Falk had halted at the booth and was looking down at his sister and the man opposite her like he wanted to drag him to his feet and question him about what he was doing here.

"Are you coming?" Callie repeated in a loud tone.

Falk threw her an impatient look, then followed her. In the corridor leading to the restrooms, he shot, "Who's that guy?"

"That's none of your business."

"So you know?"

"No, because it's none of my business either. Listen, I

see the whole thing now. How the murder was committed. Who it was and even how we can catch him."

Falk was staring over his shoulder into the room full of diners.

She caught his shoulder. "Hello? Are you listening? I want to catch the killer."

Falk focused on her. "Sorry?"

"The killer. I now know who it is."

"How?"

Callie was glad to see some focus in Falk's eyes. "The phone call to Smith's cell phone. You just said it came from the Haywood Hall number. There's a phone in the conservatory. Leadenby called Smith from there."

"Why? To ask him to come over? And then they fought, and Smith killed Leadenby?"

Callie shook her head. "Leadenby was telling Smith he was going to act. That he was going to make public what he knew. About Dorothea and Brenda. He was going to tell everything at the tea party."

Falk held her gaze. "So?"

"Don't you see? The blackmail scheme was based on Dorothea not knowing about Brenda. Brenda was supposed to sell herself as granddaughter to Stephen and Sheila, with them paying a huge sum of money to keep Brenda's existence under wraps and make sure Stephen got the Hall, as had been the plan from the start. Once Dorothea knew about Brenda being her granddaughter, the blackmail would be pointless."

Falk held her gaze, obviously not getting the drift. "So?"

"So once Leadenby talked, the money would be out of reach. Smith couldn't let that happen."

"You mean, Leadenby and Smith were in on it together?"

"Yes. They had to be. We were thinking all along that someone had killed Leadenby to prevent him from telling some secret. We thought that one of the victims of his unpleasant practices had killed him. But it was his accomplice."

Falk didn't seem convinced. "Why would Smith ever get into anything like that?"

"I don't know, of course. But I can guess. He made big promises to the other business owners. But there was no money. The fund had been squandered by Moore. Or at least we know Moore signed for those investments. But what if he made those based on suggestions from Smith? Smith seems to have muscled in on everything here in town. Mayor Moore's Christmas village got kicked out of the community center and a friend of Smith's was allowed to put up a display there. Smith was pulling the strings, probably claiming he was the better businessman. When the investments turned out to be worthless, Moore might have told Smith to find a solution."

Callie nodded to herself as it all fell into place. "Smith needed money to replace the chamber of commerce's dissipated funds. So he set up a clever scheme with Leadenby. They brought Brenda to Heart's Harbor and then tried to force her into playing along. But she refused, and Leadenby said he'd tell himself."

"But what would be the point? You just said that if everybody knew about Brenda being Dorothea Finster's granddaughter, they'd never get any money."

"Right. I don't fully understand that yet. I also don't see why Leadenby would first lie to Dorothea that he hadn't been able to find her son and then used her granddaughter to get money. Money he then had to share with somebody else. I mean, I assume Smith would have wanted to get most of the blackmail money to pump into that empty fund. Why would Leadenby cooperate at all? How did he benefit? But I'm pretty certain I'm right about Smith's involvement in Leadenby's death. He got a call that surprised him, probably because he realized it came from within the Hall. He left the tea party at once. He was away long enough to have killed Leadenby. I even saw him rubbing his hands like he had just washed them and needed to dry them off. I just thought he had been to the bathroom, but . . ."

"That's all a very nice theory, but we can't prove any of it. Just the phone call, and Smith can always just make up a story of what was being said."

"But there's the missing blackmail material. Smith might suspect it can also point the finger at him, if Leadenby made notes about their agreement, what they were going to do. If he had more than just paperwork. Maybe a recording? If you leak to Moore that you're going to search again, his wife will tell everyone. It will also get to Smith. He'll come to the Hall to look for it before you do. I'll be there waiting for him. I can talk to him and get him to confess. Then you can arrest him."

"Wait. What? I'm not letting you wait for him. What if he hurts you?"

"He won't have a chance. We need to know if there was evidence and where he hid it. It can hurt people."

Falk sighed. He thought for a few moments. "If I'm going to do this, I'm doing it alone."

"Smith doesn't take me seriously. If he's confronted with me, he'll think he can outsmart me. Please, let's give this a try. We'll never clear it up any other way. Christmas is coming, and people want to be together. Dorothea and her granddaughter."

Falk held her gaze. "Why do I sense that I'm going to let you win me over?"

He leaned back on his heels. "How am I going to leak this to Moore, anyway?"

"He's here sampling dinner options. Just stop by his table and tell him of your intentions. His wife is sitting right beside him and will hear every word of it. She'll start calling people as soon as they get home."

"And then we spend the night at Haywood Hall in the conservatory waiting to see if Smith got the message and turns up?"

"I suppose there's nothing else to do."

Falk shook his head. "I don't like it." He wanted to say more, but Peggy appeared and came at them. "Thanks a lot." Her voice was strangled. "Thanks to you, the whole thing is ruined. Why did you have to come over to the table? In uniform! Now I'll never get the job."

"What job?" Falk asked.

"Something I can do from home to make money and be there for the boys at the same time. I worked my nails off for this chance, and you just ruined it for me." Peggy stepped back, tears of frustration in her eyes. "Thanks a lot." She marched to the restrooms and disappeared into the door marked LADIES.

"Did you understand any of that?" Falk asked Callie with a bewildered expression.

"Apparently that man can offer her a job. And with you appearing at their table, he got the impression Peggy is somehow in trouble with the police." Callie tapped his arm. "Wait a sec while I go talk to her."

As she came into the restroom, Peggy was checking her makeup. She glanced at Callie in the mirror. "I don't need a lecture about how wonderful my brother is," she warned her.

"Is your prospective boss still there?"

Peggy sighed. "Yes. He didn't run screaming because a deputy stopped at our table. But he did look at me strangely, and I don't want to tell him that the deputy is my brother. It will only look worse. Like I can't take care of my own life."

"I think you're doing a great job raising two boys on your own."

"Yeah? If I'm doing such a great job, why did you have to interfere with Tate this morning?" Peggy nodded at Callie's face. "Your forehead is turning purple now."

"They were teasing him, and Jimmy wasn't there to stand up for him. I just wanted to help. That's what friends are for." She held Peggy's gaze. "You don't have to do this all alone."

Peggy looked at her. Her lips wobbled a moment. "I just want Greg to come back. This is the worst time of year. Everybody is getting together. And what can we do?"

"I don't know. But I do know that Falk cares very much for your kids. I was at his cabin to talk about the case, and he has no personal stuff there whatsoever. But he does have drawings from the boys on his fridge."

Peggy blinked. "Don't you make me cry. I have a job interview to finish."

"And Falk has a killer to catch."

Peggy froze. She looked at Callie with wide eyes. "He's just like Greg was," she whispered. "He's risking his life to keep others safe. What if he gets hurt? What if he dies? What if I lose him too?"

So that was it. Peggy didn't want to get too close to Falk, since he might also die in the line of duty. She didn't want to get hurt so deeply again. "The way you're treating him now, you've lost him already."

Peggy looked down. Her face was young and vulnerable. Then she seemed to come to a decision. She pulled her shoulders back. "I'll get that job somehow. I've already put so much time and effort into it."

"Yes, you will. Good luck."

Callie let her pass and went out after her, watching her as she walked back down the corridor.

Falk still stood there, like a silent sentry. Peggy walked

over to him and, for a moment, Callie thought she was just going to breeze past him without saying anything, acting like she was still mad. But Peggy stopped, put her arms around Falk, and kissed him on the cheek. Then she hurried on.

Falk stared after her with blank surprise.

As Callie appeared at his side, he said to her, "What on earth was that for?"

"Good luck, I guess. She knows you have a killer to catch."

Falk's eyes went dark. "You didn't tell her that, did you? She's bound to be worried sick about me."

He hesitated a moment, his whole posture tensing. "I thought about it, you know. Changing professions, doing something different than this, for her and the boys. To make sure I won't catch a bullet in the back and die on them."

His jaw pulled tight. "But I couldn't do it. I believe in my work. I believe that I was made to do this. That I would never feel as strongly about any other job."

He looked her in the eye. "Do you think that was wrong?"

Callie shook her head. "No. I think you know what you need to do. Just like Peggy knows it. Have some faith in her." She touched his arm. "Come on. We have some interesting news for the mayor."

# Chapter Seventeen

After they had dropped the news about the new search at Haywood Hall in Moore's ear—or rather, in that of his wide-eyed wife, who clearly couldn't wait to call all of her friends to talk about it—they finished their half-cold dinner and left the Golden Chef.

Iphy went home in her car, while Falk took Ben and Callie to Haywood Hall. He then left to show his face at the police station and convince anyone who was possibly watching the Hall that it would be a night like any other. He assured Callie he would return later, leaving his car well away from the house and coming over on foot.

Callie informed everybody what was up, asking them to stay upstairs, whatever they heard or thought was happening. "We don't want anybody else to get hurt."

Amber told her to be careful and hugged her, while Dorothea said she was sure she had made the right decision with her will, in leaving her legacy to people who fought for what they believed in.

The mention of the will made Callie's heart heavy again, and she lingered with Sheila on the landing. "How're you feeling?"

"I had a long talk with Dorothea. She needed to talk about Switzerland and giving up her baby. I never realized there was such a silent sadness in her life. She also explained to me about the Hall, the will, and . . . I can't be angry with her. I wanted to, honestly; I wanted to feel cheated. But how could I? I've been happily married; I had my daughter with me always. I had so much that Dorothea never had."

Sheila took a deep breath. "Yes, once upon a time I wanted Stephen for the Hall. I told myself I had to marry anyway, and it was better to marry someone with a reputation and money to come. Someone who could take me to exciting places abroad. It wasn't hard to like him, either. You know how it was."

Callie nodded with a smile. "Stephen was everybody's hero."

"And he chose me." Sheila held her gaze. "I felt like I deserved it. Later on, remembering how calculating I'd been, I . . . wasn't so sure anymore. Whether I had deserved it and whether . . . he had ever loved me. I did love him. I do love him, Callie. I realized that more than ever when we were at risk of losing everything. I love him and I love Amber, and they are the most important things in the world to me. Everything else is second rate. Yes, it means something to me to be a diplomat's wife and to have an easy life, opportunities. But when it comes down to it, they mean more. They're everything. It's just . . ."

Her expression contorted. "I can be such a busybody. Amber must hate me for planning her engagement that way. And Stephen . . . what if he never loved me at all? What if my entire marriage was a lie?"

Callie held her gaze. "You asked Amber to wear something at the tea party when you planned to have Ben propose to her. A pendant. It looked like a coin. It wasn't very . . . grand, and I was a little surprised Amber was wearing it, she told me, because you asked her too."

Sheila smiled sadly. "When Stephen asked me to marry him, we were in Athens. We were sightseeing and we ended up in this lovely little square tucked away between some houses, with kids playing and blossoming roses against the house fronts. A few paces away from us, this small coin was lying in the street. Stephen picked it up and gave it to me. As our eyes met across our hands, he . . . asked me to marry him. Just like that."

Sheila swallowed. "It wasn't planned; it wasn't a big affair like I tried to set up for Ben and Amber. It was summertime, we were enjoying ourselves, we made this find in a beautiful place and . . . it just happened."

She blinked, and her eyes shone with tears on her lashes. "I always kept that coin, had it turned into a necklace. When I decided to have Ben propose, I . . . On impulse, I wanted Amber to wear the coin. You're right that it didn't really fit her dress but . . . I just wanted her to be connected to that moment when Stephen asked me and . . ."

A tear ran down her cheek. "Amber never loved Ben. And maybe Stephen never loved me either. Maybe I just thought he did. Everything I believed during twenty-two years of marriage might be lies."

"You'll have to talk to Stephen about that. He can tell you."

"He's been so cold to me. I think he blames me for setting it all off. The tea party and the murder."

Callie grabbed her friend's hand and squeezed it. She remembered how anxious Stephen had been about the new will, claiming it had the power to change their lives. Had he sensed Dorothea wouldn't leave Haywood Hall to him? Had he been afraid that it would also mean the end of his marriage to Sheila? Sheila, who had always dreamed of being mistress here?

She said to her friend, "No, I bet you he's worried you won't stay with him now that Haywood Hall is no longer part of the deal."

"How silly." Sheila looked down the corridor to where the door to the library was. "I suppose he's hiding among the books like he used to. I'll go talk to him."

"Do that. But stay up here, whatever happens, and don't interfere with catching the killer. Let Falk and me handle that."

"Falk is a trained policeman and he has a gun. You have nothing. I can't imagine why he's letting you do this."

"I made him. I want to do it. Once upon a time, Leadenby taught us all about plants and regional history, and we cared for him. He belonged to Haywood Hall. Even with his quirks and his manipulations. He has been stolen away from us, and we have to set that right. Go to Stephen now. It will all be fine."

Callie walked downstairs and stood in the empty sitting room for a few moments, trying to prepare herself mentally for the hours ahead. Maybe nobody would come. Maybe she was wrong about Frank Smith. Maybe the killer was somebody else. Somebody they would never catch.

But as she thought of Leadenby and her promise to him, here in this room, that she would come see his orchids, a promise she had never been able to keep, she knew she had to find his killer. Like she had just told Sheila, Leadenby had been part of their story at the Hall. No matter what he had turned into as he had become older and more manipulative, once upon a time he had been a part of their childhood here, of everything she had been with Sheila and Stephen and Dorothea. Along with the tall trees and old books and secret passageways they had invented.

She closed her eyes a moment and indulged in the warmth of those memories.

A knock on the window made her snap her eyes wide open. Although she knew Falk was coming, her heart pounded, and she had to force herself to go over, push the curtain aside, and open the window so he could climb in.

Falk's leather jacket was covered in snow, and small flakes

rested in his hair and even on his eyelashes. His breathing was ragged as if he had walked fast or perhaps even run. "I came as quickly as I could. I was worried the killer would be ahead of me." His hand touched hers. "Is everything all right here?"

"I told everybody else to stay upstairs. They're slightly worried about this whole enterprise . . ."

"Then they're not alone." Falk sounded stern. "I like it less and less."

"Still, we're going to do it," Callie said before he could try to talk her out of it. "I figured out exactly how it can be done. I'll be in the conservatory with a flashlight. I'll turn it on Smith when he comes. We'll argue about him paying me money to keep silent about what I know or something along those lines. Then once he's confessed enough to be charged, you'll jump him."

"Just like that, huh?" Falk said in a sour tone. "You suddenly put your life into the hands of the man you didn't think could lead a murder investigation?"

"I already said I was sorry about that. Aren't you flattered I changed my mind and became convinced of your qualities so quickly?"

Falk shook his head. "I was at the station and I considered simply arresting Smith and keeping him in a cell until he talks."

"You know he's too smart to talk. He can guess we have nothing to go on. Especially now that you told Mayor Moore that you're still looking for evidence."

Falk sighed. "I wish I had never said that."

They went to the conservatory and took their places, Falk taking cover behind a group of potted palms. "Whatever you do," he warned her, "don't get near him where he can grab you. Once he's holding you hostage, I won't be able to jump him. And if he should manage to move you away from the house, anything can happen."

In the darkness, the ensuing silence seemed deeper than Callie had ever experienced.

Then Falk said, "Haywood Hall needs you. Keep that in mind."

\* \* \*

Callie sat on the floor, her knees pulled up, her chin resting on her knees. Her right hand closed around the flashlight. She had lost all track of time. Sometimes when she opened her eyes wider to stay awake, she wasn't sure she hadn't been half sleeping and was just waking up. Maybe Smith had come and gone already, outside the fogged-up windows.

Maybe he had already dug out the all-important papers and taken them away to burn them, laughing as he watched the incriminating evidence turn to ashes?

Suddenly there was a ray of light. A scraping sound.

Callie sat up straight, her neck hairs standing up. This wasn't a creaking beam that woke her in the night, maybe the rustle of a critter. No, it was a human being, searching for a way in. A way into the room where he had killed a man by digging a screwdriver into his chest.

Callie tried to move. Her legs were so stiff that she could barely push herself up. She rose, wincing as her knees locked. Sitting like that had been stupid. She couldn't move freely, let alone quickly. Clutching the flashlight, she rubbed her wrist over her upper leg to warm the muscles, at the same time flexing her toes and tensing her calves to get the feeling in her feet back.

A cold draft across her face told her that the intruder had managed to open the door and was on his way into the conservatory.

She listened to his careful footfalls, his subdued breathing. The ray of his flashlight played through the room, slipping over the tiles, the workbench, the many flowering plants. Callie held her breath, as if he might suddenly see her. But he was still on the other side of the conservatory, close to the doors through which he had entered.

He was now moving something, dragging it across the tiles. She had decided to wait a little and see what he was doing. He might actually find some evidence that Leadenby had stored away and which they could then use against him. Standing there, she wasn't sure that even catching him in the act would be enough to get him convicted. It felt like he was too cold and ruthless to go down.

There were soft sounds, as of earth hitting the tiles. He was emptying pots to search inside them. Leadenby might have hidden something among his beloved orchids. That made perfect sense.

Callie tried to register everything the intruder was

doing as if she could see it clearly, knowing her testimony would be all-important later on. She wished they'd had time to install a camera of some kind, to ensure they had footage of his careful search. He wouldn't be leaving any fingerprints. She was sure he would be wearing gloves.

He muttered something under his breath. Was he calling Leadenby names for having dragged him into this mess? Or was he just telling himself to be careful, to take his time, since he had only one chance to outwit the police?

Callie's left foot started to feel numb and she moved it. Something ticked in the silence.

The shuffling noise stopped. The intruder had become fully alert and was listening for what had disturbed his quiet probing.

She could just kick herself for this, and at the same time she was glad. He had to discover her presence sometime and start talking.

He continued working. More earth piled up. She could hear more pottery being moved. If she waited too long, he might slip out again, a shadow into the night. Then she'd never be able to prove he had been here.

With her free hand, she dug into her pocket and produced a nail. She had picked it up off the floor earlier for this express purpose. She held it tightly, her throat constricted with fear, counting. *One. Two. Three.*

She didn't do anything.

*You coward*, she goaded herself. *Count again and this time do it.*

*One.*

*Two.*

She imagined Falk waiting in the darkness, as tense as she was, as reluctant to have a confrontation yet as desperate to get it over with. She had to do it.

*Three.*

She dropped the nail.

It fell to the tiled floor with a sound that, to her tense mind, ripped through the silence.

The shuffling stopped at once, and the ray of light darted her way. She stepped aside and bumped into something that moved. Good. Now he would really be spooked.

The ray danced closer to her. She could hear his breathing. Then the light found her feet. Her legs. Her upper body. It shone full in her face, blinding her. She squeezed her eyes shut and turned her head to the side.

If he had a gun, he could just shoot her. But he wouldn't risk the sound of a shot in the quiet night, waking up the entire household.

Still, Callie stepped out of the ray into the protective shadows of a potted plant with large yellow blooms. Its sweet scent enveloped her.

"I have what you're looking for," she said. "I found it in the snow right after the murder. I want to give it to you. For the right amount of money."

There was a tense silence. Would he buy it?

"How much?" the voice asked, sibilant and almost unrecognizable. Was that Frank Smith? Or was it somebody else?

"Fifty thousand."

"Hah, do you think I can just produce that kind of money? If I could, Leadenby wouldn't have had a chance of pulling me into his dirty business."

"Was it his dirty business? Or was it your plan from the start?"

"It was his. You know that. If you saw the paperwork, you know that he found out about the girl years ago. The old biddy asked him to look into her long-lost son." His voice dripped with disdain. "Leadenby found him and found the girl, but he was worried Mrs. Finster would take them into her home and heart, not caring for him anymore. He was a frightened old man. Drank too much. Got all sentimental. In such a state, he told me about the son and the girl. Then I decided to get her a job here. Leadenby didn't know that. He didn't agree either, I suppose. But he had to play along. I threatened to reveal everything to Mrs. Finster. How he had betrayed her, lying to her that he hadn't found her family when in fact he had. You don't need to feel sorry for any of them. Leadenby was nothing but a pathetic loser. And dear Brenda is a terrible teacher. She should be glad I got her a job here. Nobody else would ever have given her one."

"You only wanted to use her. What kind of life is that?"

"She could have cooperated and earned some money too. We could all have been the better for it. You're smarter than she is. You see the value of money."

"I don't want to be a tour guide all of my life," Callie

said. "Cater to people who don't speak the language or can't find their way around a foreign city. It's worse than working with toddlers." She silently asked forgiveness for talking about her clients this way, but she had to sound like Smith. Certain she was so much smarter than the rest of the world.

"Show me what you have," he said.

"Not until you give me the money."

"What about Falk?"

Callie froze. Did he suspect the deputy was there? What if he did have a gun? What if it came to a shootout? "What about him?"

"He's planning to search. You were at the Golden Chef together."

"I'm pretending to cooperate with the police. He tells me everything he finds out."

The figure laughed softly. "The advantage of a pretty face."

"You were stupid to kill Leadenby. He would never have told the truth at the tea party. What good would that have done him? He wouldn't have gotten a dime."

"He didn't want money anymore. He suddenly had a conscience. Christmastime and all that. He wanted to come clean to the old biddy. He called me to tell me that. He was coming to the party to tell all. He said he'd keep me out of it and would pretend he had brought Brenda to Heart's Harbor as a surprise. Brenda would be happy with that solution and never mention the blackmail either. None of us would look bad. But I didn't believe him. I couldn't risk him saying the wrong thing or Brenda spilling the beans. Until that moment, Brenda didn't know I was the mastermind behind it all. And it had to stay that way. If Leadenby became a weak link, he needed to be eliminated."

Callie stood motionless. Leadenby, with his smile for her upon their reunion. Had he suddenly remembered how he had been before he had turned into a manipulative old man, trying to extort people into helping him? Had he felt sorry for what he had become? Had he wanted to turn back the clock? That moment of remorse had been his undoing.

In a flash, the dark figure was in front of her. He reached out for her. She remembered Falk's words: *Don't get near him; don't let him grab you.*

She dropped herself to the side, hitting the floor on her right thigh, sliding away across the tiles.

Something dark jumped the figure. There was a struggle, the sound of flesh impacting flesh. Grunting and shuffling. Pottery falling over and breaking. Scrambling, as if the killer was trying to crawl away across the floor. Impact again and a cry of pain.

More shuffling. She didn't dare shine a light on the struggling figures. Maybe it would give the killer an advantage. She had to let Falk handle this. His way.

Then cuffs clicked.

Falk's voice called out to her, "Are you OK?"

"Yes," she wanted to call back, but it came out like a whisper. "Are you hurt?"

"He kicked me, but I took it in the shoulder. It'll be fine. Are you sure you're OK?"

"Yes." It still sounded weak, more like a croak than a reassuring reply.

"Callie? Where are you?" Falk moved over to her, his aftershave washing over her first, before his silhouette leaned down to her. His hand felt for her, touched her face. His fingertips trailed down from her cheek to her chin. "Are you OK?"

"Yes," she could say, stronger now. "I'm fine."

Falk's fingers traced down her shoulder, feeling for her hand. He grabbed it firmly and pulled her to her feet. "That was close."

"I knew what I was doing."

"I bet you did."

They stood in the darkness that was no longer threatening but almost soothing. They didn't have to look at the killer apprehended on the floor. He was cuffed and could do no more harm.

They could just stand close together and breathe the sweet scent of the flowers all around them.

# Chapter Eighteen

The cheerful organ notes drifted from the open doors of the small church as the churchgoers flooded out, shrinking into their coats under the first touches of the drifting snow. They exchanged a few words here and there, then looked for their cars to go home and enjoy the rest of Christmas Eve with their loved ones.

Dorothea Finster stood straight up, Mrs. Keats by her side, tilting her head. "Do you hear it?"

Callie didn't hear much of anything beyond the organ and the buzz of voices all about her.

But then, as she really listened hard, she heard what Dorothea meant. Sleigh bells. Sleigh bells in the distance, coming closer. Her heart skipped a beat like it had when she was just a little girl.

"I rented five of them," Dorothea said with a smile. "All drawn by black horses. I do love black horses."

The first one came into view, the sleigh decorated with red and gold bows and the horse in front with his mane braided. Much time and effort had been put into the presentation of these magnificent animals and the winter wonderland carriages they were pulling.

Stephen helped Dorothea into the sleigh, then Mrs. Keats. He put the warm blankets that were provided across their legs and gave Dorothea a pat on her arm. "We're just waiting for . . . oh, here she is already."

Brenda Brink appeared beside the sleigh, her face warm and relaxed, her hair pushed back gently by the snow-filled breeze. She climbed in and sat on Dorothea's other side, slipping her arm through hers. "Dad called me from the airport. He and Mom are on their way over. They'll be at Haywood Hall later tonight."

Dorothea nodded. Nerves showed in her expression, but Brenda said, "Dad takes things with an open mind. You don't need to worry. I'll be there to break the ice."

Dorothea smiled now, and the sleigh started to move. Stephen said to Callie, "I can't believe how much Dorothea has changed now that she's been able to speak about her son. It must really have influenced her entire life."

"I'm so happy for her that she's managed to bring her family together before it was too late. Leadenby did the right thing, wanting to get the truth out in the open."

Stephen nodded. A second sleigh pulled up, and he helped Sheila get in. She looked years younger with her hair loose around her warm face. As soon as Stephen sat beside her, they grabbed each other's hands. Callie smiled to herself. Apparently the talk in the library had cleared things up. Sheila needn't have worried that Stephen had never loved her. He did love her, and she loved him. They looked like newlyweds as the sleigh glided away into the night.

The third sleigh picked up Amber and Cole Merton. He looked a bit uncomfortable with this whole luxury thing, but Amber whispered that it was so romantic, and he wrapped his arm around her and they didn't seem to see anything of their surroundings anymore.

Callie felt a twinge of sympathy for Ben, who had said he wasn't staying for Christmas but would rather spend it with his own family. He had genuinely cared for Amber, and it would take time for him to recover from the disappointment that his feelings were not returned. But on the other hand, it was better for him that he knew now and had not been forced into an engagement that would only have ended in even more heartbreak down the road.

A fourth sleigh halted, and Peggy stepped up with the boys. Tate was jumping up and down that they were going to ride in a sleigh with horses, and although Jimmy acted cool, like this was perfectly normal for him, his eyes also shone with excitement.

Peggy whispered to Callie, "It really is a bit much, but the boys love it."

"Christmas is a time when dreams come true. You just have to embrace them."

Peggy brushed a hand through Tate's hair as she seated herself, then arranged the blankets. Callie knew she would be missing her husband, especially tonight, but it was good that she would be with other people, not sitting alone, reminiscing.

The sleigh pulled away to follow the others. The air seemed full of the sound of bells.

The fifth one halted, and Callie was about to climb into it on her own when a voice said, "Do I have to walk, or is there room for a passenger on this one?"

She turned to Falk. He was dressed in a three-quarter woolen coat over dark pants. A completely different picture again from the leather jacket or the deputy's uniform. It would take time to figure out who he was, really.

Callie tried to sound casual. "Sure. Get in."

He sat down beside her, close enough for her to feel his warmth. He looked up at the skies, from which soft snow was drifting down upon them. He reached out for the blankets and arranged them over them, tucking them in together.

Callie sat stiffly for a few moments, then decided she wanted to enjoy this and relaxed in the seat and against Falk. She said, "It was a beautiful service. I couldn't help thinking of Leadenby. I felt like the words were written especially for him. That in the end you have to remember one thing: you are forgiven and you are loved." She glanced at Falk. "Leadenby decided he didn't want to go on with his blackmail because he needed forgiveness, don't you think?"

Falk nodded. "He needed it, and I think he got it. When he picked up the phone to call Frank Smith and tell him it was over and he was going to tell Dorothea the truth, he must have known deep inside that he was doing the right thing. That he was making a choice for family instead of money."

Callie smiled as she looked up at the skies, where, between the thin clouds, a single star was visible. "Speaking of family: Peggy looked a little shocked that she was invited to our Christmas Eve party at Haywood Hall. But it was Dorothea's idea, really. More people from the village are coming. She just arranged these sleighs for us."

"The boys will love it. I just have to keep an eye out that they're not taking all the candy canes off the trees."

"What did you do with that tree Mayor Moore saddled you with in the drawing?"

Falk gestured. "The roots are still on it, so I thought I would plant it outside the cabin as soon as the ground isn't frozen stiff anymore."

He glanced at her. "It was smart of Leadenby to hide his evidence under the snow. In a box so it wouldn't be ruined. He probably wasn't sure about Smith. That's why he went out and hid it before he called Smith. The wetness on the floor came from *his* shoes."

Callie sighed. "Why did he call Smith at all? If he had just walked in and told the truth, he might still be alive."

"Maybe he acted on impulse, not even considering what he was setting off." Falk flexed his fingers. "Are you wearing gloves?"

"I can keep my hands under the blankets, that's OK."

Falk nodded. "After the arrest, Smith told us all about Moore's bad investments. Of course, he denies having had anything to do with them. Unless we can prove that he actually gave him advice, Moore's signatures on all the paperwork will have him in the hot seat. I can't help but think he will have to step down as mayor now. His wife won't be happy that she's losing her position as town mother."

"Change is never easy."

Falk seemed to freeze at the mention. "Twenty-fourth today," he said. "Only a few more days left in the old year, then onto the new. I suppose you'll be traveling again."

"All booked up for months."

"Yes, of course. You can't just . . ." He looked ahead to the dancing head of their horse.

"Did you sort of gauge Peggy's feelings about her taking on Daisy?" Callie felt bad every time she thought about leaving the sweet dog behind here in Heart's Harbor, but she couldn't take her along on her travels.

"She thinks a dog is a big thing for the kids. Maybe in the summer vacation. They'll be a bit older then and have more time to spend with the dog. Besides, Daisy isn't really a dog for kids like Tate and Jimmy. She likes it quiet with lots of cuddles. She'll get the cuddles from them of course, but they'll also like to play wild games. We're thinking about a Labrador maybe. Cole Merton said he could let us know when a suitable dog comes into the shelter. Peggy would like a rescue, if he doesn't have too many issues."

Callie nodded. "That's great. I need to put Daisy someplace, though."

"She could be at the Book Tea, maybe."

"That sounds neither convinced nor convincing."

"Well, I certainly can't enlist her as a dog for the force."

Callie laughed but without really feeling it. She hated the idea of giving the dog away, but she had a job, and . . .

"I, uh . . . I have something for you." Falk reached into the pocket of his coat and produced the parcel he had won in the drawing. "My mystery gift. I think you should open it."

"But you have no idea what's in it. Maybe you'll be giving away something valuable."

"Aw, no, it'll sooner be some crocheted pillow case. I don't need anything, really."

"OK." Callie put the parcel in her lap. Here she was, traveling in a horse-drawn sleigh through a fairy-tale landscape on her way to the house she had always loved, with a new friend beside her and a present to unwrap. It felt like she had unwrapped a couple of presents that day already, seeing the happiness of the people around her. Dorothea and her newfound granddaughter, Stephen and Sheila in love all over again, Amber and Cole reunited.

She fumbled with the red ribbon, then the amply applied tape to open the paper. Her heart was pounding as if Falk had picked this present especially for her. It was just a thing he had won, she reminded herself, nothing special.

She folded the paper back. It was a gingerbread heart with colorful frosting all around the edges and forming words. She read them slowly. They were just simple English words, but still her eyes couldn't quite believe what it said.

*Welcome home.*

"You switched the contents," she said to Falk, her heart pounding violently.

"No, absolutely not. This is the gift I won with my ticket number thirty-two."

The number she herself had drawn from among all of those bingo balls.

*Welcome home.*

Home to Haywood Hall, which Dorothea wanted her and Iphy to have and preserve. Home to Heart's Harbor, where Callie had found so many fond memories alive and well. Home to her old friends and to new ones that she had quickly locked into her heart.

Home to . . . a steady life? No more traveling, but . . .

She looked at Falk. The snow was in his hair again and on his lashes, like on the night they had caught Smith together.

*Together* was a nice word.

"Thanks," she said simply.

"You're welcome. Also to cook for me again."

"I'll see if I can find a space in my schedule."

He poked her with his elbow, and she slapped him playfully. They were laughing, teasing with just a single look. The sleigh halted at the Hall, and they climbed out and threw fresh snow at each other, not caring what the others thought. Once inside, they had to take a moment to catch their breath.

Daisy ran to greet Callie, and she picked her up and cuddled her. As the dog snuggled against her, Callie knew she wanted to keep her. That giving her up was just impossible.

Iphy came over to her. She had denied wanting a part in the sleigh ride, as she'd had to be first at the Hall to see that everything was perfect for their Christmas Eve buffet. She hugged Callie, dog and all. "I'm so happy with how this all turned out."

She nodded in the direction of Amber and Cole, who were lost to the world as they stood talking, Cole brushing back Amber's wild red-golden hair. "My plan worked out perfectly."

"Yes," Callie said, "you never did tell me what the clue in the cake was."

"The Brother Cadfael story about the body found under the ice, of course," Iphy said, as if it had been obvious all along. "It's a winter story, full of snow and ice, so the cake really resembled that. But the main thing is, the lady of the story runs away with a man she believes can give her security. But in the end she realizes love is far more important, even if you have to take a risk for it." She smiled as she nodded at Cole. "I knew it was just a matter of time before Amber real- ized that the right man was under her nose all along."

Callie shook her head. "It's that easy?"

Iphy nodded at Falk, who had caught Tate in his arms and was lifting him high to see if he could reach the top branches of the Christmas tree. Jimmy was eyeing the pres- ents, which had appeared under the tree, wrapped up in sparkly paper with cute hand-drawn gift labels on them. Peggy stood watching the scene, a little forlorn still but not completely alone. She was part of this, enveloped in the light and the warmth.

Iphy said softly, "It can be that easy if you just want to see it."

Callie exhaled. Maybe she also just had to see it? See what happened to her as she returned to this place? Falk had been so right. Daisy could stay at the Book Tea while Callie wrapped up the trips she was already booked for. She just had to tell her boss she wasn't taking any new engagements. That, come summer, she'd be living someplace else. Doing something completely different with her life. Helping Iphy turn Haywood Hall into a venue for parties, a museum, a place where the history of the house and the town nearby was kept alive. Wouldn't it be fabulous if Dorothea could be a part of it? Why wait for changes until after her death when they could start on this big project together? Have Dorothea be a part of the new future she so wanted for her beloved home?

Callie looked down at Daisy and said, "What do you think, girl? Do you like it here?"

Daisy made a satisfied sound as she settled against Callie.

Falk caught her eye as he lowered Tate to the ground. Callie smiled at him, and he winked back at her.

Outside the house, the sleigh bells were fading in the darkness as the drivers steered their horses back to the stables through the thickly falling snow. Inside the Hall, it was warm and light, and there would be chatter and laughter for hours to come, excitement as presents were opened and wishes granted.

This was a place for staying.

A place to call home.

# Acknowledgments

As always, I'm grateful to all agents, editors, and authors who share online about the writing and publishing process. A special thanks to those who worked closely with me on this brand-new series: my amazing agent Jill Marsal, my wonderful editor Faith Black Ross, and the entire talented crew at Crooked Lane Books, especially illustrator Brandon Dorman for the wonderfully festive cover.

And, of course, to you, readers: thanks for picking up this Christmas story; I hope that it put festive cheer in your hearts and made you fall in love with the quirky inhabitants of small-town Heart's Harbor. You're warmly invited to join them again as Fourth of July celebrations bring an old celebrity disappearance back into the headlines and catapult Callie into a web of deceit and secrets that only persistence and help from friends can unravel.